I0688359

John Benson Rose

Comedies

Translated by John Benson Rose

John Benson Rose

Comedies
Translated by John Benson Rose

ISBN/EAN: 9783337086381

Printed in Europe, USA, Canada, Australia, Japan

Cover: Foto ©Andreas Hilbeck / pixelio.de

More available books at **www.hansebooks.com**

Phormio, Act II., Scene 3.

COMEDIES

OF

PUBLIUS TERENTIUS AFER.

TRANSLATED BY

JOHN BENSON ROSE.

LONDON:
DORRELL AND SON, CHARING CROSS.
1870.

LONDON: PRINTED BY WILLIAM CLOWES AND SONS, DUKE STREET, STAMFORD STREET
AND CHARING CROSS.

PREFACE.

" Homo sum : humani nil a me alienum puto."

IT is in accordance with that sentence that I offer Terence in another English garb.

Reader, you have reflected here the manners of the Roman Republic some 150 years before our Saviour. There are startling laws and manners shown forth in slavery and infanticide, but most strange of all the manner in which Roman youth wooed and won their wives. It may have derived from the recorded story of Romulus and the Sabines; but modes of marriage are nothing more than forms and fashions with different nations and people, and varied by circumstances and laws.

We plainly perceive the fact of a paucity of females compared with the males, brought about by the prevailing exposure of the female children, and indisposition of the Greeks and Romans to rear girls. Hence the boys snatched a wife, and there is no sign of repentance or of having made a foolish and hasty match ever expressed through the plays; on the contrary, with a power of divorce, it appears ever to be as joyful a conquest as our own hardly-won assents of free maidens.

Marriage customs and manners differ at times and places even with us; nor need we refer to Fleet marriages or Gretna Green, now both amidst the past; but our maidens of the sister Isle in this century found charms in an elopement beyond any other form of ceremony. The Calmuck damsel prefers to be mounted on horseback, and give her lover a glorious chase and capture of herself, if she so choose. The present Belgravian mode is an untimely breakfast, probably the worst mode of all. Let these, then, excuse the Roman youth for seizing their brides, following their time-honoured god Quirinus, and also the contemporary practice of the Spartans, who preferred to win their brides in darkness and by raid, although palpably connived at by the bride, than by the wearisome tedium of the hymeneal.

Neither must we confound the class of Hetairæ of the ancients with the proscribed class of the present time; for they were educated women, whilst the wife was uneducated; they were brilliant in society, whilst the wife was immured at home. We find a Thais accompanying Alexander and chief instrument in burning Persepolis; Rhodope is mentioned mythically as the builder of the third pyramid of Gheeza; Phryne who rebuilt the walls of Thebes, for the sole guerdon of her name being engraved on the walls as " Phryne the Hetaira." Pericles wedded Aspasia, and Socrates sat at her feet to learn eloquence. Plato had his Archianassa, and Aristotle his Hepyllis.

We here tread on Athenian soil, where Terence lays the scene of his dramas, and where the lost Comedies of Menander, from whence he drew his own, had their origin. They had also a religious halo, for the girls were offered in early youth or saved by dedication to Aphrodite at Corinth and elsewhere, where there were colleges or institutions where they were instructed, and where some chosen few were rich enough to visit them to their ruin. So we find Antiphila saved (Heaut. iii. 5) by the Corinthian crone. We find Simo, in the Andria, grace unbidden the funeral rite of his neighbour Chrysis. Chremes entertains Bacchis and her train in his house, whilst with an hypocrisy past endurance he will not pronounce the word *meretrix* before his wife in his son's presence, poor unhappy Sostrata, whom he has rated like a slave in Act III. scene 5, and treated with utter indignity and cruelty.

Neither does there appear to have been any poverty, or want, or disease in their order, but, like good Samaritans, they appear to be rife of charitable deeds. It may be remarked, that however Homer may vituberate his Samaritan deities, Calypso and Circe, he has drawn them more honest, true, and beneficent than his Pallas Athene and Here; in like manner, Sostrata is nobody before Thais; and whilst Bacchis can call up the contents of the cellar and fastidiously condemn them, the wife is not permitted to taste wine. These anomalies could be cited at great length, but enough has been said to show that there is no reflex of the Hetaira class with us. That which approaches it is our opera singers and actresses, who, although proscribed as servants by the aristocracy supporting them, live in luxury, and ever and anon carry off a noble scion in matrimony. It is therefore I have left the terms *meretrix* and *amica*, as also those of *psaltria, citharistria, tibicina*, &c., in their original tongue—they might be termed actresses, minstrels, harpists, vocalists, &c., but the original words are better. Also I refrain to translate *edepol* and *mecastor*, and other interjections. We have exploded oaths ourselves, and the swearing which was in vogue a century ago is now offensive to our ears, which *pol* and *papæ* are not; besides, they tend to draw us back to the scene, and to remind us we are in ancient Rome, with Davus and Parmeno and Bacchis; whilst to call the Forum, the market-place, is to blunder exceedingly: we translate far too much.

We as plainly trace Molière drawn from Terence as Terence was traced from the Grecian Menander, the loss of whose dramas appears to be a real loss.

Molière has an enormous advantage over Terence in having educated heroines to grace his wit. The age, too, of Louis Quatorze furnished materials for polished pleasantry, which the granitic age of the Roman Commonwealth did not supply. But the bare fact that Terence portrays the true manners of an age of which we know very little, whilst Molière has travestied the absurdities of his own, gives to Terence a value and an interest far above that which Molière wins from the exquisite *fooling* of his renaissance age.

Terence has no Lucile to reply to Eraste in a " *Dépit Amoureux*," nor a Marinette to make love to Gros René. Although the same play, which gives us Thais, gives us also the clever Pythias, who pegs into Parmeno, not by love, but jeering him. This is an exception in Terence, whilst female wit is the charm and the rule with Molière.

Neither does Terence ever descend to anything not possible, such as the statue of the warrior supping with Don Juan. His facts are all such as were probable, and find their main plot in infanticide; and the recognition by means of the token appended to obtain their funeral rites; and in the paucity of women, which affords a sufficient cause for a forcible abduction of the wife.

The Hecyra, or Stepmother, is not included, mainly because it does not contain any new point which is not to be found in the others; secondly, because the

events are less pleasantly told, for it was hissed off the
Roman stage. This translation skims the surface,
eschewing the depths of the scholiast, and offers to
those who will accept it a picture of Rome 150 years
before our Christian era, and before the Civil Wars
began, which degraded Rome from the peaceful and
legal position here portrayed, and which did not re-
assume the virtues with the vices, which we find
deplored, or affected to be deplored, by Horace,
Juvenal, and Persius.

Like Æsop, Terence was also a slave. We lose sight
of him at the early age of thirty-five. He enjoyed
patrician society, and his daughter married a patrician.

The frontispiece is taken from a manuscript in our
possession in the British Museum, and is printed in a
paper read before the Royal Society of Antiquaries,
plate vi., vol. xxiv., p. 144.

Samian Juno.

TERMS AND SIGNIFICATIONS WITH NO EXACT ENGLISH EQUIVALENTS.

Amica.
Meretrix.
Tibicina.
Citharistria.
Psaltria.
Fidicina.
Furcifer—bearing a log on the neck, as do the Chinese.
Crucifer.
Carnifex—hangman.
Pluvium—an open space in roof.
Pyre—funeral pile.
Oaths :—

    Faith of gods.
    Faith of men.
    Faith of gods and men.
    Pol and Edepol—Pollux and fane of Pollux.
    Castor and Ecastor—Castor and fane of Castor.
    Hercle—by Hercules.
    Me hercle—me Hercules juvat.
    Jupiter—proh Jupiter.
    I am beloved of gods.
    As the gods love me.
    Papæ.
    Atat.

Altar and intercessor.—*Heaut.*, v. 2.
    refuge for a slave.—*Phorm.*, i. 50.
    at doorway with verbenæ.—*Andr.*, iv. 4.
Babe laid at threshold.—*Andr.*, iv. 5.
Conclave—an apartment with lock and bolt.
Creaking of hinges—or warning of exit from doors which opened
externally.   The noise was made to give warning to those outside.
Daughter exposed.—*Heaut.*, iii. 5.
    discovered by ring.—*Heaut.*, iii. 5.

Dowers—ten talents.—*Andria*, v. 5.
    two talents.—*Heaut.*, v. 1.
Dionysia—feast of Bacchus.—*Heaut.*, iv. 3.
Father—power over wife and son.
    salutes his household gods.—*Phorm.*, i. 5.
Jewels—courtesans not permitted to wear them in the street.—*Eun.*, iv. 1.
Meretrix—wealth, pride, and independence of.—*Heaut.*, ii. 2.
    Thais—the best female character.—*Eun.*
Mina—about 3*l.* 5*s.*
Talent—sixty minæ; under 200*l.*
Great Talent—the same.
Omens enumerated.—*Phorm.*, iv. 4.
Orphans to be wedded by next of kin.—*Adel.*, iv. 5.
    or his descendant.—*Phorm.*, i. 2.
    or dowered at fifteen minæ.—*Phorm.*, ii. 2.
Price of girls—twenty minæ.—*Adel.*, ii. 1.
Pyre.—*Andr.*, i. 1.
Pluvium—an open space in roof; a fountain, or plot of green beneath.
Rings—*Heaut.*, iii. 7; *Eun.*, iii. 4.
    pledges for costs for dinner.—*Hecyra*, v. 3.
Slave—manumitted.—*Andr.*, i. 1; *Adel.*, v. 3.
    tortured.—*Adel.*, v. 4.
    self proposed for torture.—*Adel.*, iii. 5.
    evidence otherwise inadmissible.—*Phorm.*, i. 5.
Son—escapes authority by foreign enlistment.—*Heaut.*, i. 1.
    travelling equipage, belt, sword, and bottle.—*See Plautus.*
Wife—indignities borne by her.—*Heaut.*, iii. 5; v. 4.
    holds separate property.—*Phorm.*, v. 3.

ANDRIA.

PERSONS.

Prologue.
Simo—Father of Pamphilus.
Pamphilus.
Sosia—Freedman of Simo.
Davus—Servus of Pamphilus.
Chremes—Father of Glycerium and Philumena.
Glycerium.
Charinus—Lover of Philumena.
Byrrhia—Servus of Charinus.
Crito—Stranger from Andria.
Dromo—Servus of Simo.
Mysis—Maid of Glycerium.
Lesbia—Midwife.

PROLOGUE.

When first the poet thought to write a play,
He only hoped to win a poet's sway
Over your plaudits popular : but now
A cloud arises, he must make his bow
In prologue to avert a brother's ban,
Not to expound his fable and its plan.
Listen, I pray you, to the critic's spleen
And maledictions on this present scene.
Menander "Andria" and " Perinthia " wrote
In which there is no difference to note ;
Who knows the one needs also know its brother,
Though differing in their style from one another.
Our poet introduced, as he thought fit,
Into the Andrian the Perinthian wit ;
And hence the cause that they vituperate
That we Greek fable so contaminate.
So they in knowledge ignorance display.
For what would Nævius, Plautus, Ennius say,
Whom they accuse in thus accusing us,
With so much senseless and censorious fuss.
The author better loves their negligence,
Than such obscure and diligent pretence.
I warn them from henceforth to keep the peace,
And let their railings and their murmurs cease.
Hear ye and judge, and with calm spirit sit,
And pass your judgment on the poet's wit ;
Whether it may, from critic scorn exempt,
Win from you, admiration or contempt.

ANDRIA.

ACT I.

SCENE 1.—SIMO—SOSIA—DAVUS (*with provisions*).

Sim. Here you, take these within; stay, Sosia, stay,
  A word with you.
Sos.   About the cookery
  No doubt.
Sim.   Nay, it is something else.
Sos.   Whatever
  It may be, I'll do my best.
Sim.   It is not
  Your active but your passive operation
  That now I need; silence and secrecy;
  Virtues I ever noted strong in you.
Sos. I am all attention.
Sim.   Since I purchased you,
  A little child, I have been just to you,
  And clement in your servitude to me.
  You served me well and I affranchised you;
  So I repaid your service with the best
  Return that I could make you.
Sos.   Which I hold
  In grateful recollection.
Sim.   Nor do I
  Repent your manumission.

Sos.   I am glad ;
   And that my service is commendable,
   I am grateful also, Simo ; but my ear
   Is frightened more than flattered by this speech.
   Wherefore remind me of these benefits,
   Unless it be to blame forgetfulness ?
   Then tell me in one word your present will.
Sim. I will do so ; but first I must inform you
   The nuptials which we feign to celebrate
   Are but fictitious.
Sos.   Wherefore do you feign them ?
Sim. Hear, then, from first to last, and by that means
   Learn my son's life, and what I now design.
   When Pamphilus was adolescent, Sosia,
   I gave him licence more than, perhaps, I ought ;
   But so I learnt his true propensities.
   Unchecked by fear or magisterial hand,
   He then betrayed his bent.
Sos.   Ah ! that is so.
Sim. Boys usually have passions and desires,
   Hugging some special pastime to their arms
   As dogs and horses—or philosophy.
   For him—he follows with sobriety
   All things with prudence, so delighting me.
Sos. And good ; to my mind there is nought in life
   Superior to the adage that, " Enough
   Equals a feast."
Sim.   This was his course of life :
   Urbane unto his fellows—subjecting
   His will to theirs, his pleasures unto theirs,
   Opposing none ; it following, of course,
   He gained their praises and he made them friends.

Sos. It is a good commencement; for to-day,
   Deceit wins friendship and truth enemies.
Sim. Some three years since a certain woman came
   Hither from Andros, and here made abode.
   Want and neglect of relatives coerced
   Her to that step—she—young and beautiful—
Sos. I fear this Andrian woman brings ill-luck.
Sim. Modest and prudent at the first, and gained
   By toil a pittance by the wool and loom.
   When lovers came, their purses in their hands,
   With her as with the rest of human kind,
   Whose tendencies are prone to luxury,
   Hostile to toil—she unsupported fell—
   At first submissive but to one or two,
   And then she opened house to visitors:
   Among the rest, by others led, my son.
   Then said I to myself—behold him caught;
   Then I waylaid their servants, and I asked,
   Holloa, my lad—tell me which one possessed
   Chrysis, for so she called herself, last night?
Sos. What said they?
Sim.   They replied—or Phædrus,
   Clinias, or Niceratus; for these three
   Made court alike to her! Ahah! quoth I,
   "And Pamphilus, what doth he there?" "Eh, what?
   He sups and pays his shot." I was rejoiced,
   For still it held the same—no Pamphilus.
   And I thought him a proof—and an example
   Of wisdom in a youth, one firm enough
   To mingle in the world and in its ways,
   And not to trip—to such a one we may
   Resign the bit and let him have his fling;

And all the world would praise me open-mouthed,
Because I had a son of such good sense.
And so it followed.　Chremes hears his praise,
And straightway comes to offer me his child,
His only child—with an enormous dowry—
As wife to Pamphilus.　I was well pleased,
Accepted—and the nuptials fall to-day.
Sos. Why, then, delay them in reality?
Sim. For this—our neighbour Chrysis died.
Sos. I breathe again—I was in mortal fear
　Of that same Chrysis.
Sim.　　　　　　　•　　　　And when she was dead
　My son—and all her other clientage—
　Performed the funeral rites.　I marked him sad,
　I saw him weep—and I rejoiced and thought
　If he grieve thus for one who is a stranger,
　How would he grieve for one allied to him,
　How weep for me his father—they were signs
　To me of an ingenuous human soul,
　And so to end my tale, to please my son,
　Neither suspecting evil—I resolved
　That I would join her funeral rites myself.
Sos. What followed then?
Sim.　　　　　　　　　　　All in good time.　They brought
　Her body forth, we went.　Amidst the women
　That followed there—there was a girl—a girl
　Of most exceeding beauty—
Sos.　　　　　　　　　　Ah! no doubt!
Sim. Face, Sosia, and demeanour, exquisite,
　Modest, in deep affliction.　Marking her
　I asked the other women in the train
　Her name, and learnt she sister was to Chrysis.

My mind misgave: attat, if that is so
Hence, hence our tears; hence, hence our misery.
Sos. I dread the sequel.
Sim.   So the train proceeded.
 We followed to the tomb—they placed the corpse,
 Upon the pyre, and they raised the lament.
 The sister then incautiously approached
 The blazing pile, and doubtless was in peril.
 Then Pamphilus betrayed the secret fire,
 Hidden before, he sprung forth—caught the girl
 About the waist, exclaimed, Glycerium,
 Wherefore is this—why would you slay yourself?
 And it was evident that burst of love
 Was not the first which had ta'en place between them;
 She flung herself on him familiarly.
Sos. What did you say?
Sim.   Irate, with some ado,
 I choked my anger, for of no avail
 Had been reproaches then. He would have answered—
 What have I done, my father? I have saved
 A woman who had leapt into the flames.
 To outward sight, it was so—and was right.
Sos. Truly, for if you objurgate a man
 For saving life, what could you do to one
 Devising evils and committing wrongs?
Sim. And the next day came Chremes unto me,
 Indignantly declaring Pamphilus
 Was wedded to this stranger. I denied it—
 Said, there was no such thing; which reaverred
 By him—I straightway came away and left
 Him, in no mood to give to us a daughter.
Sos. Where is your son?

Sim.   I do not think as yet
    Proof is sufficient, to attack my son.
Sos. Why not, I pray you ?
Sim.   For he will retort.
    Father, you set a bourn to my pursuits,
    And soon compel me to submit to others—
    Let me, I pray you, live in the mean time.
Sos. What will be then sufficient cause of plaint ?
Sim. If he through love of her refuse to wed,
    That is an injury I may avenge.
    I lay a trap to catch him, by false nuptials
    Catching a true refusal ; whereupon
    I reason have to act.   At the same time
    I catch that cursed Davus, who will show
    His store of tricks and wiles, which will not lack ;
    He will lay hand and foot to work to cheat.
    He better loves, methinks, to trouble me
    Than to assist my son.
Sos.   Why so ?
Sim.   Dost ask !
    " Bad mind, bad spirit ;" but if I perceive—
    Cease this discourse, for if he prove to me
    Obedient, nor asks delay—then Chremes
    May be brought round again, on due petition.
    That which we now must do—to make appear
    These sponsals to be real : knock Davus down—
    Keep eye upon my son, and mark what they
    Will machinate together.
Sos.   Enough, I will take heed,
    Let us go in.
Sim.   Go on, I follow you.

ACT I.—SCENE 2.—SIMO—DAVUS.

Sim. I do not doubt but that he will refuse,
   I noticed Davus give a quail, when I
   Spoke of the marriage.   He comes out of doors.
Dav. I cannot make it out; what is on foot,
   That master ever lenient intends :'
   Who ever since he knew Chremes will not
   Bestow his daughter here, has held his tongue,
   Nor shows a bit of grief.
Sim.   But now who means
   To do so, and to make you know it too.
Dav. It seems to me he laps us in false joy,
   Puts us to sleep with much security,
   To swoop upon us, and at unawares
   Enforce this marriage.
Sim.   Hark to that carnifex.
Dav. He, there; I saw him not.
Sim.   Davus.
Dav.   How now ?
   Who calls ?
Sim.   Come here.
Dav.   Master, how now ?
Sim.   How now !
Dav. I mean what matter.
Sim.   What matter? the whole town
   Declares my son to be in love.
Dav.   [*Aside.*] `   The town
   Cares little about that.
Sim.   Say, do you hear
   Or not ?

Dav.   I hear, I hear.
Sim.   It is not right—
   That I, his father now, should ferret this:
   Nothing he has yet done affecting me.
   I suffered all this nonsense in due season,
   And let him have his fling.   Now, otherwise
   The time demands a change of life and manners,
   And therefore I demand—that is—I pray
   Thee, Davè, that he march in beaten track.
Dav. What does this signify?
Sim.   All boys who love
   Kick against marriage.
Dav.   Ay, ay—so they say.
Sim. If then it hap some evil counsellor
   Lure him astray—for evil counsellors
   There are, and prompt to lead the love-sick wrong.
Dav. Hercle! I understand not.
Sim.   Of course not!
Dav. Davus I am, not Œdipus.
Sim.   Do you mean
   You wish me to speak out the rest in words?
Dav. I do, assuredly.
Sim.   Then hear my words—
   If I catch you, in matter of these nuptials
   Devising treachery—in opposition—
   Or showing off your knavery—you shall have
   A thousand stripes and then off to the mill
   For life, I say—and swear that if I spare you
   I'll take your place and grind—do you understand
   Or do you need further enlightenment?
Dav. Nay, none; you have explained, indeed, the whole
   With singular intelligence and clearness.

Sim. Do you employ your own intelligence
　　Of craftiness upon some other subject.
Dav. Kind words, I pray you, master.
Sim. 　　　　　　　　　　Ah, you jeer,
　　I know you well : now don't be obstinate,
　　Nor say I did not warn you : eh, beware.

ACT I.—Scene 3.—Davus.

Dav. From what I see, my Davus, it is time
　　To wake and look about—from what I see
　　About the sentiments of this old man
　　This marriage threatens ruin to my master,
　　As well as unto me.　Now, bother it,
　　I can't see whether I had better aid
　　My master Pamphilus, or master father.
　　If I leave Pamphilus the boy will die,
　　And if I leave him not, my back must smart.
　　I cannot see my way, Simo knows all,
　　And has his eyes on me, and watches me
　　Lest I should play a trick, and if he spy me
　　Devising one—off am I to the mill—
　　And to that am I tending otherwise.
　　This Andrian, whether wife or whether may,
　　Is heavy now by Pamphilus—and they
　　Outrageous are in wild audacity—
　　Madness, not gladness, better tells their state ;
　　They mean to rear the child, or boy or girl,
　　And feign a likely story—that she is
　　An Attican—a citizen of Athens.
　　There was a certain merchant—who they say

Was wrecked on Andros, and that there he died.
The father of this Chrysis took the child
Orphan'd and wrecked, an infant—'tis absurd!
To me it seems a most unlikely tale,
To them it seems most cleverly devised.
Here Mysis comes forth from her—I will hence
Unto the Forum to find Pamphilus,
And warn him of these matters going on.

ACT I.—Scene 4.—Mysis—Archillis.

Mys. Nonsense, Archillis, what you talk about;
  What! Lesbia? Pol, a woman wine-bibber,
  And rash withal—and to commit to her
  The management in this—a first-born's birth!
  And must I bring her home?   Behold you now
  The trickery of these—contipplers both.
  Gods grant unto my mistress a good time;
  If they must blunder let it be elsewhere.
  Eh! what's the matter now with Pamphilus?
  I fear what it may be, must stop and know,
  I fear he brings us tidings of some woe.

ACT I.—Scene 5.—Pamphilus—Mysis.

Pam. Now, is this human—this vile enterprise?
  Say, is this deed paternal?
Mys.   What is what?
Pam. O faith of gods and man!   What is, I say,
  A vile indignity, if this be not—
  To marry me to-day, nor think it meet
  To ask me, or communicate the fact.

Mys. Unhappy me, what tidings do I hear?
Pam. And Chremes, who withdrew his word, nor would
   Grant unto me his daughter.   Say has he
   Turned round because I am unsuitable?
   And is he thus obdurate, to enforce
   My separation with Glycerium?
   If so, I am undone—past remedy.
   Was ever man, I ask, so crossed in love,
   Unhappy and unfortunate as I?
   O faith of gods and man!   Is there no mode
   By which I can avoid—escape this tie.
   Cursèd alliance.   And myself contemned,
   Despised, and unconsulted, find it all
   A settled thing.   Zounds!   And am sent for—why?
   Now, by my soul! I think she is deformed,
   And no one else will have her; therefore, therefore,
   They come to me.
Mys.   I am frightened of my life.
Pam. My father also— that he should transact
   Affairs of so much moment heedlessly.
   He met me in the Forum, and he said,
   To-day we marry you, my Pamphilus!
   Hurry you home.   Hurry to hang yourself,
   Methought he said to me.   I stood aghast,
   Without the gift of speech; nor could reply
   With reason good nor bad : dumbfounded quite.
   Now, had I but foreknown, and been prepared,
   And had my reasons and objections ready;
   But now I do not know what I can do,
   For cares beset me, harrowing my soul.
   Love, pity, detestation, duty to
   My father, whom I love, and hitherto

Evermore lenient.   I am beset with doubts,
Nor do I know which way to turn myself.
Mys. Nor do I know which way to turn myself.
   I must address him, must speak of my mistress,
   If he do not ask first.   When the mind doubts
   And vacillates, a pin may turn the scale.
Pam. Who speaks?   Ah, Mysis, salvè.
Mys.   Salvè, master.
Pam. How goes it?
Mys.   Dost thou ask?   She is in labour,
   And in distress of mind—for, as she hears,
   They marry you to-day unto another,
   And she in fear that you abandon her.
Pam. How can she fear so?   Can she think that I
   Would suffer she should suffer misery.
   She who has given all to me—herself,
   Her soul, loved me exceedingly—my wife.
   She, nurtured in the gentlest fantasy,
   As modest as well educated—she
   To suffer want, to bear indignity,
   By my soul, never!
Mys.   If upon you alone
   The thing depended—but you must oppose
   Coercion.
Pam.   Am I a beast—inhuman,
   Ungrateful, barbarous—that fond possession,
   Love, honour, all things binding to the soul
   Should let me break my faith?
Mys.   And one thing more,
   Her worth and merit you should not forget.
Pam. Forget her worth and merit—Mysis, Mysis,
   I have engraven on my very heart

The words of Chrysis on Glycerium.
She called me to her side, ourselves alone,
Glycerium and me.   My Pamphilus, she said,
You see her youth and comeliness, you know
The snares which will beset them with the cash
I leave to her.   By your right hand, I pray,
And by your good faith and integrity—
Never desert her, nor live separate.
If like a brother I have ever loved you,
If you by her adored have been alone,
If I upon my death-bed trust in thee,
Be unto her a husband, friend, and father:
My worldly goods do I bequeath to you
Assured of your good faith.   And then she put
Our hands in one another.   So she died.
The faith I gave to her, I mean to keep.
Mys. Gods grant it so.
Pam.   Why did you come away?
Mys. I seek the midwife.
Pam.   Hurry then, I pray.
And, Mysis, on your life, no word of marriage
To trouble and perplex her.
Mys.   Fear you not.

ACT II.

Scene 1.—Charinus—Byrrhia—Pamphilus.

Cha. What say you, Byrrhia? She given in marriage
  To Pamphilus?
Byr.   E'en so.
Cha.   How did you learn it?
Byr. From Davus in the Forum.
Cha.   Oh misery, misery.
  Long between hope and fear my spirit swept,
  And hope was uppermost and now is crushed ;
  Hope absent—it is drowned in lethargy.
Byr. Why, edepol! Charinus, though you can't
  Do what you will, up and do what you can.
Cha. Nought save Philumena is now my will.
Byr. Ah! how much better were it now to chase
  This folly from your heart, and cease to speak
  Such sentiments as only drive you mad.
Cha. All men in health can counsel who are sick,
  But when themselves are sick 'tis otherwise.
Byr. Do as you please.
Cha.   But behold Pamphilus
  I will try every effort ere I die.
Byr. And what with him?
Cha.   Entreat him and implore him —
  Tell of my love—petition for delay ;
  At least a day or two, in hopes of something.
Byr. Which something, nothing is.
Cha.   Advise me, Byrrhia,
  Say, shall I speak?

Byr.   Why not? since at the least
   You will inform him she a gallant has,
   Ready prepared to act.
Cha.   Brute, be you off
   With your suspicions.
Pam. Salvè, Charinus.
Cha.   Salvè, O, Pamphilus.
   I come unto you, hoping and expecting
   Health and assistance.
Pam.   Pol! I am not
   In a position now to grant assistance.
   But tell me what it is.
Cha.   To-day you wed?
Pam. They say so.
Cha.   If it be so, Pamphilus,
   We meet no more.
Pam.   Why so?
Cha.   I dare not say.
   Speak, Byrrhia, and tell all.
Byr.   Am I to speak?
Pam. What is it? say.
Byr.   That he loves your betrothed.
Pam. Well, tastes are different.   Charinus, tell me
   Hath there aught passed betwixt you?
Cha.   Nothing;
   O, Pamphilus.
Pam.   Would that there had been so.
Cha. Now by our friendship and by love, I pray,
   You will not wed her.
Pam.   I will help what I can.
Cha. But if you must so---if your heart is set—
Pam. My heart is set?

Cha.   Delay, delay, I beg you,
  Some days at least, that I may hence away
  Nor witness it.
Pam.   Hear me, Charinus; now
  I will not take a credit with none due;
  For I have more antipathy to this
  Than you have will towards her.
Cha.   Ah ! I breathe.
Pam. If you and Byrrhia can devise a plot,
  Invent, imagine some mode to prevent this,
  I will omit no labours on my part.
Cha. Enough, enough !
Pam.   And in a happy time
  Lo ! Davus, upon whom I set my trust.
Cha. And, hercle ! you are useless—be you off—
  You trouble me.
Byr.   I go, with all my heart.

ACT II.—Scene 2.—Davus—Charinus—Pamphilus.

Dav. Auspicious gods ! what happy news I bring—
  But where is Pamphilus ? to root out his fear
  And fill his soul with joy.
Cha.   Davus is joyful.
Pam. It is nothing, he has not heard of this.
Dav. I fancy now, if he has heard of this,
  His nuptials now prepared—
Cha.   Do you hear that ?
Dav. But where is Pamphilus ? I am half dead
  With weariness of running here and there.
Pam. Here, Davus—stop.

Dav.   Who calls? Ah! Pamphilus,
 I seek for you. Charinus, also, good.
 I matter have for both.
Pam.   I perish, Davus.
Dav. Hear me, hear me.
Pam.   I die.
Dav.   Nay, not at all.
Cha. And also I myself am like to die.
Dav. I know your wants.
Pam.   My nuptials.
Dav.   Yes, I know.
Pam. To-day.
Dav.   · Be still, I know it all, I say.
 You, master, would not; you, Charinus, would
 Wed not, and wed.
Cha.   The thing is even so.
Pam. 'Tis even so.
Dav.   This even so, is nothing.
Pam. Quick, put me out of doubt and misery.
Dav. I will do so. Chremes won't give his daughter.
Pam. How do you know it?
Dav.   Thus; your father called
 Me on one-side, and told me that he wished
 That you should wed to-day; he prattled, too,
 On this and that, all foreign to the matter.
 I cut off to the Forum to find you.
 I found you not. I climbed a pedestal,
 And looked around about; I saw you not.
 I ran then against Byrrhia—I asked him,
 But he had seen you not. I—fidgety,
 And what to do was puzzling, thence returning,
 Suspicion entered in my brain—eh, eh!

No purchases for supper, old man sad,
Babbling of nuptials—incoherently.
Pam. Get on, get on.
Dav. So I set off to Chremes,
And when I came—no porter, no one there,
The gateway void—and I began to joy.
Cha. With reason too.
Pam. Get on.
Dav. I stood awhile,
I did not see a soul. No matron there,
No decorations, tumult—not a sound.
I entered—looked around.
Pam. What signifies?
Dav. Does that resemble nuptials?
Pam. Davè, I doubt.
Dav...How do you doubt? I say the thing is sure;
And after that I met the boy of Chremes
With fishes, and an obolus of herbs.
Cha. You have revived me.
Dav. What is this to you?
Cha. Chremes wont give his daughter unto him.
Dav. What stuff you talk. Because he weds her not,
Is that a reason sure that you must wed her?
You must look out, you must beseech your friends
Or you will go without her.
Cha. Very true,
And you admonish well. I'll set about it,
Although I often failed before. Farewell.

ACT II.—Scene 3.—Pamphilus—Davus.

Pam. What does my father mean?　Why simulate?
Dav. I will tell you why.　First, he is angry now
　With Chremes and his promise now withdrawn,
　He thinks such retractation is injurious—
　Your sentiments unknown.　If you refuse
　The alliance proffered, he will transfer his wrath
　To you, and there will be a precious row.
Pam. But shall I suffer that?
Dav.　　　　　　　　　　He is your father,
　Pamphilus, and has authority; whilst she,
　Poor soul, is sole and unprotected—he
　Will soon find means to exile her from hence.
Pam. Exile?
Dav.　　　　　And quickly.
Pam.　　　　　　　　　　What, Davus, must I do?
Dav. Say you are ready.
Pam.　　　　　　　　No.
Dav.　　　　　　　　What do you say?
Pam. I ready.
Dav.　　　　　Wherefore not?
Pam.　　　　　　　　　　I never will.
Dav. Do not say so.
Pam.　　　　　　Nay, ask it not.
Dav.　　　　　　　　　　　But look,
　What will occur?
Pam.　　　　　　It will occur that I
　Shall lose the one I love, and have the other.
Dav. Not so, not so.　Your father will speak thus:
　I do desire that you shall wed to-day.

You will reply—Behold me ready, father.
He cannot scold you more, and all his plans,
Determinations, cast to all the winds.
You need not fear, for Chremes will refuse
To give her anywise ; so fear not him.
Now say it bravely, without hesitation—
Say, Father, I am ready.   For do not think
That you are master of yourself, or can
Command events by acting as you please.
He is determined now that you shall wed,
To take one dowerless, to have his way.
Consent with him, and throw him off his guard,
And he will go to sleep—and act no more ;
In the mean time, something may turn up good.
Pam. You think so ?
Dav.   Out of doubt.
Pam.   Ah, take you heed.
Dav. Be still, I say.
Pam.   Well, I consent.   But look !
    He must know nothing of the infant child.
    I have promised her to rear it.
Dav.   Madness !
Pam. She has besought, and I have promised it.
    It is a pledge, I never will desert her.
Dav. It shall be seen to ; but your father comes.
    Be careful and disguise your melancholy.

ACT II.—Scene 4.—Simo—Davus—Pamphilus.

Sim. I stroll about, to see what they are at,
    What they devise.
Dav.   The old man is uneasy,

He thinks you will refuse; he meditates
In silent solitude; and practises
A grand oration, pitiful to hear.
Prepare you ready then, it is for you.
Pam. Ah! if I can, my Davus.
Dav.   Credit me,
O Pamphilus. He will not have a word
To utter, if you say that you will wed.

ACT II.—Scene 5.—Byrrhia—Simo—Davus—Pamphilus.

Byr. My master bids me, quitting other matters,
To keep an eye on Pamphilus, and learn
His mind about this marriage; therefore, I
Follow the old man here; and here I meet
Davus and Pamphilus; that is all right.
Sim. Behold them both.
Dav.   Take care; hem!
Sim.   Pamphilus.
Dav. Look round promiscuously.
Pam.   Hem, father mine.
Dav. Well done that.
Sim.   To-day I marry you—to-day.
It is my will, I say.
Byr.   I tremble, and await
His answer—what?
Pam.   Father, I am prepared
Both now and ever to obey your will.
Byr. Eh—what?
Dav. [*Aside.*] Struck dumb.
Sim.   You do that which becomes you;
According, with much sense, what I demand.

Dav. All right!
Byr.   My master may go troop elsewhere.
Sim. Go in, and wait within till we have need.
Pam. I go!
Byr.   No faith in man; put not your trust in man.
  Truly the proverb says—That everyone
  Must take care of himself and not another.
  I know the maiden, of a faultless form,
  And, doubtless, Pamphilus is more content
  To clasp her in his arms—in lieu of other.
  Now to my master, to get my reward,
  The portion I shall have for my good news.

ACT II.—Scene 6.—Davus—Simo.

Dav. He thinks me now a-hatching roguery,
  And therefore keeps me here.
Sim.   What say you, Davus?
Dav. Ah! nothing to the purpose.
Sim.   Purpose, how?
Dav. Nothing at all.
Sim.   Yet I expected something.
Dav. [*Aside.*] He is put out.   I know it—in a rage.
Sim. Now can you speak the truth?
Dav.   Nought easier.
Sim. This marriage, now, has sorely hit my son;
  All through his intercourse with that same stranger.
Dav. Hercle! Not so; or, if he be put out,
  'Tis but a matter of a day or two.
  He will forget it; for you now perceive
  He has surrendered to run the right way.

Sim. And I am glad.

Dav.   Whilst things permitted it
And age allowed, he loved—but silently—
He was most mindful of the world's report—
His reputation. Now behoves to marry,
And now he is on fire to have a wife.

Sim. But he seemed sad, to me.

Dav.   .   But not for that,
There is a matter he is wrath with you.

Sim. What ?

Dav.   Boy's fantasy !

Sim.   But what ?

Dav.   Ah ! nothing.

Sim. Say what ?

Dav.   Ah, well ! you make no feast ;
Art niggard.

Sim.   Me ?

Dav.   You ; not ten drachmas spent.
" Upon the feast and marriage of his son,
Whom of my friends has he bid to the supper ? "
Now, by my word, you do this niggardly ;
Neither do I approve it.

Sim.   Hold your jaw.

Dav. [*Aside.*] I hit him there.

Sim.   I will take care for that.
All shall go right enough. What does this mean ?
He is a sly old fox ; if aught go wrong.
I see and know the author well enough.

ACT III.

Scene 1.—Mysis—Simo—Davus—Lesbia— Glycerium.

Mys. Pol ! Lesbia, what you say is very true.
  You may go far to find a faithful lover.
Sim. Is this the maiden of the Andrian ?
Dav. Yes, yes.
Mys.   But Pamphilus—this Pamphilus—
Sim. Eh, what ?
Mys.   Has kept his plighted troth.
Sim.   Hem, hem.
Dav. Would either he were deaf, or they were mute.
Mys. And he has given commands to rear the babe.
Sim. O Jupiter ! ·What is the thing I hear ?
  It's lost—if what she states is veritable.
Les. Now, by my credit, an ingenuous lad.
Mys. An excellent.   Now follow me within ;
  Perchance my mistress needs you.
Les.   Come away.
Dav. Davus, how now, how remedy this freak ?
Sim. Is it credible—I ask, now—credible ?
  What, from a stranger ?   Ah ! now, I perceive—
  Ah, what a dunce am I !
Dav.   What does he say ?
Sim. It is that rascal's villany, to feign
  This parturition ; there is no such thing—
  Only to frighten Chremes.
Gly. [*Within.*] Juno Lucina ! help—help I beseech you !
Sim. Oh, oh ! directly—quite absurd—so soon
  As I am at the doorway—cry away.

Davus, you have not managed the plot well,
You don't divide the acts.

Dav.   How, master, me ?

Sim. Your actors lose their cue.

Dav.   I know not what,
Master, you say.

Sim.   Ah ! if this rogue now had
Caught me in a loose moment, unprepared,
I had been nicely fooled, or if in earnest —
But now he will be shipwrecked—the whilst I
Sail into port.

ACT III.—Scene 2.—Simo—Davus—Lesbia—Archillis.

Les. Archillis ! everything as yet goes well ;
All promising a speedy convalescence.
Firstly the bath, and afterwards the potion,
Pursuant both to time and quantity.
I will return immediately.   Ecastor,
A noble boy is born to Pamphilus.
May the good gods preserve him—for so kind
And good a father, and who would not wrong
The mother by its death.

Sim.   Now who can doubt,
Hearing this stuff, but that you are its author.

Dav. Author of what ?

Sim.   Why, mark you, in the house
She held her peace, nor issued her commands ;
But thence departed,—forthwith she begins
Here in the street to bellow out this stuff.
Oh, Davè ! did you think me such a fool
To be deceived, to be outwitted thus—

Grossly and openly.   Davus, learn your craft,
That at the least you may pretend to fear me.
Dav. [*Aside.*] Hercle! he cheats himself—It is not I.
Sim. Did I not bid you lay by trickery?
And have you done so?   And with what result?
Think you I will believe this child is his?
Dav. I see his error, and I catch my cue.
Sim. Why are you silent?
Dav.   Think you would believe?
Did not some one inform you of all this?
Sim. Inform me, who?
Dav.   Eh, did you guess, yourself,
That this was all a mime?
Sim.   They mock at me.
Dav. You were informed, else how could you have had
Such a suspicion?
Sim.   How, because I know you.
Dav. You seem to think and say, it was my counsel.
Sim. Without a doubt it is.
Dav.   There, Simo, let me say
You know me not.
Sim.   How so, I know you not?
Dav. The instant I begin to tell the truth,
You think that I deceive.
Sim.   Lies!
Dav.   So, hercle! I
Dare not to open mouth.
Sim.   I know full well
No one has brought forth here.
Dav.   It may be so,
But that will not prevent them bringing here
An infant, and to lay it at your door.

I tell you, master, what will come to pass
So that it may not take you unprepared,
And that you may not think it was the deed
By trick or counsel, of this brain of mine.
Henceforth I would stand right in your opinion.
Sim. How do you know this ?
Dav.   I heard it, and believe it ;
A thousand things concur.   This woman, first,
Says she is great with child by Pamphilus.
Well, that's a lie.   Next, when she hears of nuptials,
She sends to seek a midwife, who then brings
An infant to her ; for, unless you see
The child with your own eyes, you won't believe,
Neither retard these nuptials.
Sim.   What is this ?
If you were cognizant of such a plot,
Why did you not tell Pamphilus ?
Dav.   Who, I !
Who else, save I, has weaned him from this girl !
We know the fervour wherewith he adored her,
And now he asks a wife.   Let me alone,
Let me conclude this matter.   The mean time
Do you push on this wedding, and I trust
The gods will bring it to a good result.
Sim. Well, get you in ; and wait you for me there,
And get all things in order—do you hear !

ACT III.—Scene 3.—Simo.

I know not what to think of this, or if
The fellow tells me true or tells me false.
Nor do I care ; for, what concerns me most,

My son has made the promise.   Now, I go
To find out Chremes, and to win the wife.
If he consents, I see no reason why
This marriage should not come to pass, to-day.
Altho' my son consents, there is no doubt
My rights paternal also may constrain him.
Here Chremes comes, and at the nick of time.

ACT III.—Scene 4.—Simo—Chremes.

Sim. Health unto Chremes!
Chr.   Ah ! I sought for you.
Sim. I sought for you, too.
Chr.   You come at the wish.
  I hear that you have rumoured it abroad
  To-day your son is to wed with my daughter.
  Now, are my neighbours crazy, or are you ?
Sim. Now, hear me a few words.   You know my wishes—
  You know the truth of what you now demand.
Chr. Speak then, I am attention.
Sim.   By the gods,
  I do entreat you, Chremes : by that friendship
  Which has existed from our early boyhood,
  And which has grown with years.   I do entreat you, by
  Your only daughter and my only son,
  Whose happiness is now within your hands,
  Aid and consent to this ; and suffer now
  This marriage, promised, and then broken off.
Chr. Nay, ask it not, I say ; and do not deem
  That this can be accorded unto prayers.
  Think you that I am other than I was,
  When I consented to their nuptials ?   If

They are consistent with their happiness,
Then call them hither, let them marry straight.
If, on the other hand, they bode for ill—
Evil to both—I pray you pause a while;
Let us take counsel in this case together,
As if she were your daughter, he my son.

Sim. Therefore I wish it, therefore I demand it;
Ah, Chremes! if it were not evident
For good, I would not ask it.

Chr.   Well, how so?

Sim. Glycerium and my son have fallen out.

Chr. Well:

Sim.   And irretrievably, as I believe.

Chr. Fables!

Sim.   Nay, it is fact.

Chr.   Hercle! e'en thus:
"Quarrels of lovers but renew their love."

Sim. Ah, Chremes! aid us, whilst the time avails;
Whilst passion is the prey of contumely;
Before the harlot tears convert to smiles;
Before the angry humour change to love,
Grant him the wife; won by connubial bliss,
And conversation with a worthy wife,
He will retrieve himself from depths of ill.

Chr. It may seem so to you, but not to me;
I have no faith in his so fickle love;
Nor will I trust it.

Sim.   But how can you tell,
Unless you make essayal?

Chr.   Essayal, by the hand
Of my dear daughter—no—that were unjust!

Sim. The utmost inconvenience could arise

Would be their disagreement—Gods avert it !—
And separation.   On the other hand,
Mark the great gains : first, you reclaim a son
For me, your friend ; you gain a worthy son—
Your daughter, too, a husband not unworthy.
Chr. Do you believe so ?   If you so believe,
  I am unable to refuse your plea.
Sim. Chremes ! I ever loved you, very dearly.
Chr. But—
Sim.   But what ?
Chr.   How know you they have quarrelled ?
Sim. Davus, who knows, revealed it unto me ;
  And begs besides to hurry on the match.
  Think you that he would do so unadvised,
  Or contrary to wish of Pamphilus ?
  Nay, you shall hear it with your very ears.
  Eh, Davus, hither !   Ah ! here Davus comes.

ACT III.—Scene 5.—Davus—Simon—Chremes.

Dav. I sought you.
Sim.   Eh, what now ?
Dav.   Where is the wife ?
  Where are these tardy nuptials ?
Sim.   There, you hear.
  Davus, I own I held you in distrust,
  Suspected you, that like to other servants
  That you would serve my son, betraying me.
Dav. That I was such a one ?
Sim.   Ay, I believed it ;
  Therefore I hid, what now I will reveal.
Dav. What ?

Sim. I now put confidence in you.

Dav. You know me now, at last.

Sim. Those nuptials were
Only a feint.

Dav. Look now, I never could
Unfold that mystery. Ah, bah! What depth
Of cleverness.

Sim. Listen, I will tell all.
Now, when I bade you to go in the house,
Chremes I met outside.

Dav. [*Aside.*] Then we are lost.

Sim. I told him what you told me.

Dav. [*Aside.*] Bother it !

Sim. I asked him for his daughter, and he grants her.

Dav. I am knocked down.

Sim. Eh, what is that you said ?

Dav. I am enchanted, quite.

Sim. No obstacles
Existing on his side.

Chr. And I will hence go home,
Get matters forwarded, and then return.

Sim. And Davus, since through you this happiness
Hath come to pass—

Dav. Yes, truly so, through me.

Sim. Try and control my son.

Dav. Ay, if I can.

Sim. Whilst that his soul is irritated—urge—

Dav. Depend on me.

Sim. Off then, where is he now ?

Dav. Most probably at home.

Sim. I'll keep him there,
And tell him of these things now come to pass.

Dav. I'm in a mess.   Now, with the right foot forward,
Sent to the mill.   Prayer will be useless now.
I have upset all—I have deceived my master,
Hurled him into a marriage that he hates—
And hurried on, despite of the old man,
Against the will of Pamphilus.   Zounds, I'm astute!
If I had never meddled—never made,
This had not come to pass.   Ah! Pamphilus
Himself; I sink—I faint.   Oh, that there were
A precipice whence I might cast myself!

ACT III.—Scene 6.—Pamphilus—Davus.

Pam. Where is that villain who has ruined me?
Dav. I am undone!
Pam.   And I need blame myself.
Incredible stupidity! to trust
One's dearest fortunes to a stolid slave!
I reap the fruits of my absurdity,
But he shall not unpunished so depart.
Dav. If I get out of this, I need not fear
The future pranks of fortune.
Pam.   What can I
Say to my father; that I will not marry—
When but an hour since I gave consent.
With what face can I say so?   I know not
What I can do.
Dav.   Nor I—howe'er I search;
And yet not so, for I have a device,
Which now I must impart to him, and will.
Pam. Oh!
Dav.   He spies me.

Pam.   Eho ! thou honest man !
  Do you acknowledge where your counsels led me ?
Dav. I labour now to extricate—
Pam.   To extricate ?
Dav. Truly so, Pamphilus.
Pam.   Ay—even as before.
Dav. Not so, I trust, but with a better fortune.
Pam. Think you—I will believe you, furcifer !
    Can you restore a thing that 's lost and gone ?
    Oh ! from a state of happiness, to be
    Cast down to depths of married misery !
    I told you it would be so.
Dav.   You did so.
Pam. And what do you deserve.
Dav.   Deserve the cross—
    Grant me a moment, let me think a while—
    Devize some plan.
Pam.   I have no leisure now
    To punish, nor to think of punishment.
    I must see to myself—my own affairs
    Have now the sway o'er me and mastery.

ACT IV.

SCENE 1.—CHARINUS—PAMPHILUS—DAVUS.

Cha. Oh! is it credible, or to be found,
　Or did one ever hear of treachery,
　Innate in the black heart, to match with this—
　To gloat on ills of others and to reap
　From thence advantages?　Ah, even so,
　There is a race of man so treacherous,
　Who first blush to deny you—yet fall off
　At the first show of false necessity
　Unwilling for a while—then yielding to
　Their interests—and straightway launching out
　In impudent and insolent discourse—
　Who are you? and, what may you be to me?
　Or, what are mine to you?　I am myself,
　My nearest relative; but if you ask,
　Oh! where then is good faith? they do not blush.
　When there was no occasion, then they blushed;
　And now there is occasion they blush not.
　What shall I do—shall I go find him out,
　Expostulate, and overwhelm with words?
　You will reply—what good can come of that?
　Much—he is troubled and I am avenged.
Pam. Charinus, I have lost, unwittingly,
　Thee and myself, unless the gods assist us.
Cha. How, lost unwittingly?　You find a cause
　Sufficient, and you break your word.
Pam. What cause sufficient?

Cha.   Cease now to delude
  With further words.
Pam.   Charinus, what means this?
Cha. I told you I adored her—and away.
  You love her also—my unhappy chance
  To judge of other's natures by my own.
Pam. Wrong—you are wrong.
Cha.   Was not your happiness
  Sufficiently complete, unless you had
  Another's misery to triumph o'er.
  Go, wed her!
Pam.   Wed her? Ah! you do not know
  The misery in which that carnifex
  Of mine has now involved me hopelessly!
Cha. Not wonderful, when he obeys his lord.
Pam. You would not say so if you knew the truth,
  Nor if you knew my heart.
Cha.   I know them well.
  You long opposed your father: he was wroth,
  So wrathful, that to-day you have submitted,
  Consenting to espouse.
Pam.   It was not so.
  You do not know the truth: this marriage was
  Only a feint—a stratagem to prove me—
  There was no wife.
Cha.   And you coerced yourself.
Pam. Wait, hear the rest.
Cha.   The rest is that you marry.
Pam. Why will you kill me with your bitter thoughts?
  He never ceased to press me to this deed,
  Submission to my father—and to yield,
  And I at last consented.

Cha.   Who is *he?*

Pam. Davus.

Cha.   Davus.

Pam.   Davus has done the wrong.

Cha. Wherefore?

Pam.   Methinks the gods were wrath with me.
 I know not else why I obeyed his counsels.

Cha. Davus, did you do this?

Dav.   I did.

Cha.   Then why?
 May the gods' curse light on you for the deed.
 Tell me—if every bitter enemy
 Had counselled so, what worse they could have done.

Dav. I was deceived; but I do not give in.

Cha. That, I believe.

Dav.   The project has gone wrong,
 We must essay another. Do not think
 Because we are rebuffed that we are beaten.

Pam. So much the contrary, I am convinced
 That if you manage well as heretofore,
 Out of one marriage you may make me twain.

Dav. Pamphilus, I am your slave—and I am bound
 To labour day and night on your behalf,
 To peril life itself to profit you.
 And it behoves you, Pamphilus, to bear
 The event, as it may turn out, good or bad.
 I do not spare myself—I do my best,
 Find but another better, and dismiss me.

Pam. Most readily—but it is requisite
 You leave me where you found me: where I was.

Dav. I will.

Pam.   But now, at need.

Dav. Hist! hark a while,
The hinges of Glycerium's portal creak.
Pam. But that does not concern you.
Dav. I will see.
Pam. Well, and your plan?
Dav. Master, my plan is this.

ACT IV.—SCENE 2.—MYSIS—PAMPHILUS—CHARINUS –
DAVUS.

Mys. Wherever he may be, be sure I'll find him
And bring him hither. Do not fret,—my soul,
And trouble so the flesh.
Pam. Mysis—how now?
Mys. Ah! Pamphilus,—met at a happy time,
I come to seek you.
Pam. Well, and what is it?
Mys. My mistress wishes most impetuously
To see you, Pamphilus: she prays you go,
If that you love her, go!
Pam. This evil grows.
I am undone, undone—behold your work.
She in her misery now supplicates,
Because she hears the rumour of this deed.
Cha. How happy in quiescence had you been,
Had he been quiet.
Dav. Go on—enrage him more—
As if he had not woes enough to bear.
Mys. Ah! edepol she has, and that afflicts her,
Her spirits are depressed and miserably.
Pam. Mysis, I swear, by the great gods I swear,

I will desert her—never.   Come what may,
The enmity of all the world, I care not;
For I besought her love, I have her love,
We love each other well—no force shall part;
Nothing, save death, shall separate us twain.
Mys. I breathe again.
Pam.   Apollo's oracles
  Are not more sure than this—this will I do.
  If that my father can be made believe,
  I am not the obstruction, that will do.
  If he will not—then I declare myself
  Unwilling and recalcitrant, Charinus.
Cha. Equal are we in misery.
Dav.   I seek a remedy.
Cha. And you are capable, methinks, to find one.
Dav. And I have an impediment prepared.
Pam. It must be now, directly.
Dav.   And it shall.
Cha. What is it?
Dav.   Lest you blurt, I shall not tell.
  This is my master's matter.
Cha.   Be it so.
Pam. Tell me the matter.
Dav. '   Is the day so long
  That I have time to stand and prate about it,
  I must be up and doing.   Go away—
  Go both of you—your presence hinders me.
Pam. I will go see Glycerium.
Dav.   And you.
Cha. Shall I tell truth?
Dav.   Confound it—some long story.
Cha. What will become of me?

Dav.   Be off with you.

   You must be now contented with reprieve

   Hereafter for your wooings.

Cha.   But, Davè—Davè.

Dav. Well, what?

Cha.   Win her for me.

Dav.   Ridiculous!

Cha. But come and tell me, if your plot succeeds.

Dav. Why so? and if I fail.

Cha.   If you fail not.

Dav. Why then I will.

Cha.   And I shall be at home.

Dav. Mysis, do you stop here and wait for me.

Mys. How so?

Dav.   You must.

Mys.   Well, hurry then.

Dav.   I will.

ACT IV.—Scene 3.—Mysis.

Is mortal happiness e'er durable?

   Faith of the gods! I thought that Pamphilus

   Was the best blessing could befall my mistress,

   A friend, a lover, and a husband, all

   Combined, to make her happy—and, behold!

   Oh, what a load of human misery!

   Assuredly less pleasure than of pain

   Has fallen to her lot by loving him.

   Davus comes out—my man! hollou, I say,

   Where do you bear that babe?

ACT IV.—Scene 4.—Mysis—Davus.

Dav. Now, Mysis, waken wits, and look alive:
　I want your aid, your wit, and self-possession.
Mys. What is it all about?
Dav.　　　　　　　　Quick—take the babe,
　And go depose him, now, before our gate.
Mys. Upon the ground?
Dav.　　　　　　　　Snatch the verbena there
　From off the altar—make a bed of those.
Mys. Why not do that yourself?
Dav.　　　　　　　　If I must swear
　To our old master, that I did not do it,
　I shall make oath with a more liquid conscience.
Mys. I see. Oppressed by new religions qualms.
　Give me the babe.
Dav.　　　　　Now set about it quick,
　And ask me afterwards the reasons why.
　Proh Jupiter!
Mys.　　　　　What?
Dav.　　　　　　　　The father of the bride,
　He comes—I change my mind—stop.
Mys.　　　　　　　　Wherefore stop?
Dav. Mysis, I now am come from the right hand,
　So I declare; support me with your word,
　Don't contradict, say nothing but at need.
Mys. I understand you not, but what of that?
　If I can serve your turn in anything,
　And you see more than I—I will assist,
　For fear to cast obstructions in your path.

ACT IV.—Scene 5.—Chremes—Mysis—Davus.

Chr. I want to get things ready to return,
  Now they are all prepared; but what is this?
  Hercle! a boy babe. Woman, say, did you
  Depose him here.
Mys.   Where is he, where?
Chr. Why not respond to me?
Mys.   Where is he, where?
  What, run away and left me? fie for shame!
Dav. Faith of the gods! why, what a turmoil reigns
  Now in the Forum! How men litigate,
  And how all things are dear! Ah! what to think of things
  I do not know.
Mys.   But why leave me alone?
Dav. What do you prate about? Holloa! How now,
      Mysis, whose babe is this? Who brought it here?
Mys. Eh? Are you mad, or what—to ask me that?
Dav. Who can I ask else? You alone are here.
Chr. I wonder whence he is.
Dav.   Reply, will you,
  To what I ask.
Mys.   Ah!
Dav. [*to Mysis.*]   Jump on this right hand.
Mys. Are you mad—yourself?
Dav. [*to Mysis.*]   Now, if you speak a word
  Save in reply to me—I say, beware!
Mys. You menace me?
Dav.   Whence is he? Speak out plain.
Mys. From home.
Dav.   Ah, ah, ah!—impudent beyond belief!
Chr. This is the Andrian's damsel, as I think.

Dav. What do you think to play upon us so:
  Are we such likely persons to be duped?
Chr. I came here in good time.
Dav.   I say, my girl,
  Just carry off this brat before the gate.
  [*Aside.*] Don't move a jot; stand just now as you are.
Mys. May gods uproot you!   How you frighten me!
Dav. Is it to you I speak, or not?
Mys.   Eh, what?
  What do you want?
Dav.   A pretty question that—
  Who owns the brat you laid there, tell me that?
Mys. As if you did not know.
Dav.   As if I did not know—
  Answer me straight.
Mys.   Well, then, of your—
Dav. Your who?
Mys.   Your Pamphilus.
Dav.   Our Pamphilus
  How so?
Mys.   How so—say, is it not so?   Eh?
Chr. With reason I have ever feared this match.
Dav. Oh! libel, libellous and actionable!
Mys. Why bawl you so!
Dav.   Did I not yesterday
  See you bear this thing home?
Mys.   O villain, rogue!
Dav. But it is truth.   Why, I saw Canthara
  With bundle 'neath her robe.
Mys.   Pol! I am glad
  Matrons freeborn * were present at the birth.

------

* Slaves could not bear testimony.

Dav. You know not him on whom you play these pranks.
  You think if Chremes saw before these gates
  That baby, that he would not give his daughter.
  He would give her the more quickly.
Chr.   Hercle, no!
  That would I not.
Dav.   Now, I tell you what—
  If you don't take him off at once, I'll roll
  Him in the street, and you into the gutter.
Mys. Pol, you are drunk!
Dav.   One roguery, you see,
  Capped by another; now the rumour runs
  She is a citizen of Attica.
Chr.   Hem!
Dav. And consequently, by the law, his wife.
Mys. Ah! I beseech you, is she not his wife?
Chr. Faith, I have nearly been the laughing-stock
  Of all the town.
Dav.   Who speaks?   O Chremes, here!
  You come when needed.
Chr.   I have heard it all.
Dav. What, heard it all?
Chr.   Commencement to the end.
Dav. What heard it all? The wicked one! we must
  Have her interrogated on the cross.
  You thought that you were only fooling me,
  But he was here.
Mys.   Unhappy I! My master,
  I told the truth.
Chr.   I know it all, I know—
  Is Simo now within?
Dav.   Simo is now within.

ACT IV.—Scene 6.—Mysis—Davus.

Mys. Do not come near me—keep away—you beast,
  Pol! If Glycerium knew what you have said—
Dav. Hist! silly one! Do you not see our drift?
Mys. What drift? Not I.
Dav.   He is the sire-in-law,
  And in that manner, don't you see, we have
  Informed him what we wanted.
Mys.   Hem! But you
  Should have forewarned me.
Dav.   Ah, nay, not at all!
  That which is done in nature, out of hand,
  Is better than premeditated art.

ACT IV.—Scene 7.—Crito—Mysis—Davus.

Cri. Chrysis, they tell me, lodges in this street,
  Who better loved dishonest luxury
  Than a good name with honest poverty.
  All her effects, by law, belong to me,
  For she, I hear, is dead. I must inquire,
  Eh? salvè.
Mys.   Whom do my eyes behold, eh?
  Is this not Crito, cousin unto Chrysis?
Cri. O Mysis, salvè!
Mys.   And salvè also Crito!
Cri. And so, poor Chrysis, eh?
Mys.   Ah! the poor soul
  Has left us wretched.

Cri.   And ye, how do you live?
How are you off for means?
Mys.   Who, we? Alas!
We live, as saith the proverb, how we can,
Who can't live how we would.
Cri.   Glycerium,
Has she found out her friends?
Mys.   Ah, would the gods—
Cri. Not found her friends. With inauspicious foot
Do I come here. Ah! had I only known,
I had stayed where I was. She ever passed
For sister of our Chrysis, and, no doubt,
Inherits all the chattels that she left.
I am a stranger here—to go to law,
Other examples I have witnessed, prove
The trouble and the cost. Besides, I think
She has a friend to aid her—for, look here,
She lives in style. Besides, I shall be deemed
A sycophant, a mendicant, in search
Of her inheritance; and, last of all,
I cannot rob the child.
Mys.   O welcome guest!
Pol! Crito—with a heart as good as ever.
Cri. Since I am here, take me to see her face.
Mys. Most willingly.
Dav.   And I will follow too,
And so keep out of my old master's way.

———————————

ACT V.

Scene 1.—Chremes—Simo.

Chr. Enough—enough now, Simo; I have run
    Myself in peril, in my wish to aid you.
    Cease to entreat me more: in pleasing you
    I nearly sacrificed my daughter's peace.
Sim. But, Chremes, I entreat more earnestly,
    Ah! with increase of vehemence, to fulfil
    Your promise given!
Chr.   Your wishes blind you, Simo.
    You set no bounds to one's benignity.
    You have cast off your reason: if you thought,
    You would perceive you sought what is unjust.
Sim. How so?
Chr.   Ah! dost thou ask? Entreating me
    To grant my daughter to a man engaged,
    Absorbed in other love, and hating marriage,
    To wed her to dissensions, and divorce.
    We are to medicate with our repose,
    Disorders of your son. I gave my word,
    I went to forward things whilst I believed
    The marriage possible. I find it not.
    She is a citizen—a child is born—
    Dispute not further.
Sim.   By all the gods! I say,
    Do not believe a word those creatures say,
    Who do not wish my son to be reclaimed.
    All lies and fictions to break off this match,

And so soon as we win him from their toils,
  They, too, will cease to sue and pester him.
Chr. You are deceived yourself. I chanced to hear
  The maid-servant and Davus at hard words.
Sim. All fable.
Chr.   Not a bit: they were at strife;
  Nor one nor other knew that I was present.
Sim. I do believe it: Davus had forewarned me
  That so it was to be; also to warn you—
  I marvel I was so oblivious.

ACT V.—Scene 2.—Davus—Chremes—Simo—Dromo.

Dav. Now I ordain that all be silent here.
Chr. Hem, Davus—here.
Sim.   Whence doth the fellow come?
Dav. And all attend to me and to this stranger.
Sim. What roguery's this!
Dav.   I never knew a man
  Arrive more opportunely at a time.
Sim. Scoundrel! whom praise you?
Dav.   Matters now are all
  Safely on shore.
Sim.   I will have at him now.
Dav. Master, by Jove!
Sim.   O salvè! honest Sir!
Dav. Hem, Simo and our Chremes, all is laid
  Ready now for you.
Sim.   You have been diligent.
Dav. Whene'er you bring the bride.
Sim.   Ah! very good.
  We only lack the bride. But hark you now!

Reply to what I ask you.　Tell me what
You do within there.

Dav.　　　　　　Who, me?

Sim.　　　　　　　　Ay, you.

Dav. Who, I?

Sim.　　　　You, you I say.

Dav.　　　　　　　A moment since,
Only, did I come here.

Sim.　　　　　I did not ask you when,
But wherefore?

Dav.　　　　With your son.

Sim.　　　　　　　What doth he there?
I am on thorns.　Did you not tell me, sirrah,
That they had quarrelled?

Dav.　　　　　　Ay, that was so.

Sim. Well, then, what doth he there?

Chr. [*With irony.*]　　　What doth he there?
He quarrels with her.

Dav.　　　　　More, O Chremes! more,
An insolence unheard of.　An old man,
Who or from whence I know not; an old man,
With a front bold and sly, who seems to think
Well of himself—with face of formal cut,
And words of candour.

Sim.　　　　　Well, what stuff is this!

Dav. Nought; save for what he said.

Sim.　　　　　　What did he say?

Dav. Glycerium is an Attic citizen.

Sim. Hey, Dromo! Dromo!

Dav.　　　　　What's the matter now?

Sim. Dromo!

Dav.　　Hear!

Sim.   Speak not a word.   Eh! Dromo.

Dav. Hear, I entreat you.

Dro.   Master!

Sim.   Haul him hence;
Haul him within directly.

Dro.   Whom?

Sim.   Him—Davus.

Dav. Wherefore?

Sim.   Because I choose: haul him within.

Dav. What have I done?

Sim.   Haul! haul!

Dav.   If I have told a lie,
Then murder me.

Sim.   I will not hear you, but
Give it you, soundly.

Dav.   But I spoke truth.

Sim. See that he be well bound; and, hear you, hear!
Bind him by hand and feet.   Pol! if I live,
I will shew you, my man, that peril lies
In treason to your master, and to me,
The father.

Chr.   Nay, be not in a passion.

Sim. Chremes! is this then filial piety? is this
Respect due unto me? or shall I care
For such a son? oh Pamphilus, I say,
Come forth, come forth and blush.

ACT V.—Scene 3.—Pamphilus—Simo—Chremes.

Pam. Who summons me? My father, I'm undone!

Sim. What dost thou say? Of all—

Chr.   ' Forbear, I say ;
  Speak calmly to him, without rhapsody.
Sim. If it were possible with what he has done —·
  Say is Glycerium **a** citizen ?
Pam. They so affirm.
Sim.   They so affirm ; do they ?
  A most outrageous impudence—is there
  A falter in his voice—blush on his brow ?
  Is there a sign of penitence or shame ?
  Ah ! can it be ? so impotent of mind,
  So callous to the laws, so hostile to
  His filial obedience—father's hopes—
  To wed to ignominy and disgrace.
Pam. I am most wretched.
Sim.   Do you, Pamphilus,
  Learn that to-day ?—You should have wretched been
  Before you gave unbridled passion reins.
  Now truly may you say you're miserable.
  But wherefore do I trouble so my soul—
  Wherefore torment my mind—excruciate
  My old age—weary me to madness—
  Shall I endure the penalties for him ?
  No ; let him troop and go and—live with her.
Pam. My Father !
Sim.   Ay, my Father ; as though you
  Needed a father : you have house and home
  And wife and child, and all against his will.
  You bring your sycophants to prove that she
  Is a free-born of Attica.   I yield.
Pam. Father, will you permit me a few words ?
Sim. Wherefore—what words ?
Chr.   Yet, Simo, let him speak.

Sim. I hear him? wherefore, Chremes, should I hear?
Chr. Nay, suffer him.
Sim.   I suffer him; speak on.
Pam. Father, I do avow I am in love,
  And, if that be a crime, am criminal.
  But, father, I submit; impose on me
  Your pleasure, what you will; for if you wrench
  Me from her arms I love, I must submit.
  But do not think I have suborned this man
  To do you wrong; and let me bring him here.
Sim. Him here!
Pam.   Oh, suffer it, my father.
Chr.   Do;
  For what he asks is just.
Pam.   Oh do, I pray.
Sim. I suffer it: Chremes, I would comply
  With what you wish, avoiding all deceit.
Chr. However great the errors of a son,
  Sufficient is rebuke from hands paternal.

ACT V.—Scene 4.—Crito—Chremes—Simo—Pamphilus.

Cri. Beseech no more; sufficient were one cause
  Of three impelling me, yourself, the truth,
  And love I bear Glycerium.
Chr.   Do I behold—
  The Andrian Crito?
Cri.   Health be unto you, Chremes.
Chr. And what do you at Athens?
Cri.   Wherefore I—
  But is this Simo?
Chr.   Ay.

Sim.   Doth he seek me?
  Do you affirm that this Glycerium is
  A free-born Attican?
Cri.   Do you deny it?
Sim. Do you come hither thus prepared?
Cri.   Prepared!
Sim. Prepared: to play the rogue, delude our youth,
  And with impunity to spread your nets
  And lures for generous youth; with promises
  And vile solicitations, snaring them.
Cri. Are you insane?
Sim.   From meretricious loves
  To bind a marriage?
Pam.   The stranger is upset
  By these reproaches.
Chr.   Simo, you know him not.
  He is not what you say; he worthy is.
Sim. Or worthy or unworthy, how comes it
  That he arrives at this unlooked for hour,
  When I would wed my son unto another,
  And heretofore unknown. Is that a tale
  To be believed? say, Chremes.
Pam.   If I did not fear
  My father's wrath—ah! I could prompt a word.
Sim. A sycophant!
Cri.   Ah!
Chr.   Ah! pardon, Crito, pray,
  He is angry.
Cri.   Be it so—but he
  Must curb his tongue, or I shall say in turn
  What may displease him. What have I to do
  With your disorders—what are they to me!

It seems to me you need the equal mind
To bear your ills. For me, I speak the truth.
There was an Attican was shipwrecked on
The Isle of Andros; with him was this girl.
He chanced to light upon the father of
Our Chrysis—in extremity of ill.

Sim. Fables.

Chr.   Let him speak.

Cri.   But wherefore interrupt?

Chr. Proceed.

Cri.   Her father was my relative,
And in his house he died, declaring he
Was Attican.

Chr.   His name—his name?

Cri.   Was Phania.

Chr. Ah, I am slain.

Cri.   Doubtless, 'twas Phania,
Moreover of the burgh Rhamnusium.

Chr. Oh, Jupiter!

Cri.   It is well-known in Andros.

Sim. And grant it may be so. Now tell me, Crito,
What did he say of her? Was she his child?

Cri. No.

Chr.   And whose?

Cri.   His brother's.

Chr.   And my daughter!

Cri. How—what!

Sim.   What!

Pam.   Lift up your ears, O Pamphiló.

Sim. Do you believe this, Chremes?

Chr.   Yes. Phania—
He was my brother.

Sim.   True ; I know him well.

Chr. He fled from hence and war.   He followed me
　To Asian shores, where then I was.   He led
　My daughter with him, daring not to leave her.
　And lo ! the first that I have heard of her.

Pam. I am beside myself, with spirit stirred
　By fears and hope and joy.   I am o'erfraught
　With gladness, and with unexpected wonder.

Sim. Chremes, I am glad ; for many reasons glad,
　That you have found your child.

Pam.   Surely, my father.

Chr. But one doubt troubles me—one doubt remains.

Pam. Confound your stupid doubt.   I hate the man
　Seeking for doubts where there can none exist.

Cri. Pronounce it.

Chr.   IIer name was not Glycerium.

Cri. Assuredly, she had another name.

Chr. What was it ?

Cri.   Ah ! if I can call to mind.

Pam. What, shall I suffer a bad memory
　To blight and blast my joy, when I myself
　Have the remedial knowledge ?   I will not.
　Chremes, her name was Pasibula then.

Cri. It is.

Chr.   It is.

Pam.   We often call her so.

Sim. Chremes, I give you joy, I give you joy.
　You credit me ?

Chr.   I do assuredly.

Pam. My father, now——

Sim.   My son, the late annoyance
　Becomes a blessing now.

Pam. My dearest father,
  If Chremes now consents and grants his daughter.
Chr. Nay, I am willing, if your father is.
Pam. Ah! surely.
Sim. I consent.
Chr. And, Pamphilus,
  Her dower is ten talents.
Pam. Most content.
Chr. I hurry to my child. Ah, Crito, come!
  Come with me, for she knows me not!
Sim. Wherefore
  Not bring her home?
Pam. True, true; I will find Davus.
Sim. He cannot.
Pam. Who?
Sim. For he has business
  Imports himself more nearly.
Pam. What is that?
Sim. He is bound.
Pam. He is unjustly bound.
Sim. I so commanded.
Pam. Oh, bid the contrary.
Sim. So be it then.
Pam. Without delay.
Sim. I go.
Pam. O happy and O most auspicious day.

ACT V.—Scene 5.—Charinus—Pamphilus.

Cha. I sought for Pamphilus, and lo, behold him!
Pam. Another one might, perhaps, imagine now
  That I am full of fond imaginings,

And in a fool's elysium.   Now am I
Persuaded that the gods immortal are,
Because their joys have immortality.
And I, too, am immortal in my bliss,
If no mischance step on my happiness.
Oh! for a friend I love the best, to be
My partner in this joy and ecstacy.
Cha. He is rejoicing surely.
Pam.   Davus, ah!
I want you, Davus; no one more than you,
For none more vividly reflects my joys.

ACT V.—Scene 6.—Davus—Pamphilus—Charinus.

Dav. Where then is Pamphilus?
Pam.   Behold! 'tis I.
Dav. O, Pamphilus.
Pam.   Dost know my happy fortune?
Dav. No; but I know my own bad fortune, since
  We parted last.
Pam.   And I—I know it, too.
Dav. The lot of mortals; quicker is the flight
  Of tale of woe than tale of happiness.
Pam. Ah! my Glycerium has found her friends—
  Her father.
Dav.   That is well done.
Cha.   Hem!
Pam. Her father is our friend.
Dav.   Who?
Pam.   Chremes.
Dav.   Good.
  I am rejoiced.

Pam. Nothing forbids the marriage.
Cha. Doth he not dream, and waking, grasps a shade ?
Pam. And the boy, Davus—
Dav. Trouble not yourself ;
  The gods love only him.
Cha. And I am saved,
  If what they say be true. Now will I hail
  And ask.
Pam. Charinus, in a happy hour—
Cha. And I rejoice.
Pam. Oh ! have you heard?
Cha. I have—
  I have heard all; and now that you are blest,
  Aid, and forget me not, I do implore you.
  Chremes is now your relative, and will
  Grant whatsoe'er you ask him.
Pam. And I will.
  But we cannot wait here, Charinus, now
  Until he comes forth from Glycerium.
  Come you with me and seek him. Davus—you,
  Go seek the men to bear her to our house !
  Why do you tarry ? Go!
Dav. I go, I go.
[*To the audience.*]
  Now do not wait until they reappear,
  Whate'er is to be done, will be done there.
  There may be more to do than we can tell ;
  And so applaud us, sirs, and fare ye well.

HEAUTONTIMORUMENOS.

(THE SELF-TORMENTOR.)

PERSONS.

CHREMES—An Elder.
MENEDEMUS—The Self-tormentor.
CLITIPHO—Son of Chremes.
CLINIA—Son of Menedemus.
SYRUS—Slave of Clitipho.
DROMO—Slave of Clinia.
BACCHIS—Meretrix.
ANTIPHILA—Maiden.
SOSTRATA—Matron.
NURSE.
PHRYGIAN DAMSEL.

PROLOGUE.

Lest any of you wonder why the poet
Sends me, an old man, forward, I will show it.
This day we act a drama from the Greek—
Heautontimorumenos—and seek
To make its single plot a double one:
Therefore our comedy is new, or none.
Who wrote the Grecian comedy—you know;
That is one point I have no need to show.
But wherefore am I here, you ask again:
Pleader am I, your suffrages to gain.
Ye are our judges.   We seek your applause
So I, and not the prologue, plead the cause;
And though some tongues malevolent declare
The Grecian plots contaminated are
Whence he indites his Latin, nor doth he
Deny the charge nor will defend the plea.
He can produce authority to show
That greater bards have done so long ago.
Another charge malevolence adduces,
That he with music now your ears seduces,
Instead of his own talents.   We submit
That to your judgment; you must settle it.
Shut up your ears to slanders we entreat you,
And open them to hopes in which we greet you;
Listen to us who weave fair novelties,
Not like the breathless slave who ranting cries,

" Give place, make room,"* and hurling folk about.
Why should he careful be for such a lout ?
Better to quash his crudities than follow
So bad a master; let him cease to holloa.
And now attend and listen to the play,
Whilst I, uninterrupted, say my say ;
Nor rack my legs and lungs upon the stage,
As running slave, or old man in a rage,
Or greedy parasite or sycophant
Or pander merchantman ; but rather grant
Remission from such labours unto me.
For they who now indite the comedy
Demand my aid when they have somewhat dry ;
If volatile to volatiles they fly.†
But this is declamation pure—its zest
Lies in its moral—let me do my best.
I am not overweening, but I fain
Am your applauses and your praise to gain.
Then make me an example, so that they,
Who work to please you, on a future day
May find a beaten track and trodden way.

---

* A cut at the Amphitryon of Plautus, where Mercury, as Sosia, comes dashing on—" Give place, make room," &c."—*Act* III. *sc.* 4. The slave would have been flogged for so doing.

† The *stataria* or *motoria fabula*, stationary or mobile acting : the first to the old men, the second to the slaves.

HEAUTONTIMORUMENOS.

(THE SELF-TORMENTOR.)

ACT I.

Scene 1.—Chremes and Menedemus.

Chr. Neighbour, though yet unknown, for only since
  Your purchase of yon farm our neighbourhood
  Dates its brief space; there something is besides,
  Either your worth or neighbourhood, for they
  Stand next to friendship in my poor conceit,
  Impels me with familiar—nay, bold speech
  To admonish—that your present mode of life
  Is unbeseeming of your age and state.
  For—faith of gods and man!—what do you do?
  What do you hope, desire? Some sixty years,
  As near as I can guess, are on your back;
  You hold the best farm that lies round about,
  Money enough, and slaves; and yet you slave
  As if, forsooth, you were devoid of both.
  Early and late, at dawning morn, and eve,
  Ever at work, for ever fardel-laden,
  No sparing, pity for yourself. You say
  Your slaves are idle; be it so, but you
  Would find your interest more to make them work,
  And be their overseer.

Men.   My neighbour, Chremes,
     Does your superfluous leisure give you time
     To mind, and interfere in deeds of others?

Chr. I am a man; and nought pertaining to
     Humanity is alien unto me.
     For my advice or curiosity,
     I would myself follow a course, if right,
     Or, I would warn another in the wrong.

Men. I do what pleases me, do thou the like.

Chr. But does it please to crucify yourself?

Men. It pleases me.

Chr. I know not what afflicts you,
     Or what great woe may warrant such infliction.

Men. Ah, me! Ah, me!

Chr.   Nay, sigh not so, but say—
     Confide in me, fear not, and let me try
     By sympathy or counsel to console you.

Men. Have you such wish?

Chr.   Truly I have, to aid you.

Men. Then shall you know it.

Chr.   Then lay by that rake,
     And sit you down at ease.

Men.   No!

Chr.   Wherefore no?
     Why not permit yourself a minute's ease?

Men. Leave me alone; I do not ask for ease.

Chr. 1 will not suffer this, I say.

Men.   I say—forbear!

Chr. That heavy rake!

Men.   It should be heavier,
     To counterweigh my fault.

Chr.   Well, say you on.

Men. I have one only son: what do I say?
  I had one only son.   Ah, Chremè, ah!
  Whether I have or not, I do not know.
Chr. Say on.
Men.   I will do so.   From Corinth came
  An ancient dame, and poor: my son became
  Enamoured of her daughter, and desired,
  Beyond controlment, to have her to wife.
  'Twas told me privately; and I began
  To work with all the rigour and oppression,
  Regardless of the mind's infirmity,
  Which parents use to do on such occasions.
  Him I reproached incessantly: you fool,
  Think you that I will suffer in my life
  Authority deposed, that you may live
  With an amica, as with wedded wife?
  You err if so you think.   I tell you, Clinia,
  You do mistake me much: you are my son
  Whilst you do worthily; if you transgress,
  Behoves it then that I do what I ought.
  This dalliance comes from too much idleness,
  And, at your age, I never dreamed of love.
  Well, I was poor, and off I went to Asia,
  To conquer glory and acquire wealth.
  So I went on; until the poor, poor lad,
  O'erwearied by resistance, gave it up.
  He yielded to my age, obedience;
  He thought me wiser than he was himself.
  Ah! Chremes, he has gone to serve the king,
  A soldier, into Asia.
Chr.   What dost thou say?

Men. Clandestinely to Asia; three months since.
Chr. You both did wrongly; and yet he betrayed
  A noble spirit, and a heart of gold.
Men. Those in his secret, after he was gone,
  Informed me then. I wandered homeward bound,
  Bent with my grief; nor knew I what to do.
  I cast me down: slaves drew my slippers off,
  And hurried in the supper. There I lay.
  They did their very best in serving me.
  Their sympathy caused me to muse myself—
  What then was I? Behold how many slaves,
  How many damsels, how impressed to serve
  For me alone! And he, my only son,
  He who should share with me these cares and home,
  Him have I driven forth. And shall I live
  In luxury, and he in want? I will not.
  Unjustly banished; I will be the same;
  And whilst he lives in toils, so I will toil
  And labour, spare, and heap: revenge my boy.
  I put it in effect; I sold my house,
  Vases and vestments, handmaidens and men,
  Excepting labourers; those who could work
  And gain our means; so I raised fifteen talents.
  I bought this farm, and labour night and day;
  For I deem, Chremes, I alleviate
  The injury done, by sharing it with him.
  Nor will I taste of pleasure or repose
  Until the time I share them with my boy.
Chr. Indulgent father, and an upright son.
  Ah! I perceive—misunderstanding, all;
  And, when it is so, everything goes cross.

You hid the depth of your paternal love;
He hid, in turn, his filial confidence;
And thence and thence all this entanglement.
Men. It is too true, and I avow my faults.
Chr. But, Menedemus, things shall all come right;
Here shall he reappear, all sane and sound.
Men. May the gods grant so!
Chr.   Ah! they will, they will.
Come, this is Dionysia; come and sup—
Come, sup with me, and let us keep the feast.
Men. No!
Chr. Why, no?   This " no " will never do;
Your son will blame it, absent though he is.
Men. It were unrighteous, when I have a vow
To labour, I should flee the vow and feast.
Chr. So you resolve?
Men.   Even so.
Chr. Farewell then.
Men.   Fare you well.

ACT I.—Scene 2.—Chremes.

Chr. Pol! I am weeping; he has made me weep.
But the time flies; behoves it me to go
And bid my neighbour Phania come to sup.
It is a long time since he crossed my door.
Be he at home, no need bid him to come.
Then, home to my convives.   Holloa! how now?
Who issues from my house?   I wonder who.
Some one comes forth; I will hide here and see.

ACT I.—Scene 3.—Clitipho—Chremes.

Clit. Fear nothing, Clinia, there is nought to fear;
  They will obey your messenger and come;
  So cast away confounded hopes and fears.
Chr. Whom has my son got there?
Clit.   Ah! here is one.
  My father, as I wished: My father, hail!
Chr. What's this about?
Clit.   Do you know, Menedemus,
  Who lives by here?
Chr.   Yes, well?
Clit.   Has he a son?
Chr. He has, in Asia, one.
Clit.   In Asia, no!
  My father, he is here.
Chr.   What dost thou say?
Clit. I met him now, as he came off the ship;
  I brought him home. Oh! it is very long
  That we have known each other; we, old friends.
Chr. I am right glad to hear it. This is news
  Gives me much pleasure. Bid Menedemus now
  To join our supper. I shall be right glad
  To see his happiness.
Clit.   Do nothing of the sort,
  I do beseech you.
Chr.   Why, nothing of the sort?
Clit. He is all in the clouds, and dreading all;
  His father's anger he is most afraid of.
  Look you, he is in love, most miserably;
  He sailed, and he returns, for sake of her.

Chr. I know it.

Clit.   He has sent a varlet lad
  To her in town ; so I sent Syrus with him.

Chr. What does he say ?

Clit.   He says he is unhappy.

Chr. Unhappy ! stuff ! how can he be unhappy ?
  What hinders him to have all heart's desire—
  His father, country, both in good estate ;
  Friends, birth, relations, riches ?   It is true
  That those possessing these things own them not ;
  Those who possess them not, know well their want ;
  Blessings well used—curses when cast away.

Clit. But this old man, aye, was importunate
  And savage with his son : he fears his father
 · That he will ——

Chr.   He need fear him not—so, so !
  I had best hold my tongue, and leave the lad
  In wholesome filial fear.

Clit. What do you whisper ?

Chr. I was about to say—however wrathful
  May Menedemus be—it is his duty
  To go and see his father ; he will find him, perhaps,
  More angry than he wishes : he must bear it—
  It is his duty ; if he hear not him,
  Whom will he hear ?   Which, think you, is most just —
  A father to submit unto his son, or son
  Unto his father ?   Harshness ! oh yes, harsh !
  I know a little of a father's harshness.
  Hard to forbid—this, that, and t'other thing ;
  Refusing money for the civic lurements,
  And forcing virtue on them.   For if vice
  E'er get firm hold, it holds inherently.

And lay this maxim to your heart, my son—
Let other's wreck teach you to shun the shoal.
Clit. Good faith! I will.
Chr.   And I will now within;
And mind that you are here at supper time.

ACT I.—Scene 4.—Clitipho.

Clit. How unjust are all fathers to their sons!
We should be born with beards; should ne'er be young;
Never have youthful passions—passionless.
They would forsooth have all resemble them.
If e'er I have a son, I will be just;
He shall confide in me, and I in him.
Not like my sire and me, whose constant prate
Is about other's wrecks.   It makes me mad
When he is in his cups; and fain to brag
Of youthful days and deeds; and now, he says,
Take warning, boy, and do not thou the same.
A likely joke, to which my ears are deaf.
My ears hear well enough my mistress' words,
"Bring me," and "give me;" nor dare I reply.
Now Clinia is far better off than I.
He loves a damsel, modest, well brought up—
No meretricious mind—the whilst my dame
Is haughty and presumptuous, full of greed,
Calling for money; and I fain to hide
That I have none—ay, none.   I bear my grief
In solitude.   My father knows it not.

ACT II.

Scene 1.—Clinia—Clitipho.

Cli. If there were tidings good of my beloved,
   I surely should have heard ; for absence saps
   The faith of woman, and a thousand ills—
   Her age and opportunities—the dame,
   Her mother – caring but for gold.
Clit.   Clinia !
Cli. What now—more woe ?
Clit.   Take heed you are not seen
   By anyone, leaving your father's house.
Cli. I will—I have presentiment of ill.
Clit. Now don't prognosticate—we soon shall know.
Cli. Good news comes swiftly—had come long ago.
Clit. Why, it comes now.
Cli.   Now—when ?
Clit.   Well, give it time :
   A girl must dress her hair—adjust herself;
   You know not woman—half a year to dress :
   Look out ; here Dromo and here Syrus come.

ACT II.—Scene 2.—Syrus—Dromo—Clitipho—Clinia.

Syr. Ah ! say'st thou?
Dro.   Verily.
Syr.   But how is this ?
   Whilst we have chattered, they have dropped in rear.
Clit. She cometh, Clinia—dost thou hear ?

Cli.   I hear,
  And I begin to breathe and live.
Dro.   I say,
  Where have they got to? what detains them now?
  Ah! it's that troop of girls.
Cli.   Girls! how should she
  Possess a troop of girls—I perish.
Clit.   . Wait—
  I'll speak to them.
Syr.   We ought not to have left
  Them, and their chattels.
Cli.   Chattels—do you hear!
Syr. Gold, jewels—and the night is coming on,
  And they know not the way.   Dromo look out—
  Run back again—you stand there like a fool.
Cli. There go my hopes anew; unhappy me!
Clit. Well, what's the matter now? what dread you now?
Cli. What dread I now!—servants and jewels—clothes ;—
  And when I left her, she had one young girl.
  Whence then this wealth?
Clit.   Ah, ay, I see!
Syr. Ye gods auspicious! what a troop of girls—
  Our house will never hold them.   Meat and drink!
  And my old master in a rage : ah, here
  Are those I wished to find!
Cli.   Oh Jupiter!
  Where, then, is faith? whilst I fled from my home
  For love of you, Antiphila, and bore
  The ills of exile; you enriched yourself,
  And leave me in my woes ; and you the cause
  That I am blamed by all, and disobeyed
  My father, as I ought not to have done.

I die of shame and passion, when I think
Of all his admonitions—all in vain.
No admonitions tore me from your arms.
Now to retrace my miserable steps,
Obedient, and too late.

Syr.   He heard our talk,
And now he goes and blunders.   Clinia,
Your love and mistress are all fair and true;
She is unchanged—unchangeable, if all
That we have seen and heard of her is sooth.

Cli. What have you seen?   Oh say, oh tell me, tell—
That I suspect her most injuriously!

Syr. Well, first, that you may truly know the whole,
The dame is dead, and she was not her mother.
Now, that I heard by chance upon the road,
From her own lips.

Clit.   Whom told she that?

Syr. Have patience, Clitipho, I must begin
Before that I can end.   We'll come to that.

Clit. Well, well, get on.

Syr.   At first we found her house;
Next Dromo came and knocked upon the door,
And an old woman answered.   Opened doors,
In Dromo pushed, and I pushed after him :
The old dame drew the bolts, and took her wool.
Now, Clinia, now, at such a time and tide,
You learn most surely what a woman is;
You catch her at haphazard, and you learn
How she lives in your absence; her you find
At ordinary occupations—tasks
Which mark their inclinations and their lives.
Well then, we found her busy at her loom,

Arrayed in mourning garb, no doubt for her,
The old dame dead.   She wore no ornament,
Nor gold, nor gem; was very meanly clad;
Her locks at liberty—all negligent—
All unadorned in beauty.
Cli.   Ah, Syrus; pray
Do not delude me with fictitious good!
Syr. The old dame spun: there was one other girl—
A little girl—unwashed, unclothed, who worked
At the same loom as worked Antiphila.
Clit. Clinia, if this be true—and I believe it—
You are most fortunate.   A sordid damsel
Is a sure proof of a reproachless dame,
Where servants are not pampered, 'tis a rule
That they receive no presents—are not bought
To make assignments for their mistresses.
Cli. Syrus, go on; but say no more than sooth.
O' flatter not!   Say what did she reply
Learning of my return ?
Syr.   I told her that,
And that you prayed her instant company.
She dropped her shuttle, and her eyes were charged
With gathered tears; she hurried—we could see
That she was all impatience to behold you.
Cli. Oh happiness: I am beloved of gods!
I know not where I am, so much I feared.
Clit. I knew all would be well, my Clinia !
Now Syrus, of the other, what of her ?
Syr. Well, we bring you your Bacchis.
Clit.   Bacchis—bring—
Why zounds ! you villain, do you bring her here ?
Syr. To take her home with us.

Clit.   My father's house?
Syr. The very one.
Clit.   Oh, impudence unheard of !
Syr. Master: you cannot do things great and tall
  Without some peril.
Clit.   Sirrah, mind what you do:
  You gain no glory, mind, at my expense ;
  Now if you blunder I am surely lost:
  What will you do with her ?
Syr.   But ——
Clit.   But what, I say ?
Syr. Well, suffer me to speak.
Clit.   I suffer you.
Syr. The thing is thus—that is—the thing is so—
Clit. You quibble, or you seek some subterfuge.
Cli. Speak, Syrus, truly ; come now to the fact.
Syr. I can't do otherwise : he is unjust.
  Clitipho, I can no more put up with you.
Cli. By Hercules, be quiet ! Let him speak.
Clit. Well, let him speak.
Syr.   You are in love ; you want
  To gain a mistress, and I find the means.
  Money you want ; you don't want any risk.
  Well, you are not a fool—that is to say,
  If you don't ask what is impossible ;
  You must take this with that, or go without.
  Will you accept the peril, or renounce
  The prize ? I have devised things well,
  All, all is safe enough. You shall possess
  Your mistress safely in your father's house.
  Moreover, find the money that you owe her.

Money—I'm deaf with your long bawling for.
What want you more?

Clit.   I am content with this,
    Provided—

Syr.   Ay, provided: will you try?
Clit. Yes, yes; but tell me what you now propose.
Syr. Bacchis to counterfeit Antiphila!
Clit. Oh, excellent, in faith! but what of her?
    Will she pass off as his?   Methinks that one
    Will be perplexing and enough for him.
Syr. I take her to your mother.
Clit.   Eh, for what?
Syr. Now this is tedious, Clitipho.   I know
    My course of action: you must trust in me.
Clit. Ah, fables, fables!   I can nothing see
    Of reassuring in your rigmarole.
Syr. Wait, then—I have one more expedient
    Which you shall both confess not perilous.
Clit. For heaven's sake, yes; one not perilous.
Syr. Most easily; I will go meet the dames
    And send them back.
Clit.   What is it that you say?
Syr. Rest you contented: they shall both go back,
    And you shall go to bed and go to sleep.
Clit. Here's a dead lock!
Cli.   I think that we should take—
Clit. Eh, Syrè! tell me now—look up at me—
Syr. Be off with you; to-morrow you may wish,
    And wish too late.
Cli.   But we consent, you see;
    I don't think we shall find another chance
    So good as this.

-

Clit.   What, Syrus, ho!

Syr.   Ah, cry and bawl!
   I'm off—I am.

Clit. But, Hercle! you are right—
   Syrus, I say—ho, Syrus! Stop and hear.

Syr. He grows red hot.   Well, what?

Clit.   Well what, return!

Syr. Well, here am I.   Say on, what is your will?
   For I can nought propose that pleases you.

Clit. Not so, my Syrè!   Ah! now, leave us not!
   My love and honour I confide to thee.
   You know the best; only take care of falls.

Syr. Pooh, pooh: do you admonish, Clitipho!
   Have I not more to fear by far than you?
   Now, if this plot of mine should not succeed,
   You will get off with a rough word or two;
   I shan't escape so well, but bear rough stripes.
   Guess then if I shall not take care of falls.
   But ask of him: will he dissimulate,
   Accepting Bacchis?

Cli.   Truly will I so,
   If needful is to do so, as we stand.

Clit. I thank you truly, Clinia.

Cli.   Tell me now,
   Can we trust Bacchis?

Syr.   She is shrewd enough.

Clit. I am surprized—surprized that she consents,
   She who rebuffs so many with her scorn.

Syr. I caught her at the tide—the very tide—
   The very turn of tide: a soldier there
   Besieging her: and she was making terms,
   Terms of surrender; but with such address

Inflaming and rejecting him, until
She made his passion uncontrollable,
And then abruptly swamped it to please you.
I say, beware! where you imprudent run.
Your father is astute, has open eyes;
And you, I know you too: confusing words,
Twisting your head, groaning, and hemming, grinning—
I say, beware!

Clit.   You flatter me.

Syr.   Take care.

Clit. You make me proud.

Syr.   Ah, ah! here come the women.

Clit. Where; where? Zounds! stay me not.

Syr.   Now, don't you see—
You must not know them now.

Clit.   Stuff—but I may,
When they arrive—

Syr.   I tell you, no.

Clit.   I will.

Syr. You shall not.

Clit.   But I will.

Syr.   But I forbid it.

Clit. Only one kiss.

Syr.   Now don't be such a fool.

Clit. I go—and Clinia?

Syr.   No, Clinia must remain.

Clit. Thrice-happy Clinia!

Syr.   Now, be off—be off.

ACT II.—Scene 3.—Bacchis—Antiphila—Clinia—Syrus.

Bac. Now, edepol, I vow, Antiphila,
  I praise and hold you very fortunate.
  Your beauty, with your manners in concurrence
  I wonder not that men run mad for you.
  May the gods prosper me! your very talk
  Betrays to me the beauty of your mind.
  Ah! when I think upon the wife's career;
  Living for one alone—I marvel not
  To find conjoined with it, such excellence.
  That is forbidden us in our careers;
  Our gallants buy our beauty, when that goes,
  Away go they—and purchase where they can—
  And therefore we must needs be mercenary.
  'Tis not so with the wife, the wedded wife.
  With love and equal age and sentiment,
  Devotion ever growing more and more,
  To such a love time does not put a bourn.
Ant. I do not know nor can dream of another,
  My heart is all concentred, all in one.
Cli. [*Aside.*] 'Tis that, Antiphila, attracts me home.
  Of all the woes that on the exile wait,
  None is so great as absence from his love.
Syr. No doubt, no doubt.
Cli.   Syrus, I can't hold out.
  Zounds! to stand here and never welcome her.
Syr. Ah! then, you can't hold out.   Your father soon
  Will give you other things to think about.

Bac. Who is yon youngster who is ogling us?

Ant. Help, hold me up!

Bac. 　　　　　　　　　　What is the matter now?

Ant. I faint, I perish.

Bac. 　　　　　　　　Antiphila, how now?

Ant. Speak! is it Clinia?

Cli. 　　　　　　　　All hail, my soul!

Ant. Oh, my expected Clinia!　All hail!

Cli. My sweetest love!

Ant. 　　　　　　　　I joy to see you safe.

Cli. And do I hold you fast, Antiphila?
　How have I longed and pined—

Syr. 　　　　　　　　　　Now get you in,
　The old man in the house is waiting too.

————　—　----

ACT III.

Scene 1.—Chremes—Menedemus.

Chr. The morning dawns.   Then why do I delay
    To beat upon his door, and tell the news—
    The son's return—and cheer the father's heart ?
    The youngster does not wish it ; but the grief
    Of the old man who loves so fervently—
    No ! I cannot delay to soothe his grief,
    The whilst it cannot hurt the boy at all.
    I must—I must—I will aid this old man,
    The boys know one another—they are friends,
    Interchange thoughts and wishes—why not we ?
    Let old men unto old men do the like.

Men. Or, I was born for woes and miseries
    Past mortal lot, or else the proverb's false
    That time soothes grief; time only adds to mine.
    Each day that's fled adds to the period of
    My boy's departure, with increasing grief,
    As the time flies.

Chr.   Ah ! here he comes.
    I will address him : Menedemus, hail !
    I have news for you—news that will make you glad.

Men. News of my son, O Chremes ?

Chr.   He is well.

Men. Where is he, I beseech you ?

Chr.   Well, with me,
    At home, there.

Men.   What, my son ?

Chr.   Is come.
Men.   Is come?
Chr. Yea, truly.
Men.   Clinia! is my Clinia come?
Chr. I said so.
Men.   Hence, then, lead me quick, I pray!
Chr. But he would rather that you should not know
   Of his return; he trembles at his deed,
   He doubts the moderation of your wrath.
Men. Did you not tell him, Chremes, of my mind?
Chr. No I did not.
Men.   And wherefore did you not?
Chr. Because you, also, now are blundering.
   It is not good for him to go unpunished;
   It is not good for you to seem so weak.
Men. Nay, it is right, I have been harsh enough.
Chr. Ah! Menedemus, you are marring all;
   You go from one extreme unto another.
   From reticence to prodigality—
   Two paths which lead unto one precipice.
   Some little licence when this love began,
   And with that woman it had soon burnt out;
   Unless, indeed, she kept that modesty
   Content with little, which now is all gone
   And merged in desperate extravagance.
   Necessity has cast her on the world,
   And now she must be purchased at her price,
   And you are ready. Learn, then, what that is.
   Why, her establishment is ruinous!
   Ten girls in vests of gold. A satrap would
   Shrink from the charges which you would incur.
Men. Is she with you?

Chr.   Is she with me—why yes !
  I know it sensibly.   I found the supper
  For her and all her troop ; another such,
  And I am ruined.   Casting wine away
  With mouth fastidious : Father ! this is rough ;
  Go seek some sweeter.   All my jars are pierced,
  She stove them all.   My men had much ado
  To bring them up, and all this in one night.
  How would you manage that now, every day ?
  As the gods love me, but I pity you.
Men. She shall do as she will.   Shall mar or make ;
  Shall spend and cast away ; do what she will,
  So long as she will come and dwell with me.
Chr. If so you will, methinks that it were well
  He should not know, that it is you who do it.
Men. How shall I act ?
Chr.   Do anything but that
  Which you propose ; do it vicariously,
  Pretend that you are cheated by his slave,
  For that is their intent.   I quickly saw
  Their private machinations ; 'twill soon appear,
  For Syrus is at hard work with your servant
  Earwigging one another, and the boys
  They are in conference deep,   'Twere better lose
  A talent to them thus than grant a mina.
  We must not now mind cash, but give a lesson
  To this young fellow, and yet save ourselves,
  If so we can.   If once he spy your weakness
  That you would hazard all—your peace and purse—
  To keep him here, you open then a door
  To his destruction ; his sin upon your head,
  For we can none of us withstand temptation.

He will launch out in all extravagance,
Thoughtless and reckless, and you must look on,
And see your property and see your peace
Take flight; or, if you gird up to resist,
Off, off--he quits you: that is, he will threaten.
Men. I do believe that what you say is truth.
Chr. Now in good sooth, I have not closed my eyes
The livelong night in communing to aid you.
Men. Give me your hand. I pray you, Chremes, follow
The plan you now advise me.
Chr.   I will do it.
Men. But know you what I wish?
Ch .   Say, what you wish.
Men. Why, since they machinate some roguery,
Hasten it on. I want to pleasure them,
I want to see my boy.
Chr.   And so you shall.
I must find Syrus, and exhort him to it.
Hush! who comes from my house? I pray you go
Back to your house; let us not be seen together.
I too have business. Simus and Crito, two
Neighbours of ours, chose me for arbiter.
I will bid them defer it from to-day,
And be back in a minute.
Men.   Do so, I pray you.
O faith of gods! behoves it that all men
Are blind to things pertaining to themselves,
Lynx-eyed to those of others. It happens thus
In all our own affairs, that joy and grief
Deprive us of our judgment. Chremes now
Can act for me better than I myself;
My judgment is not free. Here Chremes comes.

ACT III.—Scene 2.—Syrus—Chremes.

Syr. All hurry-scurry, running here and there
  For money, and to circumvent the Seniors.
Chr. [*Aside.*] Ah! I was in the right to "circumvent"—
  That slave of Clinia's is somewhat dull,
  And, therefore, they've commissioned Syrus. Ah!
Syr. Who speaks? Ah me, he heard me speak of money.
Chr. Syrus.
Syr.   Ahem!
Chr.   - What are you after here?
Syr. All right. But, Chremes, wherefore up so early,
  You banquetting so late?
Chr.   Not overmuch.
Syr. Not overmuch! then yours is the old saw—
  Youth of an eagle!
Chr.   So—so!
Syr.   Ah! that woman,
  Of easy, merry mood; this meretrix.
Chr. Yes, I have found her so.
Syr.   And exquisite—
  Hercle! an amorous form.
Chr.   So—so, so—so!
Syr. Ah, yes! not like you know the dames of old,
  But fair withal. I do not, I confess,
  Marvel that Clinia loves her fervently;
  But there's a certain father, a true screw,
  A dried up miser, do you know the man?
  Our neighbour there : rolling in riches—ah!
  Rolling in riches, and he drives his son
  From house and home. Eh! do you know the man?

Chr. How know him not? a man that should be sent
  To turn the mill.
Syr.   Hem! who?
Chr.   That slave of his—
  That knave—
Syr. [*Aside.*]   Syrè, I fear for thee.
Chr.   That knave
  That suffered this to be.
Syr.   How could he help it?
Chr. How! do you ask?   He should have told some tale,
  Some lie, to win the money from the father,
  And aided so their loves; he would have served
  The old man well, and done him a best service.
Syr.   You chaff me!
Chr.   I do not, such is my mind.
Syr. Eh! do you praise the slave who cheats his master?
Chr. Well, that depends on time and place.
Syr.   That's true.
Chr. For very often fraud spares mighty ills—
  Ills without remedy. This only son
  Had stayed at home now, had the slave been shrewd.
Syr. [*Aside.*] Is he joking or in earnest, I know not,
  But this incites me onward in my fraud.
Chr. And where now, Syrus, is this dunce, this mule,
  That cannot serve his master in his need,
  Nor frame a lie to take in one old man.
Syr. Ah, 'tis a mooncalf.
Chr.   Wherefore do not you
  Lend him some wit.
Syr.   I will so willingly,
  If you will give me orders. By my word,
  It is the very thing I best am fit for.

Chr. Hercle! and I esteem it.
Syr.   For to cheat
  Comes native to me.
Chr.   Then to it.
Syr.   Master mine,
  You will remember that I do your bidding ;
  You will remember, should it ever happen,
  That Clitipho, your son, who human is,
  Perchance may do the like.
Chr.   Well, I trust—not.
Syr. I trust—not, too, 'twas all surmise.   I ne'er
  Saw that in him as yet, as *yet*, I say.
  You see the age he has, Chremes, beware !
  If that should come to pass, you wont blame me.
Chr. Go to, go to, if that should come to pass
  We'll see to it; now follow up this cue.
Syr. I never heard my master speak so well;
  I have full liberty to cheat and lie,
  To work then with impunity.   They come.

ACT III.—Scene 3.—Chremes—Clitipho—Syrus.

Chr. Why, how now? Clitipho; what means then this ?
  What manners pray are these ?
Clit.   What have I done ?
Chr. Your hand beneath her robe, upon her bosom ;
  I saw it with these eyes.
Syr.   Then our game's up.
Clit. Who—mine ?
Chr.   Deny it not.   I say it—I.
  Is this the way that you insult your guest—
  Not hold your hands off! 'tis the last affront

That you can do him, to caress his mistress!
Your conduct yesterday was overbold,
Immodest at the supper.
Syr.　　　　　　　　　　　Ah, that it was!
Chr. Importunate to her.　Now, as I live,
　May the gods love me, as I feared a scene.
　I know the touchy jealousy of youth:
　They wont put up with it—that, I can tell you.
Clit. But, father, my good friend knows well enough
　That I would ne'er do him an injury.
Chr. So be it; but they don't want company.
　You should leave them alone, for lovers have
　A hundred things to say.　I know it well.
　I tell you, Clitipho, that no one would
　Unbosom all his heart to his best friend,
　For self-respect forbids it: shame forbids.
　'Twere foolishness, or 'twere effrontery.
　The same with Clinia: you ought to know
　The right of time, and place, and courtesy.
Syr. Do you mark this now, what he says.
Clit.　　　　　　　　　　　　I die!
Syr. That, Clitipho, is what I said to you:
　The proper office of a man, I said,
　Was temperance, self-control—
Clit.　　　　　　　　　　Be silent, then.
Syr. You hear, Sir.
Chr.　　　　　　Syrus, I am ashamed!
Syr.　　　　　　　　　　　　And I,
　Though I am not his father, am ashamed.
Clit. Will you be silent?
Syr.　　　　　　　I speak my sentiment.
Clit. Can't I approach them?

Chr.   What stuff you ask!
  You must approach them in all decency.
Syr. [*Aside*] It is all up: now will he all betray
  Or ere I've got the money. Chremes, Sir,
  Will you take counsel of a fool?
Chr.   Say on.
Syr. Then order him away.
Clit.   Where shall I go?
Syr. Go where you please, but please to go away.
  Go, walk.
Clit.   Walk where?
Syr.   Oh! there are walks enough:
  Go here, or there, or where you will, but go.
Chr. He counsels well.
Clit.   May gods uproot thee, Syrus!
  Chasing me hence.
Syr.   Learn not to interfere.

ACT III.—Scene 4.—Syrus—Chremes.

Syr. Now, by my faith! what do you think of this?
  May the gods help thee, Chremes, if you fail
  To admonish and chastise.
Chr.   I will take care.
Syr. Master, 'tis now—now to take heed and act!
Chr. So be it.
Syr.   If you please; for day by day
  He flouts my counsels more.
Chr.   Now, Syrus, you—
  What have you done, devised on our behalf?
  Have you devised a plan or have you not?
Syr. Ah! of our plot. Hist, hist, I know of one.

Chr. That's my good Syrus, say.

Syr.   I will, in sooth,
  As things go in a chain, and oft fall out—

Chr. What is it, Syrus?

Syr.   This Bacchis is a—

Chr. So it appears.

Syr.   Ah! subtle—that she is.
  She tells this likely tale: a dame of Corinth,
  To whom she says she lent a thousand drachmas—

Chr. What then?

Syr.   Is dead, and left a child—a girl—
  Now held in pledge by her, and for that debt.

Chr. Well—well!

Syr.   She brought her here, and now she is
  At home, and with your wife.

Chr.   Well, and what more?

Syr. Bacchis of Clinia asks a thousand drachmas,
  And offers to enfranchise this young girl
  On touching it, but still to be a gift.

Chr. She may demand!

Syr.   Yes, that is past a doubt.

Chr. What now do you propose?

Syr.   What I propose:
  To find out Menedemus, and to tell him
  This damsel is a Carian, noble, rich.
  Let him redeem her, and make profit by it.

Chr. Ah! you mistake.

Syr.   How so?

Chr.   I will reply
  In place of Menedemus: " I refuse."

Syr. Nay, say not so.

Chr.   Because there is no need.

Syr. No need!
Chr.   No, none.   I pray thee wait a while.
   I will tell you presently : just let me see
   What all this racket is before my doors.

ACT III.—Scene 5.—Sostrata—Nurse—Chremes—
Syrus.

Sos. Unless my eyes deceive me, this same ring,
   I have no doubt about it, is the one
   With which my daughter was exposed.
Chr. Syrus, what is this?
Sos.   Look, if it be not so.
Nur. Truly I say, now that you show it me,
   It is so, and the same.
Sos.   Look at it well;
   Look at it well, my nurse.
Nur.   Good sooth ! it is.
Sos. Go you in-doors, and see if she has bathed;
   Be thou my messenger.   I will wait here
   And meet my husband.
Syr.   It is you she wants.
   Go, see now what she wants.   She is sorrowful;
   I know not for what cause; some cause there is;
   I dread what it may be.
Chr.   What it may be ?
   With much ado to tell me some great stuff.
Sos. Hem ! husband mine.
Chr.   Hem ! also, wife of mine.
Sos. I sought for you.
Chr.   Well, say then what it is.

Sos. I pray thee, first of all, you will not think
   Against your edict; I have moved in this.*
Chr. Go on—must I believe the incredible?
   But though incredible, I will credit it.
Syr. Some fault in such purgation surely lies.
Sos. You well remember when I was in labour,
   How oft we reasoned, and how you insisted
   The child, if 'twere a girl, should be exposed.
Chr. I see : you had her nourished; is that so?
Syr. My mistress, if you did so, you did wrong;
   You wronged your lord.
Sos.   I did not in the least.
   There was a dame Corinthian, trusty dame;
   I gave the child to her to be exposed.
Chr. O Jupiter! that you should so have done.
Sos. I perish! should do what?
Chr.   Eh, can you ask?
Sos. Dear Chremes, if I sinned I knew it not.
Chr. Wife, I believe it; all you say and do
   Is done in inscience, for imprudently
   You think and act. How many faults arise
   In this one act of yours! First, disobedience—
   When I commanded, you should have put to death,
   Not simulated words, and did it not.
   I forgive that—maternal weakness—nature—
   Compassion—well, they conquered you, I grant.
   What had you in your head, what in your mind,
   What purpose had you—any—had you any?
   Abandoning a daughter to a crone—

-----

* Sostrata means in redeeming the girl he in his paternal power had
exposed, or rather devoted to death.

To be a slave—a harlot—bought and sold.
I know well what you meant—you only thought
To let her live—to live—that was enough.
What can we do with women who know not
The just, or honest, or expedient—
Good, better, bad or worse, 'tis all the same
To her who only cares to please herself.
Sos. Well, I did wrong: I own it, my own Chremes,
But I beseech you, older and more wise
Than I, to pardon me what I have done.
Chr. I must excuse it.   What is done, is done.
I fear my much indulgence is your ruin.
Say, Sostrata, wherefore did you do this?
Sos. Foolish and superstitious women are.
When I abandoned her, I drew a ring
From off my finger, saying, as I did it,
" That if exposed and perishing, yet she
Should be endowered with part of our wealth."
Chr. And you did well ; guarding yourself and her.
And she survives ?
Sos.   Lo! now, here is the ring.
Chr. From whence ?
Sos.   From her, the girl, by Bacchis brought.
Syr. Ahem!
Chr.   And what said she ?
Sos.   She bade me hold
The ring for her, whilst she was in the bath.
I took it from her heedlessly, but when
I saw—I knew it, and I ran to you.
Chr. What makes you think 'tis she; what proof have you ?
Sos. None other : you yourself must ask her more—
From whence she had it, and discover her.

Syr. I am murdered : for it is most surely her.
   In faith I wish it were not so.
Chr.   Does she
   To whom you gave the infant yet survive?
Sos. I know not—I—
Chr.   What did she say she did.
Sos. That which she was commanded.
Chr.   And what was her name,
   I will go search her out.
Sos.   She was named Philterè.
Syr. 'Tis she! 'tis she herself, and I'm undone.
Chr. Come, Sostrata, come in!
Sos.   Oh, how beyond
   My utmost hopes—how different are you
   From the hard heart, O Chremes, that you had
   When you bade me expose her to destruction!
Chr. We are not what we would be : necessity
   Does not permit it : the times are altered now.
   I should love, Sostrata, a daughter now.

ACT IV.

Scene 1.—Syrus.

Syr. Unless my mind deceives me—'tis a mess
  That we are in.   I can see no escape,
  No modo to hide the fact what Bacchis is—
  To screw out money, or to take him in.
  To hope so were a folly—all I hope
  Is to save bag and baggage.   Confound the thing –
  To lose the titbit from my very jaws!
  What can I do—what plot—what machinate ?
  I must begin again—the motto says,
  " Nought is so lost but it may be retrieved
  By searching duly."   Well, then, to the search !
  Bah ! that's no go—nor that, nor that, nor that.
  Courage ! I have a plan, it ends in this,
  That I must catch and get that thousand drachmas.

ACT IV.—-Scene 2.—Clinia—-Syrus.

Cli. Oh ! how all things go happily : how free
  From all annoyances—how glad am I,
  I yield me to my father ; nor can wish
  A happier lot than he accords to me.
Syr. I see it all : this girl is recognized,
  So far as I perceive.   I am right glad,
  O Clinia, your affairs are prosperous.
Cli. My Syrus—do you know?

Syr.   Know, wherefore not,
  Since I was present!
Cli.   Have you ever known
  A greater happiness?
Syr.   None.
Cli.   As the gods love me,
  None; but I joy most for her.   Ah! Syrus,
  She is deserving, worthy of all honour.
Syr. I think so truly: but now, Clinia,
  Behoves to think and act for others also.
  Attend to me, your friend is now beset;
  We must land him in safety.   The old man
  Must be hoodwinked on Bacchis.
Cli.   O Jupiter!
Syr. Now cease to rhapsodize.
Cli.   Antiphila!
  My love, my wife!
Syr.   You do not listen to me.
Cli. Bear with me, Syrus, I am in delights.
Syr. Hercle! and that is true.
Cli.   Ah! in Elysium,
  A life we'll lead.
Syr.   I tarry here the while.
Cli. Speak, for I hear.
Syr.   Oh, no—do you go on!
Cli. I listen, faith.
Syr.   The matter now on hand
  Is Clitipho.   We must make him, too, safe.
  Now if you walk away and leave us Bacchis,
  Our master here will recognize his mistress;
  But if you lead her hence away—she goes
  Forth as she came, as yours.

Cli. But that knocks up my marriage—knocks it up
   You understand not, Syrus, what you say—
   How can I meet my father on this plea,
   A mistress following me!
Syr.   Why not?
Cli. But how? what pretext frame?
Syr.   Oh! none at all.
   No pretexts: tell the truth.
Cli.   What do you say?
Syr. Say that you love Antiphila to wife,
   Say that he loves—and Bacchis is the mistress.
Cli. Not a bad plot, and easy to be done,
   And then to bid my father hold his tongue,
   And not to blurt to him.
Syr.   Quite contrary:
   Go tell him the true tale.
Cli. Syrus, you are mad or drunk; you but betray him.
   How would that make him safe?
Syr.   Ah! 'tis my cue—
   My palm of victory! I hug myself
   In admiration of my own astuteness.
   Cunning is power—go and tell him the truth,
   And so deceive them both. When your old man
   Tells our old man, Bacchis is his son's mistress,
   He'll not believe it.
Cli. Ah! but you knock my marriage on the head.
   When Chremes thinks that Bacchis is my love,
   Will he grant me his daughter? But it seems
   You fight for Clitipho—nor care for me.
Syr. Confound you—do you think I want an age
   To do my work—one day will do for me—
   Just time to get the money—and no more!

Cli. Ah! but a day.   Yet there is one thing more,
  What if his father finds it out—
Syr.   What if—
  What if—what if the heavens fall?
Cli.   I fear.
Syr. You fear! and how to extricate our necks
  I fain to learn—go to, and tell the truth.
Cli. Go, go, and bring me Bacchis!
Syr.   Good, here she is.

ACT IV.—Scene 3.—Bacchis—Clinia—Syrus—
Dromo—Phrygia.

Bac. Pol! now, but Syrus has bamboozled me,
  With promise unperformed of thousand drachmas.
  It happens once, but shall not happen twice,
  The next time that he sues—'twill be my turn,
  I will promise and not keep it: and your back
  My clever Syrus shall bear my revenge.
Cli. Hear you her promises?
Syr.   Think you she jokes?
  It is no joke she meditates.
Bac.   They sleep,
  They sleep, but Pol! I will arouse them up.
  My Phrygia, hark ye.   Do you recollect
  The dwelling of Charinus.
Phr.   Yes, I remember.
Bac. Next to our right hand neighbour.
Phr.   I remember.
Bac. Go in a trice: there dwells a captain, keeping
  This Dionysia.
Syr.   How now? how now?

Bac.   To him.
  Tell him that I am here against my will,
  A captive bound; but I will break the bonds
  And visit him.
Syr.   Hercle! I perish: Bacchis,
  Stop, stop, I do beseech you, bid her stop.
Bac. No, go.
Syr.   I have the money.
Bac.   Then I stay.
Syr. I will bring it directly.
Bac.   That's all right,
  And all I want.
Syr.   But we want you to do—
Bac. What?
Syr.   To visit Menedemus in your pomp,
  With all your train.
Bac.   What trick is this, you rogue?
Syr. Why, I coin money—all to give to you!
Bac. Think you that I am one to play upon?
Syr. I do not that.
Bac.   What business have we there?
Syr. To give you what is yours.
Bac.   Hence let us go.
Syr. Follow me here: Oh, Dromo!
Dro.   Now, who cries?
Syr. Syrus.
Dro.   What now?
Syr.   Lead all the girls of Bacchis
  Home to your house.
Dro.   Wherefore?
Syr.   Nay, never ask,
  But lead them there and all their rattle-traps.

When our old man shall witness their departure,
He'll rub his hands, glad to escape their keep.
I will make him pay more—but Dromo, hey!
Do you be wise and not know aught about it.

ACT IV.—Scene 4.—Chremes—Syrus.

Chr. As the gods love me, I 'plain Menedemus,
  He bides this storm : this woman and her troop ;
  He will not kick at first ; but bye-and-bye
  When the first gladness for his son hath passed,
  He'll kick at this expenditure, and wish
  His plaguy son in Asia back again.
  Ah! here comes Syrus very opportunely.
Syr. Why don't I tackle him ?
Chr.   Syrè !
Syr.   How now ?
  Ah! is it you? you I was seeking for.
Chr. What have you done with the old Menedemus.
Syr. Did I not tell you so !   Soon said, soon done.
Chr. Good faith ?
Syr.   Good, hercle !
Chr. I can't resist it, I must pat your head,
  Syrus ! I must reward you for this action,
  And joyfully.
Syr.   Ah ! if you knew how cleverly.
Chr. Bah ! you are bragging now before the fact.
Syr. No, hercle, no !   It is the truth.
Chr.   Then, say.
Syr. Clinia has told his father, Bacchis is
  The mistress of your son ; that he has led
  Her there, in fact, to deceive you—yourself.
Chr. Most excellent.

Syr. Most excellent, you think so?

Chr. I do—I do.

Syr.   Ah! if you knew; but listen—
  The plot that follows.   Clinia will tell his father
  That he has seen your daughter, and admires,
  And wants her as a wife.

Chr.   She—newly found?

Syr. Yes; she herself.   His father to demand her.

Chr. I can make nothing of this, good nor bad.

Syr. Eh! master, you are dull.

Chr.   Ah! that may be.

Syr. His father now will open wide his purse
  For nuptials, wedding-clothes.   Eh! do you take—

Chr. To fit them out?

Syr.   Exactly so.

Chr.   But I
  Will neither give nor grant, nor gold, nor girl.

Syr. No: and why not?

Chr.   Why not, do you ask me?
  What! to a man—

Syr.   Just so; nor did I say,
  Or think, to give her out and out; but to
  Do so dissembling.

Chr.   I am no dissembler;
  Look you—manage your matters by yourself
  And leave me out.   What! I betroth my child
  Unto a man I scorn!

Syr.   I quite agree.

Chr. You but deceive yourself.

Syr.   Belike I do;
  Nor had I meddled now in this affair
  But that I was incited by yourself.

Chr. Well, that is so.

Syr.   And Chremes, for the rest
  I will do as you like.

Chr.   You may go on,
  But leave me out; devise some other way.

Syr. So be it.   Let us seek one; but the money
  I told you of, your daughter owes to Bacchis,
  That must be paid.   Nor are you one of those—
  As many—to take refuge in a quibble,
  "What's that to me?   Have I to do with that?
  And is that debt, to that old woman, mine;
  Or could she pledge for debt a child of mine?"
  Ah, Chremes! the old maxim is most true,
  "Law to the letter is not equity."

Chr. I will not do so.

Syr.   Lawful to the world,
  Unlawful is to you; for your good fame
  Exists in your benevolence and riches.

Chr. I go to bring it straight.

Syr.   Eh! do not so;
  But send it by your son.

Chr.   And why by him?

Syr. Because, forsooth! they think him caught by Bacchis.

Chr. What matters that?

Syr.   It matters a great deal.
  It will make it seem apparent; it will aid
  Me in my task.   Ah! here is Clitipho.
  Go, I beseech you, and bring us the cash.

ACT IV.—Scene 5.—Clitipho—Syrus.

Clit. An easy matter becomes difficult,
  When prosecuted with a sullen heart.
  This walk enforced on me; the task was light,
  Yet it has wearied me beyond belief.
  Now I return, and here I stand in dread
  To be put forth again, in fact from Bacchis.
  Now gods and goddesses confound you, Syrus;
  Curse your conceptions and intentions all.
  Your machinations have no further end
  But to deceive and crucify myself.
Syr. Go to the ——, where you ought to go, I say;
  Knocking one's plots down in sheer stubbornness
Clit. I wish I had, by Jove! and served you right.
Syr. "And served me right;" how so? I am right glad
  To hear you say so, ere I render up
  The money I have got you.
Clit.   I don't believe it.
  You go away—you bring me Bacchis—then
  You bar me from her presence.
Syr.   I am cool.
  Know you where Bacchis is?
Clit.   At our house.
Syr. Quite wrong.
Clit.   Where then?
Syr.   She is with Clinia.
Clit. I perish!
Syr.   Be of good cheer: go seek her there,
  And give the promised money.
Clit.   Babbler! the money: whence?

Syr. Your father.

Clit.   You deceive me.

Syr.   Not at all.

Clit. Happy, thrice happy I.   Syrus, I love thee !

Syr. Your father comes, now don't bawl with surprise
   Howe'er it come to pass ; don't contradict,
   Whate'er he bids you, do ; and hold your tongue.

ACT IV.—Scene 6.—Chremes—Syrus—Clitipho.

Chr. Now, where is Clitipho ?

Syr. [*To him.*] Say, Here I am.

Clit.   Father, lo! I am here.

Chr. Have you informed him ?

Syr.   Of the greater part.

Chr. Then take this money, and bear it to her.

Syr. Take it, you stone! take it, I say, and go.

Clit. Ah! give it me.

Syr.   Then follow me and quickly,
   Master ; whilst we are absent for the moment,
   Await the moment here.

Chr. [*Alone.*] There go a thousand drachmas for my daughter
   For nutriment ; another thousand, clothes
   And ornaments ; two talents for her dowry ;
   "Oh, how unjust and how depraved is custom ! "
   My leisure and affairs I must resign,
   And find the money ; farewell hoards of mine !

ACT IV.—Scene 7.—Menedemus—Chremes.

Men. O my dear son ! I am most fortunate ;
   You are retrieved from ruin !

Chr.   Self-deception!
Men. Chremé! I sought you now: I do entreat you
  To save my son, myself, and mine—you can.
Chr. I pray you, how?
Men.   To-day, restored your daughter.
Chr. What then?
Men.   Grant her to Clinia for a wife.
Chr. I pray you, wherefore so?
Men.   What do you mean?
Chr. Have you forgotten all about that money;
  That trick they were to play you?
Men.   I remember.
Chr. That is their object now.
Men.   What do you say, O Chremes?
  How you knock down my hopes and happiness.
Chr. And Bacchis is—mistress of Clitipho,
  They tell you so?
Men.   They tell me so indeed.
Chr. And you believe it?
Men   I believe it all.
Chr. And Clinia would marry—that I should give
  My child and dowry—you the gems and vesture
  Due to espousals.
Men.   It is even so,
  Gifts to his mistress!
Chr.   His mistress, even so.
Men. O futile joy, precursor of such ill;
  And yet, despite of all, I dare not lose him.
  What answer shall I make him, of your part,
  That he may not perceive and wail his loss.
Chr. That he may not perceive and wail his loss!
  O Menedemus, you are very weak!

Men. O bear with me, the matter is begun,
    Do not desert me, Chremes, ere the end.
Chr. Say that you sought me, and proposed the marriage.
Men. What else?
Chr.   That I am willing; and admire
    The bridegroom much; and add, if so you please,
    I grant my daughter.
Men.   But that is all I wish.
Chr. That he may ask the needful, and that you
    May get rid of it, too.
Men.   That I desire.
Chr. Well, I have witnessed the expenditure.
    He will absorb a lot.   If I were you,
    I should not let him have it all at once.
Men. Nor will I.
Chr.   Go, and see what he will ask;
    You will find me within, if you have need.
Men. Good: I will take advice of you at need.

ACT V.

Scene 1.—Menedemus—Chremes.

Men. I know right well that I am not a wizard,
   Nor very quick of sight : all that I know.
   But this adjutor, monitor, admonisher,
   This Chremes is a dunce.   I don't deny
   My epithets of folly—ass, stone, block,
   And lump of lead —these am I, one and all ;
   But he, tropes fail to indicate his folly.
Chr. Zounds ! wife, don't break the rest of all the gods
   With thanks reiterated for your daughter,
   Unless you deem their wit to be like yours
   With need of drumming in a hundred times.
   Where tarry Syrus now, and Clitipho?
Men. Who tarry, Chremes, of whom do you ask ?
Chr. Ah! Menedemus, you—I pray you tell !
   What have you said to Clinia?   Is all told ?
Men. Ay, all.
Chr.   And what says he ?
Men.   Well, he rejoiced,
   As if he were in earnest.
Chr.   Ah, ah, ah !
Men. Why do you laugh ?
Chr.   The subtleties of Syrus
   Came in my head.
Men.   How so ?
Chr.   The knave, he paints
   The man, to very life.

Men.   Because my son
Rejoices, do you say so?
Chr.   I do.
Men.   'Tis strange.
The thought identical—came in my mind
Chr. Ah, the old rogue!
Men.   Ay, deeper than you deem,
As you will soon find out.
Chr.   How so, I pray?
Men. Hear then.
Chr.   Nay, wait, first answer me I pray.
What have you lost; for when you told your son
The bride was granted to him—Dromo straight
Was ready with demands for gems and vestments,
Damsels, and what not, dragging forth your gold.
Men. No; not at all.
Chr.   How, not at all?
Men.   In faith.
Chr. Neither your son?
Men.   Quite the reverse, O Chremes.
All his impatience is to marry soon—
This very day.
Chr. You astonish me: and, Syrus,
Did he say nothing?
Men.   Nothing.
Chr.   How might that be?
Men. I know not in good sooth.   I marvel too,
That you who know so well affairs of others,
Know not your own.   Syrus has so well served
Your son, that now it is self-evident
Bacchis is none of Clinia's.
Chr.   Why, how so?

Men. For kisses and embraces go for nought.
Chr. For nothing, when they but dissimulate.
Men. Bah!
Chr.   What is it?
Men.   Listen, there is a room
  Apart in a recess—with couch and bedding,
  Lies all apart—alone.
Chr.   Well, what of that?
Men. Well, Clitipho went there.
Chr.   Alone?
Men.   Alone.
Chr. I tremble.
Men.   Bacchis followed him.
Chr.   Alone?
Men.   Alone.
Chr. I die!
Men.   Entered they barred the door.
Chr.   Ahem!
  Did Clinia suffer that?
Men.   He witnessed it—
  We witnessed it together.
Chr.   Ah, Menedemus!
  Then Bacchis is his mistress.   I am slain!
Men. How so?
Chr.   Ten days will eat me up, my house, and home.
Men. How so? you know he only served his friend.
Chr. He served his mistress.
Men.   That remains to see.
Chr. To see—to see!   Do you believe a man
  Would look on patiently and see another
  Bed with his mistress.

Men.   Ha, ha, ha ! why not ?
  He only cheated me, you know, to win her.
Chr. Zounds ! Menedemus, you are mocking me,
  Oh ! I could go to buffets with myself.
  The proof was plain enough ; I was a stone.
  Not unavenged, I will take charge of that !
  I will upset that game, and presently !
Men. Now moderate and cool—I do entreat you.
  Say, am not I example great enough ?
Chr. Nay, Menedemus—I will be revenged.
Men. A sage like you should not talk of revenge.
  Remember the advice you gave to others ;
  Avail yourself of some of it yourself.
Chr. What shall I do ?
Men.   The like that you advised me.
  " Reveal the depths of your paternal love,
  And he will give you filial confidence."
  So shall he come to you in all his needs,
  And you shall succour him, and he shall love you.
Chr. Ah ! he may go to the world's end for me,
  Ere he reduces me to penury
  By his flagitious practice.   Menedemus
  If I give way to him and serve his means,
  I must assume that rake you carried yesterday.
Men. Neighbour beware you do yourself no ill !
  You will be stern of mood : then pardon him,
  And lose his gratitude.
Chr.   Ah ! you feel not
  My grief.
Men.   Do—do then as you like.   But now
  Give answer unto me about your daughter,

May she espouse my son?   Have you another
Alliance in your mind?
Chr.   None; and the son-in-law
Contents me well.
Men.   What dowry shall we say?
What! no reply?
Chr.   What dowry?
Men.   Yes.
Chr.   Ah! ah!
Men. Chremes: fear not to utter it—if small.
It is not that we ask for.
Chr.   Two talents are
The dowry, I had fixed on in my mind;
But it were wise to say—to save my son
And save myself—I give all to my daughter.
Men. Do no such thing!
Chr.   Let me so simulate,
And ask him why it is I use him so.
Men. And in good sooth, I need to ask of him,
For I myself see no good reason why.
Chr. None, why?   To save a soul from luxury,
From lust, I will take care of that: I will—
He shall not turn himself without my leave.
Men. Take care.
Chr.   Take none, but just let me alone,
Let me to action.
Men.   You mean so.
Chr.   Ay, I do.
Men. So be it, then.
Chr.   At present tell your son
To lead away his wife: and for my son

He shall receive his due: in words, I mean.
But Syrus—
Men.   What for him?
Chr.   Ah! what for him?
     If I survive to do it, I will flay him,
     He shall remember it: remember me:
     Scoundrel! to make a jest of me—the knave—
     As the gods love me, I did not believe
     That he had dared to treat a widow so.

ACT V.—Scene 2.—Clitipho—Menedemus— Chremes—Syrus.

Clit. O Menedemus, is it even so?
     What! in so short a period, has my father
     Wholly forgotten ties of blood? of nature?
     What have I done, that every young man does not?
     All do the same.
Men.   Doubtless you feel it deeply,
     And so do I—obduracy of heart!
     I know not why I feel it—except it be
     My friendship for you.
Clit.   And, where is my father?
Men. Behold him.
Chr.   Why, Clitipho, accuse me?
     What have I done, that is not for your good?
     When I beheld your follies and excesses,
     Your love of pleasure, carelessness of cost,
     And thoughtless loss of future, then I sought
     Expedients to save you from yourself,
     And save your substance. As I could not do so,

Seeing that you disdained to be my heir,
I sought your nearest relative, and gave
Them power o'er the property—so you
Will be nourished, fed, and clothed.
Clit.   Ah, me!
Chr. 'Tis better far, than you to be the heir
  And spend it all on Bacchis.
Syr. I am undone! what mischief have I brewed!
Clit. Would I were dead.
Chr.   You must first learn to live.
  When you know that, then may you wish to die.
Syr. Master! may I speak?
Chr.   Speak.
Syr.   Without rebuke.
Chr. Say on.
Syr. What madness and injustice, this?
  I did the wrong for which you punish him.
Chr. Stuff! meddle not in this; it is not you:
  No one accuses you—you need not seek
  Altar or intercessor.
Syr.   But what do you?
Chr. Nothing but what is right.   And what I do
  As good for him, ought not to trouble you.

ACT V.—Scene 3.—Syrus—Clitipho.

Syr. He is off—and gone.   I was about to ask—
Clit. Ask, Syrus, what?
Syr.   Where I must find my prog
  Now we are chased abroad.   From what I see
  Your sister has to feed us.

Clit.   Ah, indignity!
   Or, beg for bread.
Syr.   Provided we don't starve,
   I see a hope—
Clit.   Of what?
Syr.   Of appetite—
   Excellent appetite.
Clit.   Zounds! do you jest
   When you should be devising remedies.
Syr. My sole employ is devising remedies.
   I was devising whilst I talked to him,
   So far as I can see or comprehend—
Clit. What?
Syr.   Matters draw near an end.
Clit.   An end?
Syr. An end I say—I think you're not their son.
Clit. Syrus, how now : are you in your true wits?
Syr. Judge you of that, I speak but my idea.
   Whilst you alone were their's, and their delight,
   Indulgence, and full means they lavished on you :
   They find their daughter, and they chase you forth.
Clit. It is very like indeed.
Syr.   Can you believe
   This matter could stir up much deadly wrath?
Clit. I do not think it could.
Syr.   Consider well—
   When sons go wrong the mother pleads for them ;
   They always take their part against the fathers ;
   We do not see your mother, now, do so.
Clit. It is very true : what shall I do, my Syrè?
Syr. Demand an explanation of the thing.
   Tell your suspicions ; bid them answer them.

Now, if you are their son, they will go weep
And pardon you offhand.   If you are not
Their son, you will know that.
Clit.   Most excellent !
I will do it.
Syr. [*Alone.*]   And happily devised :
The worse his anguish, greater their remorse.
Then they embrace, and reconcilement made,
They then will make him marry, and methinks
Bear no good will to me—what signifies !
Here comes old master, I will cut and run.
I marvel, after all, they have not sold me.
To Menedemus now, for he must be
My intercessor ; for I distrust my old man.

ACT V.—Scene 4.—Sostrata—Chremes.

Sos. By yea and nay, my husband, pray beware !
You will do mischief—you will grieve your son.
How such a notion got into your head,
I cannot think, my husband.
Chr.   Ah—listen now !
Hark to a woman !   Have I ever done
A thing without your hindrance ?   When I ask
What there is wrong, and how, you hold your tongue,
Nor can say why ; go to—you are a fool.
Sos. I can't say why ?
Chr.   Oh, I am wrong, you can.
I rather say you can, then hear again
The eternal tale.

Sos.   It is iniquity,
 If I must hold my peace in such a matter.
Chr. I do not ask what is impossible,
 So speak, and I will do.
Sos.   You are resolved?
Chr. I am resolved.
Sos.   And do you not perceive
 That Clitipho will think him not our son.
Chr. That he is not our son—not possible!
Sos. He will so think, my husband.
Chr.   Reply, 'tis true.
Sos. Ah, I beseech you! what is it you say?
 May that be for our foes: shall I reply
 Unto our son, that he is none of mine?
Chr. Eh! do you fear, the saying so will make it.
Sos. Is this because our daughter is retrieved?
Chr. Not so; but for another better reason
 It is right plain he is his mother's son:
 Like manners—obstinate—as like to like;
 Endowed with all your faults, and I believe
 None other than yourself now could have bare him.
 Ah! here he comes; ah! how demure he looks—
 He looks the very hypocrite he is.

ACT V.—Scene 5.—Sostrata—Chremes—Clitipho.

Clit. Mother! if ever you felt hope and joy
 In calling me your son, or if your ear
 Has e'er been pleased to hear me call you mother,
 Have mercy on me now; for I would know
 Who are my parents—who my parents are.

Sos. My son, I do beseech thee entertain
  Nor doubt nor thought but we thy parents are.
Clit. I must do so.
Sos.   I am most wretched then.
  What prompts such strange demand ?
                                        Ah, may you live,
  My dearest son, to close our eyes, as sure
  As you are our son ; and never let your tongue
  Utter again such doubt in words, I pray you.
Chr. And I reply, take you good care that I
  See you cast off your faults, or fear you me !
Clit. What faults ?
Chr.   Ah ! would you know them—hear them—
  A babbler, lazy, idle, gluttonous,
  A prodigal, debauched—go credit that,
  Nor doubt the fact that you are either's son.
Sos. Are these a father's words ?
Chr.   No, Clitipho.
  Had you leapt from my head, caparisoned,
  As did Minerva, child of Jupiter !
  You should not e'en then dishonour me
  By such disgraceful living.
Sos.   Now ! may the gods—
Chr. I do not know the gods; but for myself
  I will do all I can to hinder him.
  You want to know your father and your mother,
  And you shall know them ; I am present here.
  You, on the contrary, cannot produce
  Virtues to please your father, nor possess
  Manners to use inheritance of wealth
  Won by hard labour. Did you never blush
  To bring a——, but I refrain to speak

The turpid word before your mother's ear;
But you blushed not to do the turpid deed.
Clit. I am confused, and know not what to say.
    I have excuses none to offer you.

ACT V.—Scene 6.—Menedemus—Chremes—Clitipho—Sostrata.

Men. Now, really, Chremes, you are too severe;
    You crucify your son, and therefore I
    Come as a mediator.   Here he is.
Chr. Ah! Menedemus, wherefore do you not
    Lead home my daughter, and the dowry, which
    We have agreed upon?
Sos.   My husband, no!
    Do not so, I implore you.
Clit.   Father, I
    Implore you, also.
Men.   Chremes! so do I.
Chr. What, that seeing, knowing, unbeguiled, that so
    I give my wealth to Bacchis?   I will not.
Men. Nor would we suffer that.
Clit.   My father, I
    Implore you, pardon!
Sos.   Pardon him, Chremes mine.
Men. Nay, be not so obdurate.
Chr.   But you see
    I must renounce my project—my conviction.
Men. And most worthily.
Chr.   Well, upon one condition
    I will do so.
Clit.   I will obey you, father.

Chr. Wedlock.

Clit.   Father—

Chr.   Wedlock, and nothing less.

Men. I will respond for that.

Chr.   I do not hear
A response from himself.

Clit.   I perish—I—

Sos. Accept, dear Clitipho.

Chr.   Does he accept?

Men. Yes, he accepts.

Sos.   My Clitipho, marriage,
You dread so in your dreams, is happiness
When recognized in fact.

Clit.   I am consenting:
Father, I yield.

Sos.   My son, my son,
And I will choose a damsel for thy wife—
Daughter of Phanocrates.

Clit.   Homely girl:
Father, I cannot.

Chr.   Eh! so particular;
How came you by a taste so superfine?

Sos. Another I—

Clit.   Forbear! If I must wed
I must choose for myself and please myself.

Sos. I praise you, and you please me. Who is she?

Clit. Daughter of Archonides.

Sos.   Oh, happiness!

Clit. Father, one thing remains.

Chr.   And what, my son?

Clit. Pardon for Syrus—obedient unto me.

Chr. So be it. Ye, applaud us, and farewell.

Temple of Vesta.

ADELPHI.

(THE BROTHERS.)

PERSONS.

Micio—Signifying gentle.
Demea—Signifying plebeian.
Sannio—A merchant of girls.
Æschinus.
Syrus—A slave from Syria.
Ctesipho.
Sostrata—Matron.
Canthara—Nurse.
Tibicina.
Geta—Slave from the Getans.
Hegio—An old friend.
Dromo—Slave.
Pamphila—Nurse.

Acted at Rome at the funeral games of Æmilius Paulus, B.C. 158.

PROLOGUE.

The poet when he saw his muse traduced
By partial critics, and beheld abused
The play we now present you—pleads his cause.
You are his judges, and decide the laws
With condemnation, or conferring praise.
Synapothnescontes, amidst the plays
Of Diphilus, by Plautus was translated
As *Commorientes ;* but a maiden mated
To a young Grecian lover, who had torn
Her from a dealer, Plautus held in scorn.
Our author seized that incident to be
The subject of " The Brothers," that which we
Now represent and offer in this play.
If that be theft or plagiary—say.
What Plautus left unoccupied we took,
And seized, by him forsaken, the void nook.
Whatever the malevolent may deem
*Great men of the Republic aid the theme.
And work away with us with main and might,
Grievous to them, but giving me delight.
Proud to please those, the Roman commons prize,
For peace and war and state diplomacies—

---

* Scipio Africanus, Lælius, and Furius Publins.

And all performed with gracious modesty.
Now listen to the plot, which by and by
The old men and the young men will portray,
As we unfold the action of the play.
And let your favour on the poet light,
And your applauses urge him on to write.

ADELPHI.

ACT I.

Scene 1.—Micio.

Mic. Storax, last night, no Æschinus came home
   From where he supped, nor either did his slaves.
   True is the ancient adage, when we say—
   If you are absent long time, better far
   The maledictions of a wife in ire,
   Than thoughts of those who love most tenderly.
   Your wife is jealous, if you stop away
   She deems you dally, drink, divert yourself,
   And seek amusement whilst she sits at home.
   But I, what thoughts do not pass thro' the soul
   When Æschinus is unreturned; that he,
   Perchance, is frost-nipped, tumbled in a pit,
   Broken his leg, or arm.   Bah! How is it
   A man can so involve his very heart,
   And care more for another than himself?
   This urchin is not mine; my brother's, he
   Dissimilar in all things to myself.
   I live in civic idleness and ease,
   I herd with bachelors, and shun a wife;
   And he pursues the system contrary,
   Lives in the country; moils and toils all day,

Is married, has two children—whereof one,
The elder of the twain, I have adopted
And brought him up from childhood.   Him, I love,
As if he were mine own ; he knows it well,
And that I seek his love reciprocal.
I give, and I forgive—am lenient,
Exert not my authority, nor blame ;
So that all actions, sons so sedulously
Hide from their fathers, should not be so here.
No falsehoods or deceits to palm on me.
Believing as I do ingenuous youth
Are more restrained by honour than by fear.
My brother now deems otherwise, he blames
This course of licence—" How now, Micio !"
He passionately says, " you ruin him
Drabbing and drinking, dressing sumptuously,
And you encouraging all this—unwise."
He is himself too strict and too obdurate,
And widely errs, at least, I fancy so,
Who thinks that his dominion is more firm,
Founded on force than on benevolence.
I think not so myself, but reason thus—
He who is righteous by constraint and fear
Will play the hypocrite ; but let alone,
He will return to what is natural.
But treat him with benevolence, and he
Will naturally act and strive to please ;
Absent or present he will be the same.
It is a father's part to lead his son,
And not to drive him ; and it is therein
That fathers differ.   They who act the master
Know not the manner how to educate.

Ah! here he comes himself—'tis Demea,
Black as a thundercloud; to objurgate
As usual, be assured,—my brother comes.

ACT I.—Scene 2.—Micio and Demea.

Mic. O Demea, I rejoice to see you well.
Dem. Ahem! most opportunely, you I sought.
Mic. Why are you sad?
Dem.   The reason I am sad,
  Do you demand, when Æschinus is here?
Mic. I guessed so much, and what may he have done?
Dem. What hath he done!   He who can blush at nought;
  He, who fears nothing, and who thinks the laws
  Do not apply to such as he.   I may pass by
  His by-gones; for to-day—to-day he has
  Done an unheard-of action.
Mic.   What is it?
Dem. Broken the doors, and entered in perforce
  Another's house; has beaten nigh to death
  The master and his family, and snatched
  A woman thence, his mistress.   All exclaim
  Against a deed of such indignity.
  Micio, how much reproaches have I borne
  From neighbours, coming hither; all are wroth,
  Nor doth he good example lack; his brother
  Frugal, industrious, labouring at home;
  Who never did an action similar.
  Micio, these words apply to both of you—
  To you and him, for you encourage him.
Mic. How stupid and unjust is such a man,

As looking round, can only see himself;
And judges from his modicum of soul!
Dem. Why do you say that?
Mic.   To you, Demea,
And your misapprehensions. It is no crime
In a young man to foin, drink, and break doors.
If you and I did not so in our youth,
It was that we were poor and could not do it;
And will you merit take for what we did
From poverty and from necessity?
Why that were hypocritical; the fact
Is, we had not the means. Were Demea wise,
He would permit young license to his son,
Rather than let him wait until his death,
And then run wild in riot in his age.
Dem. Proh Jupiter! the man will drive me mad.
What do you say?   'Tis no flagitious deed
In a young man—
Mic.   Now do not break my head,
But listen, will you! ·Your eldest son is mine
And by adoption. If he offend in folly,
I must repair it, and must bear the brunt;
He eats, he drinks, he perfumes at my cost:
He scatters money 'mid his mistresses.
When he has none, then they will shut him out;
He breaks their doors down, we must set them up;
He rends their garments, we must mend again;
Thanks to the gods, we have the means enough!
Now cease to bother me, or, if you will,
Choose we an arbiter to put you down.
Dem. Nay, rather take instruction from a father
How to control a son.

Mic.   You are the physical—
  I am the mental counsellor and father.
Dem. What mental counsel—
Mic.   Stop, or I am off.
Dem. And do you use me thus?
Mic.   And do you ever
  Stun me with the same stuff.
Dem.   The pain is mine.
Mic. The pain is also mine. Now, Demea,
  I do entreat you, make a just division—
  You one and I the other. If you care
  For both, you take back your own gift and rob
  Me of my own.
Dem.   Ah, Micio!
Mic.   Well, I think so.
Dem. So be it then; if it so pleases you,
  Let him go to the dogs—or sink or swim.
  I wash my hands; I will not utter word.
Mic. Demea, you now wax wroth.
Dem.   No bit of it.
  Deem not that I will ever ask him back;
  But I have part in him—I am no stranger.
  If I object— Well, well! I hold my tongue.
  You wish me to take care of one: I will.
  Grace to the gods, he is all that I wish
  Unlike to him, as you will some day find
  Hereafter—Well, well! I will hold my tongue.

ACT I.—Scene 3.—Micio.

It is not wholly true, nor wholly false,
  This which he now objects; it troubles me,

And yet I veiled my trouble before him.
He is a nuisance. If I would appease him,
I must oppose him and o'erpower him
Nor then convince him. Were 1 to anger him,
1 should be stolid stupid as himself,
Or just as mad. Yet true it is that Æschinus
Now wrongs me, in this matter. What meretrix
Has he not visited, and has not fee'd?
And yet he lately spoke of marrying.
I hoped the effervescence of his youth
Was yielding to satiety ; I joyed,   .
And lo ! another outbreak. I will seek
And know without delay—so to the Forum.

ACT II.

Scene 1.—Sannio—Æschinus—Parmeno—Tibicina.

San. Help, fellow-citizens! help, help, I pray you!
 A rescue from injustice and oppression.
Æs. [*to Tib.*] Fear not; there nothing is to fear, I say.
 Why do you look so frightened?   Be assured,
 He shall not lay a finger on you, here.
San. I will, despite of all, lay hands on her.
Æs. Brute as he is, I tell you he has had
 Enough correction.
San.   Now, hearken Æschinus,
 A slave-merchant* am I.   You know it well.
Æs. I know it.
San.   Of unblemished reputation.
 You will excuse yourself, and think that I
 Accept apologies!   But I will sue
 For damages by law.   You shall not pay
 These blows by words.   I know what you will try,—
 Say you are very sorry and repent them,
 That I more worthy am of better treatment,
 When I have suffered these indignities.
Æs. [*to Par.*] Sharp is the word—hasten and ope the door.
San. Not so; I will not suffer it.
Æs. [*to Tib.*] Enter, I pray.
San. I say again—I will not suffer it.
Æs. Parmeno, stand here: here, close at hand—

---

* A privileged order, on account of the revenue.

Between us—and now fix your eyes on mine;
And when I give the signal, break his jaws.
San. I should like to see him do it.
Æs.   I say,
Let go the girl [*Parmeno hits him.*]
San.   Oh! great indignity.
Æs. Do you need more—another?   .
San.   Ah, what wrong!   .
Æs. [*to Par.*] I never gave the signal, Parmeno;
But you have erred upon the right side.   Now,
Will you be off!
San.   Are you despotic here;
Is this your kingdom, Æschinus?
Æs. If I were king you should have your deserts.
San. What have you to do with me, I say?
Æs.   Nothing.
San. Know you who I am?
Æs.   No; nor wish to know.
San. Say, have I aught of yours?*
Æs.   Ah! if you had,
It would be your misfortune.
San.   By what right
Do you bear off a girl whom I have bought?
Answer me that.
Æs.   'Twere better for thee not,
Nor make a turmoil here before the house,
Or I will have you dragged within the house,
And punished without stint.
San.   Punished—I am free.
Æs. I will.

* Am I your debtor, or have you the power of a creditor o'er me?
(Donatus).

San.   Dishonest man! where, then, is justice, say—
   Where, then, is liberty? common, they say, to all.
Æs. Slave merchant!   Now, if you have raved enough,
   Listen to me.
San.   You have raved more than I,
   Also at my expense.
Æs.   Come to the matter.
San. What matter?
Æs.   Why, on your own affairs.
San. Speak with regard to justice, then.
Æs.   Hark, now!
   A pander talk of justice.
San.   I am so—
   I own it, one pernicious unto youth—
   Perjured—a common nuisance.   With all that
   I never did you wrong.
Æs.   Zounds! if you had so.
San. Well, Æschinus, return to our affairs.
Æs. With twenty minæ did you purchase her?
   A plague upon you for it.   You shall have
   Your purchase-money back.
San.   And say that I
   Do not desire to sell; do you constrain me?
Æs. Nay, not at all.
San. Yet that was what I feared.
Æs. My own belief is, she cannot be sold—
   That she is free.   You may accept the money,
   Or fight it out at law.   I give you time;
   Now to deliberate thereon, a while.

ACT II.—Scene 2.—Sannio.

San. By supreme Jupiter! astounded, I
 No longer stand, that injuries drive mad:
 Broken my doors, and beaten me, and robbed,
 Stolen away my slave, and broke my jaws;
 And after all these outrages, demands
 To have the girl at simply the cost price.
 And I must let him have her. Ah! no doubt,
 This is but as it ought to be, and just.
 I wish I had the money; nevertheless,
 That may prove Sibyl's leaves: he purchases,
 Produces witnesses, and proves the sale—
 Off goes the silver—call again to-morrow.
 I wish I had the money: nevertheless,
 That would be gross injustice. Yet must I
 Ever remember this—who plies my trade
 Must suffer injuries, and hold their tongues.
 Confound the youth, I shall get nothing sure!
 I count my chickens, and they are unhatched.

ACT II.—Scene 3.—Syrus—Sannio.

Syr. Cease, let me go and find him; I know how
 To make him willingly accept the cash,
 And say he's much obliged. Eh! Sannio,
 Now, what is this about? I hear it said
 That you and that my master are at cars.
San. I never saw a more unequal fight;
 We fought till both of us were out of breath.
 He killed with beating, I with being beaten.
Syr. It was your fault.

San.   And how was it my fault?

Syr. You ought to bear respect to this young man.

San. What could I do—did I not lend my jaws?

Syr. Go to, go to; I come to counsel you.
  It often is a source of greatest' gain
  At just conjunctures to hate filthy lucre.

San. Hui! [*whistles.*]

Syr. You were so precious careful of your rights,
  So resolute not to concede a jot.
  O, void of wisdom, as if what you lent
  Would not have been restored unto you double.

San. I do not purchase, neither sell with hope.

Syr. You are a simpleton, unfit to trade.
  Why, Sannio, you know not how to cajole!

San. Perhaps so—indeed it might be better known.
  Yet, Syrus, I was never so astute
  As buy in hard cash, and to sell in hope.

Syr. Go to, I know your generosity.
  Now, twenty minæ, what are they to you?
  Taken to please my master. By the by
  They tell me also you are off to Cyprus.

San. Hem!

Syr.   And you have bought your venture and the cargo,
  Freighted a vessel, all which bothers you.
  Well, let us put this off to your return.

San. [*Aside.*] Hercle, now may I perish if I budge
  A foot from hence, I shall be humbugged else.

Syr. I've galled him to the very quick. He frets.

San. Accursed brutes, to catch me on the hip.
  The very fact. I have bought many women
  And other merchandize consigned to Cyprus.

Now if I fail this sailing, I have loss,
And if I quit this matter I have loss.
When I come back 'twill be past remedy.
I shall be humbugged.   Why have I delayed?
Where have I been? et cetera.   Yes! I must
Sacrifice something, for I cannot stay,
Neither will this thing wait for my return.

Syr. Have you cast up the sum, and do you know
Exactly now what gains you have in Cyprus?

San. Now is this conduct worthy, then, of Æschinus?
Now, ought he force and carry off the girl?
Now, is it not oppression?

Syr.   He is riled.
I have another proposition, see
If that may please you.   Sannio, rather
Than leave you in uncertainty and fear,
What do you say now about going halves—
Splitting the difference—ten minæ each?

San. Do I not touch your pity—do I not?
Has he no blushes? he has broke my jaws,
Raised bumps upon my head, and smitten me,
And now he wants to rob me of my money.
I will not budge.

Syr.   Well, as that pleases you,
Have you aught else to say, for I am off.

San. Hercle! I pray thee, Syrus, lend me help.
Well, if I must, rather than go to law,
Let me have only back her purchase-money.
Syrus, I grant I never yet bestowed
Bounty upon you; but be well assured
I shall remember you for service done.

Syr. I will do my best.   Ah! I see Ctesipho
  Beaming with love.
San.   Will you do as I ask?
Syr. Wait—wait a minute.

ACT II.—Scene 4.—Ctesipho—Syrus—Sannio.

Cte. Welcome to men in need are generous hands;
  But benefits are doubly pleasing when
  Falling from them we love.   O brother, brother,
  How can I render thanks and love enough.
  Every encomium would fall short of sooth,
  Which I am fain to render unto thee,
  As the most generous and best of men.
Syr. O Ctesipho.
Cte.   O, Syrus, where is Æschinus?
Syr. Waiting here for you.
Cte.   Ah!
Syr.   What's the matter?
Cte. The matter, Syrus; by his gift I live.
Syr. He is beneficent!
Cte.   He ne'er consulted
  His interests or leisure when behoved
  To succour me: the maledictions, fame,
  My passion, and my faults, assuming all—
  All on himself.   Hark, for the doorway creaks.
Syr. Stay—it is he.

ACT II.—Scene 5.—Æschinus—Sannio—Ctesipho—Syrus.

Æs. Where is he? sacrilegious beast!
San.   He seeks me.
  Has he the cash? I perish, he hath none!
Æs. Ah! opportunely : it was you I sought for.
  What do you, Ctesipho? for all goes right :
  Look then not glum.
Cte.   I have ceased, Æschinus,
  To look so since I have you for a brother.
  O my dear brother, O my Æschinus,
  I hardly dare to thank you to your face,
  Lest you should think my tropes were flattery—
  Not from the heart.
Æs.   Away—you trifler—
  As if we knew not one another long.
  I only grieve I was informed so late,
  Of love, and wants, and wishes, and came late
  To lend an aiding hand in happy time.
Cte. I was ashamed.
Æs.   We call that foolishness,
  Not shame, my Ctesipho! What, for a freak
  To fly the country! Fie! the gods forbid
  That we be cursed by such simplicity.
Cte. I was mistaken.
Æs.   What says Sannio ?
  Eh, Syrus!
Syr.   Very gracious.
Æs.   I will away

Unto the forum and defray his debt.
Go in unto her—Ctesipho—within.
San. Stop! Syrus.
Syr. [*to Æs.*]   Let us depart at once, for he
Is most impatient to be off to Cyprus.
San. Not a bit; I can wait here for ever.
Syr. Fear nothing—he will pay.
San.   Will he pay all?
Syr. All, all! be quiet now and follow us.
San. I follow.
Cte.   Heus! Syrus, Syrus.
Syr.   What now?
Cte. Hercle! I pray you, pay this villain knave,
And quickly, too, lest he kick up a riot,
And that should reach unto my father's ear,
And I be crushed for ever.
Syr.   Ah! never fear,
Pluck up your spirit—nevertheless, I say,
Get you indoors—and look you—have prepared
The couches for the supper—when we come
Home from the forum, we shall be sharp set.
Cte. And glad am I to hear it—let this day
That promises so happily, be merry.

ACT III.

Scene 1.—Sostrata—Canthara.

Sos. Nurse, I beseech you—how do matters go?
Can. Go! edepol! right well; but penalties
    Are only just commencing; whilst you quake
    And tremble now—as if you never knew
    Yourself now—pains of labour.
Sos.   I am perplexed,
    Nurse—all alone—we are but two. Geta
    Is absent, too; no one have I to call
    The midwife, nor to send to Æschinus.
Can. Pol! he will soon be here—for day by day
    He never intermits—he ever comes.
Sos. My only comfort in much misery.
Can. Now in good sooth this accident could not
    Have happened under happier auspices,
    Though hard to suffer wrong—yet Æschinus
    Is handsome, generous, rich, of family.
Sos. Pol! that is true—may the gods grant it so.

ACT III.—Scene 2.—Geta—Sostrata—Canthara.

Get. Things are so wrong, that counsel were in vain,
    And health of no avail and help unaiding,
    To mistress and her daughter and to me, ·
    So many ills fall souse upon our heads.
    I do not see how we may thence emerge,
    Force, want, injustice, solitude, and shame.

Oh! iron age—oh! wickedness—oh! man—
Vile, sacrilegious, villainous, impure!
Sos. I tremble, what is it—troubling Geta so?
　Why is he running hither in such haste?
Get. Nor faith, nor law, nor pity—pitiless;
　Although my mistress draws towards the birth:
　She, whom he treated so indignantly.
Sos.　I cannot catch the drift of what he says.
Can. Sostrata, I beseech you—hide ourselves.
Get.　I am unhappy—scarcely in my mind,
　In grief and wrath—my soaring wish just now
　To cross him in his path and fulminate
　My wrath, whilst it is vivid, at his head,
　And all his race—I would extinguish first
　The old man's soul—him from whose loins he sprung,
　And next that villain knave and accessory—
　Syrus, and rend him piecemeal limb by limb—
　To raise him up aloft—to dash him down—
　To break his skull and smear the street with brains,
　And from the master spirit rend the eyes,
　Then cast him from a rock—and all the rest
　To seize, to maul, to pound, to prosternate.
　Instead of which I must go tell my mistress.
Sos. Let me call, Geta!
Get.　　　　　　　Nay, never stay me now,
　Whoe'er ye be.
Sos.　　　　　　But I am Sostrata.
Get. Where is she?　Sostrata I wished to see.
　Ah! mistress, very opportunely you
　Meet me inopportunely.
Sos.　　　　　　　Why are you
　So troubled?

Get.   Ah, me! ah, me!

Sos.   And whither hastening,
  Geta! take courage man.

Get.   We utterly—

Sos. How utterly? and why?

Get.   Lost utterly—we are.

Sos. But speak—I ask you, now.

Get.   Now?

Sos.   Ay! now, I say.

Get. Æschinus—

Sos.   What doth he?

Get.   Abandons us,
  An alien evermore.

Sos.   Ah, I perish! why—

Get. Love for another one.

Sos.   Ah, misery mine!

Get. Ay! undisguised, and openly—he raids
  His mistress, from the slave dealer, by day.

Sos. Ah! is this truth?

Get.   Most true—I saw it—I,
  With these my eyes.

Sos.   Ah! I am lost indeed,
  Who would believe it? Upon whom rely?
  Our Æschinus! our life, our only hope,
  Our strong support, defence, our comfort, wealth,
  Who swore he could not live a single day
  Without my child—who promised at the birth
  To bear the infant to his father's bosom,
  Beseeching him to grant her for his wife.

Get. Mistress—eschew these tears, and let us think
  How to employ our time in usefulness,
  Should we submit, or seek forensic help.

Sos. Ah, ah ! my man, are you in your right wits ?
  How can we publish to the world such tale ?
Get. I am unwilling so, for truly he
  Is alienated in his love ; the facts
  Proclaim the fact indisputably clear.
  If we assert, straightway will he deny—
  Away go reputation and our honour.
  And were it otherwise, he loves another
  To grieve your daughter—turn which way you will
  Our welfare seems to be in secrecy.
Sos. No, no, I say again, no secrecy.
Get. What will you do ?
Sos.   Will plead.
Get.   My Sostrata—
  Dear mistress—now consider.
Sos.   Things cannot
  Be worse than now they are, for, first of all,
  She has no dowry—secondly, she lacks
  That which itself is dowry—maidenhood.
  If he deny, we must produce our proofs :
  The ring he gave her.   Lastly, let me say,
  We sought not this misfortune—that no blame
  Attaches unto us—nor avarice nor pride—
  Unworthy motives.   I will plead it, Geta.
Get. I must submit to better arguments.
Sos. Go, quickly as you can to Hegio.
  He is related to us—tell him all,
  He was the friend of Simulus of old,
  He always loved us well.
Get.   And he, moreover,
  The sole who cares for us.

Sos.   Haste, haste, and you
   Dear Canthara—go seek the midwife straight,
   Let her, at least, be ready at our need.

ACT III.—Scene 3.—Demea.

Lost, lost! I hear that Ctesipho, my son,
Accompanied with Æschinus, when he
Bore off that girl.   Misfortune lours upon me ;
For he, on whom I trusted, as a staff
Turns out a good for nought.   Where shall I seek,
At taverns for him, or at worse.   Ah! Syrus—
He can tell surely—hercle! will he tell?
He is one of the herd, and if he sees
Me anxious—carnifex! he will not speak,
I must look jauntily.

ACT III.—Scene 4.—Syrus—Demea.

Syr. We have divulged the tale, from first to last,
   Told it in sequent order—and the senior
   Chuckles outright.
Dem.   Proh Jupiter, the fool!
Syr. Applauds his son—to me, who gave the counsel—
   He gave me thanks.
Dem.   Zounds !
Syr.   Counted the money down,
   And cast down, for the penny, a half mina.
   I have dispensed it after my own heart.
Dem. Hem ! if you want your business done—behold
   The man to do it.

Syr.   Ah! Demea, pardon;
  I did not see you.   How go matters, sir?
Dem. How matters go!   I am in admiration,
  Beholding how you act.
Syr.   Well, clownishly;
  Nothing to brag or boast of—Dromo, ch!
  Gut me these fish—this mighty conger now
  Must purge itself in water.   I will return
  And see about the cooking, hurry not.
Dem. Flagitious deeds.
Syr.   Ah! I approve them not—
  I rail against them much.   Stephanio,
  Unsalt and rub these well.
Dem.   Faith of the gods!
  Doth he then hold it righteous to debauch,
  And look for praises for my ruined son?
  I am aghast; methinks I see the day
  When he, for want, will flee and be a soldier.
Syr. Demea, methinks that constitutes a sage;
  Not merely to perceive things at your nose,
  But see far off the things invisible.
Dem. This Psaltrian then is with you?
Syr.   Ay, within.
Dem. And to inhabit there?
Syr.   Well, I believe so;
  He is crazy, sure.
Dem.   Now, is this credible?
Syr. A foolish license—sufferance depraved—
  Paternal.
Dem.   I blush and grieve alike
  To see my brother's folly.

Syr.   The difference
Is wide and deep between you, Demea.
I do not say so for to flatter you,
But you are wise now— wise to the backbone.
He dreams, he is a dreamer.   Would you allow
Such goings on, I ask ?

Dem.   I—I allow !
Should I not nose and catch him in the intent
Months ere it came to pass ?

Syr.   No need to teach
Me—of your vigilance.

Dem.   If he would bide
Just as he is now, I should be content.

Syr. Ah ! as we wish them, oftentimes they prove.

Dem. Have you seen him to-day ?

Syr.   Seen who ! your son ?
[*Aside.*] Where shall I send him to ? [*Aloud.*] He is at home,
Ploughing the glebe, methinks.

Dem.   But are you sure ?

Syr. I walked with him half-way.

Dem.   Why, that is good !
I feared that he was here.

Syr.   He went in anger.

Dem. How so ?

Syr.   He quarrelled with his brother
About this Psaltrian.

Dem.   In faith ?

Syr.   In good faith !
Wherefore disguise ?   We counted out the cash ;
He came upon us unawares, and cried,
O, Æschinus, for shame ! is it possible
You do such deeds unworthy of your name !

Dem. Ah! I could weep for joy.
Syr.   It is not money
   You cast away, it is your name and fame.
Dem. Ah! may he thrive and grace his ancestry.
Syr. He does so.
Dem.   Syrus, I say, he is replete
   With such good maxims.
Syr.   Could it be otherwise?
   He who has ever lived at home—to learn.
Dem. I taught him sedulously—never ceased;
   Accustomed him to virtue—bade him mark
   Man in his courses, as a mirror's face—
   To follow or to shun.   Do this, said I—
Syr. Good!
Dem.   Do this, and that avoid—
Syr.   Good, good!
Dem. Such thing is laudable—
Syr.   No doubt, no doubt!
Dem. That is detestable—
Syr.   Why that is excellent.
Dem. Afterwards—
Syr.   Hercle! I have no leisure
   Longer to listen; I have other fish,
   A dish of fish, to fry.   I must take care
   They are not spoiled in cooking, Demea;
   A fault as heinous now in one of us,
   As to omit good counsel is in you.
   I also preach and parley with my man--
   Too salt, too burnt, too sodden, or all right;
   Remember now, and recollect next time.
   I teach them sedulously, never cease;
   Accustom them to virtue, I can teach

To regard dishes as a mirror's face,
And warn them what to follow, what to shun.
I feel that this is insignificant ;
But what of that, if it be my vocation.
Do you desire aught else ?

Dem. Some wisdom for you.

Syr. You are bound for the fields ?

Dem. Immediately.

Syr. Why should you stay here in the naughty town,
Where no one either needs or heeds good counsel.

Dem. I need not stay, since he for whom I came
Has hence returned, he is my care and joy ;
I love but him ; since that my brother plots
That Æschinus, the other, should please him.
But who comes here afar ? 'tis Hegio,
Him of our ward ; I have known him from a boy,
One of my very friends—the right true stuff.
Ah ! how the ancient citizens grow scarce.
Word better than his bond ; a man, I trow,
Of antique faith and virtue ; who can yet
Blush at the voice of scandal.   I must stop
And greet, and have a bit of chat with him.

ACT III.—Scene 5.—Hegio—Geta—Demea—Pamphila.

Hey. By the immortal gods, a shameful deed !
Geta, can this be true ?

Get. It is too true.

Hey. In such a worthy house to do such wrong.
Ah ! Æschinus, your father taught you not
To do such deeds.

Dem. He is talking of the Psaltrian.

It irks him now, although he is a stranger ;
It irks his father not ; would he were here
To hear his speech of ruth.
Heg.   If they brazen it,
They may find it a worse matter than they think.
Get. You, Hegio, are our only hope and trust ;
You are our only patron—only father.
Our master, who is dead, commended us
To your protection, without which we are nothing.
Heg. You need not press me, I cannot desert you ;
I hold it as an act of piety.
Dem. I will accost him.   Health and happy day
To Hegio !
Heg.   I sought for you yourself.
Hail, Demea !
Dem.   How so ?
Heg.   Your eldest son,
Adopted by your brother—Æschinus
Has done a deed, unfitting to his rank
And to his honour also, most unworthy.
Dem. And what has he done ?
Heg.   Do you remember
One Simulus, our neighbour and old friend ?
Dem. What then ?
Heg.   He hath abused his daughter.
Dem.   Hem !
Heg. Demea, there is matter yet behind
Of graver import.
Dem.   What of graver import ?
Heg. Much graver.   One, though wrong exceedingly,
Was yet excusable—by night—wine, love
And youth concurring all—a man may err.

When he discovered the wrong he had done,
He went in tears and suppliant to her mother,
And pledged his faith, and promised to espouse her.
They trusted, pardoned him, and sued him not.
The girl conceived, the tenth month hath come round,
And he hath bought a Psaltrian to his taste,
That he may live with one and quit the other.
Dem. Are you quite certain?
Heg.   The mother and the girl
 The fact—speak open mouthed, and, Geta, here—
 Honest, as servants go, hard working, who
 Supports the family by industry—
 Here take him, bind him, make him tell the truth.
Get. Hercle! make haste to torture me, to know
 That this is truth; or ask it him himself,
 He will deny it not.
Dem.   I blush—nor know
 I what I ought to do, or what respond.
Pamphila within.] Juno Lucina, help and aid, I pray you!
Heg. Hem! Is she in labour pangs?
Get.   Yea! doubtless, Hegio.
Heg. Demea, this damsel now demands your justice;
 Grant her in generosity, what law
 May grant in rigour, and, I do beseech you,
 Act with the probity becomes your name.
 If you deem otherwise, I bid you know
 That I stand here defender of this girl,
 In memory of my departed friend.
 He was my kinsman—we were boys together:
 In peace and war, we ever were allied;
 We bore our poverty and woes together;
 Therefore, I will not slur her rights, nor sleep.

I will plead for her rights, and die before
I will abandon them.   Do you demur?
Dem. All that I, Hegio, can do to-day
  Is to go find my brother.
Heg.   Demea,
  Remember this! proportioned to your rank,
  Your wealth, position, happiness; whate'er
  The points wherein you are deemed fortunate;
  In like proportion are you bound to be
  Honest and true in matters like to this.
Dem. Go, go, I hope to do the thing that's right.
Heg. And that is worthy of you.   Geta, go
  And lead me to your mistress, Sostrata.

ACT III.—Scene 6.— Demea.

My mind misgave me there was something wrong—
I would this may be all; such license leads
To deeds like these which plunge in seas of wrong.
I go to seek my brother and to chide.

ACT III.—Scene 7.—Hegio.

Be of good comfort, Sostrata; console
The afflicted damsel.   I will go and find
Micio, now in the Forum, and relate
All that has happened.   If he do his duty
Then all is well, and if he do it not,
Behoves it then to me to up and act.

ACT IV.

Scene 1.—Ctesipho—Syrus.

Cte. My father off—gone home?

Syr.   Long time ago.

Cte. Nay, but good sooth?

Syr.   By this time he is there,
  And hard at work.

Cte.   Pray fates that it be so,
  And that he labour, that, except his health,
  He may repair his frame three days in bed.

Syr. Just so; and something else, and better perhaps.

Cte. Fain would I finish, as it hath begun,
  This festal day, and fain that this my joy
  Should meet no cross. One reason that I hate
  That rustic home is, that it is so near.
  If it were further off, the night would come,
  And distance bar return. He finds me not,
  And straightway he returns, and when we greet
  For the first time to-day, and he asks where
  I have bestowed myself, what shall I say?

Syr. Can you not feign a cause?

Cte.   Nay, I cannot.

Syr. Poor boy! what nothing! Client, friend, or host—
  Nought plausible.

Cte.   We have all such; what then?

Syr. Aid and assistance asked and given at need.

Cte. That were untruth, and may not be.

Syr.   But must.

Cte. Well, that will do for daytime; what for night?
   Prompt me to that, my Syrus.
Syr.   Ah, forsooth!
   I would it were the fashion to lend aid
   To friends by night. Ah! well, well! let it be.
   I know the way to lull him into rest
   When rough as Adria.
Cte.   How?
Syr.   By praising you.
   He listens to your praises half bewitched.
   You are my genius, and I chant your praise.
Cte. Mine?
Syr.   Yours! virtues and attributes; and he
   Weeps like a baby in excess of joy.
   Hem! here he is.
Cte.   Who?
Syr.   Wolf in the fable.
Cte. My father?
Syr.   Ay, himself.
Cte.   Syrus, what must we do?
Syr. You cut and run in-doors—leave me alone.
Cte. If he asks for me, say you have not seen,
   And do not know—
Syr.   I say, will you be off.

ACT IV.—Scene 2.—Demea—Ctesipho—Syrus.

Dem. I am of men the most unfortunate;
   I cannot find my brother: and a man
   Returning from the farm, assures me that
   Ctesipho is not there. I am all astray.

Cte.   Syrus.

Syr.   Well.

Cte.   Does he seek me?

Syr.   Ay.

Cte.   I am
Undone.

Syr.   Pshaw! keep up a good heart.

Dem. Child am I of misfortune. Methinks I am
Doomed to misfortune from my birth and star.
Evil descends on my head, first of all
It lights on me. I feel it—bear the news
Round to my neighbours, who make light of it.
My shoulders bear the weight.

Syr.   Exceeding guy!
He thinks he only knows; he is the sole
Who nothing knows.

Dem.   I seek my brother now.

Cte. Syrus, take care he does not pounce in here.

Syr. Lie still and trust to me.

Cte.   I do not dare
To trust in my own strength. I will go seek
Some secret cell and bar ourselves within.

Syr. Do so; but for all that he enters not.

Dem. The villain, Syrus—lo!

Syr. [*Aloud.*]   Hercle! unbearable!
What state of things is this; I fain would know
How many masters have I—Tell me that!

Dem. What is he growling—grumbling at? Eh! you,
Hark ye my man. Is my brother there within?

Syr. Hark ye, my man! What do you mean by that?
I say, I cannot bear it.

Dem.   What is the matter?

Syr. What dost thou ask ?   Why, Ctesipho has thrashed
  Me and the Psaltrian.
Dem.   What do you say ?
Syr. Nay, look you, he has cut right through the lip.
Dem. And wherefore ?
Syr.   He says it was I who gave
  Counsel to purchase her.
Dem.   You said that he
  Had gone unto the farm.
Syr.   And so he had,
  And has come back again—come back enraged.
  Doth he not blush to beat a man so old !
  I dandled him when he was three days old.
  Look you the size of that.
Dem.   Ah ! Ctesipho :
  I praise you heartily ; you follow me ;
  A man in judgment, he.
Syr.   You praise him, you !
  If he be wise, he will not smite so hard.
Dem. He has done well.
Syr.   Done well to strike a woman,
  And an old man, a slave like me, who dare not
  Retaliate—he done well !
Dem.   He could not do
  A better deed, I say : he thinks you are
  The head and front of this most vile proceeding.
  Say, is my brother in ?
Syr.   No.
Dem.   Do you know where ?
Syr. Yes, I know where, and do not mean to say.
Dem. Hem ! What is this ?
Syr.   You see.

Dem.   I will tell you what—
 I will break your head.

Syr.   But I don't know the name;
 I know the place, but do not know the man.

Dem. Tell me the place.

Syr.   You know the portico
 Before the market-place—down here behind.

Dem. I do.

Syr.   Well! pass the portico, then cross
 The market-place, and when you get across,
 There are some steps—a short declivity—
 Jump down it, after that there is a chapel,
 And then a narrow lane.

Dem.   A narrow lane!

Syr. Ay! with a tree—a wild fig—with big trunk.

Dem. I know it.

Syr.   Well, then, go on.

Dem.   That can I not;
 It is no thoroughfare.

Syr.   Ah! that is true.
 Oh, what an ass! Ah! what a beast am I!
 Come back again unto the portico:
 We must start off afresh a shorter way.
 Know you the dwelling of rich Cratinus?

Dem. Yes.

Syr.   Well! pass his dwelling-house, and afterwards
 Turn to the left hand, and then go straight on.
 When you come to Diana, take the right;
 Then on unto the fountain and a baker's,
 And opposite a workshop—carpenter's;
 Well! he is there.

Dem.   What doth he there?

Syr.   He orders

  Legs for a table, turned with feet of oak,
  To eat off out of doors.
Dem.   Or say, to drink—
  You are given more to drink; well! I am off.
Syr. Right, you do right.   I'll exercise your legs
  To-day, I will, my busybody.

                        Where's Æschinus ?

  He should be here—confound him—dinner spoils !
  There's Ctesipho all love.   I must look out
  And take care of myself—to eat the fat
  And drink the sweet—Ah ! and to empty pots
  And cans, and to be merry whilst we may.

ACT IV.—Scene 3.—Micio—Hegio.

Mic. Now, by my word of honour, Hegio,
  I am delighted.   I will make all straight;
  I will repair all injury we've done.
  Although, perchance, you deemed me one of those
  Who, having done an injury, take affront
  And quarrel rather than make reparation.
  I cannot lay a claim to thanks for this,
  Nor need you thank me, Hegio, as you do.
Heg. Nay, not for that: I never deemed you, Micio,
  Other than what you are ; but I entreat you
  Come, calm the mother of the maiden's heart.
  Tell her that our suspicions were ill-founded,
  And that the Psaltrian was not bought for him,
  But for his brother.
Mic.   If you think it right,
  Hence let us go.

Heg.   You will do all a kindness,
  Relieving the poor soul in doubt and dread,
  Whose spirits need it too; you will be glad
  When you have done it.   If you think not so,
  I will go there alone and tell the news.
Mic. Nay, I will go myself.
Heg.   You will do best;
  For the unfortunate are jealous, too,
  And doubtful of the world; they ever dread
  It, contumelious upon poverty.
  And the best way to calm their throbbing hearts
  And justify her husband, is to go.
Mic. Ah! that is true.
Heg.   Come, let us go together.

ACT IV.—Scene 4.—Æschinus.

Æs. I am half driven wild: a thunderbolt,
  To fall from heaven, thus at unawares,
  Not dreaming of such thing—I am at sea.
  My members all are quivering with fear;
  My mind is all bewildered with its dread;
  My soul is all in doubt and cannot think.
  How shall I clear myself of all this cloud
  Of treasons and of thoughts unmerited,
  For Sostrata believes this Psaltrian
  Purchased for me? The old dame tells me so.
  I met her on the way—she sought the midwife:
  I asked her of the health of Pamphila—
  If she were in the pangs—when she began
  Exclaiming, Ai! Ai! Æschinus—I pray
  Mock us no more, with words and broken faith.

How now? I asked, amazed.   Away! she cried.
Go to your mistress—her, who pleases you!
Then I perceived the fact, but held my peace.
I kept my brother's secret from her ears.
What shall I do?   Shall I go and proclaim
His secret that this Psaltrian is his own,
Which he entreats me not to do?   Away,
Notions of their connivance and consonance!
For they would disbelieve me and my tale.
'Twas I abducted her; I paid the price ;
I led her home.   Well, it was all my fault,
I ought to have told my father, have besought him,
And gained his leave to wed with Pamphila.
Still, still am I asleep.   Up, Æschinus!
Go, justify yourself; knock at their door.
I cannot, panic fears lay hold of me
Before I knock.   Open; 'tis Æschinus.
Some one comes forth.   I must go hide myself.

ACT IV.—Scene 5.—Micio—Æschinus.

Mic. Do what I tell you, Sostrata, for me
   I go find Æschinus to tell him all.
   Who knocks upon the gate?

Æs.   My father—Ah !

Mic. Æschinus.

Æs.   Ah ! what can he do here ?

Mic. Did you knock, Æschinus?   He answers not.
   Suppose I banter him a bit—all fair;
   For wherefore did he not confide in me ?
   ·You answer not.

Æs.   I knocked not that I know of.

Mic. Just so; for what, by possibility, could you
    Have to do here? He blushes red: good sign.
Æs. And what have you, my father, to do here?
Mic. Nought for myself, good sooth, but for a friend,
    Retained to lend my aid.
Æs.   Father, what aid?
Mic. Well, listen. Here do certain women lodge,
    Not over-rich; of course you know them not.
    It is not long they have resided here.
Æs. What next, I pray you?
Mic.   There is a maiden dwells
    Here with her mother.
Æs.   Oh! continue, pray!
Mic. Orphaned as to the father. As my friend
    Is next of kin, the law obliges him
    To wed the maiden.
Æs.   I am undone.
Mic.   Eh! what?
Æs. Nothing; go on.
Mic.   He comes to lead her off,
    He of Miletus is.
Æs.   What, to lead her off?
Mic. Ay.
Æs. What, to Miletus?
Mic.   Ay.
Æs.   I am undone.
    What do the women say—what do they say?
Mic. What should they say! They can say nought at all.
    Only the mother owns there is a child,
    And by some man, and whom she will not say,
    Claiming a right for him, and that her daughter
    Cannot be his.

Æs.   And doth it not seem so?
  Is not that law?
Mic.   No.
Æs.   Will he lead her home,
  I pray you?
Mic.   Why should he not lead her home?
Æs. But you have done a deed—inhuman,
  Savage, brutal—most unworthy; I say
  it, beyond contradiction, base.
Mic. How so?
Æs.   Ah! can you ask? Imagine, pray!
  The state of that man's torture, who hath lived
  A life of joy, who dotes upon her charms.
  What will become of him? Ah! what a lot!
  To see his wife borne off before his eyes!
  It is an action infamous—my father.
Mic. But wherefore so? Who gave the girl away?
  Or who consented? Wherefore when he wedded
  Did he take one belonging to another?
Æs. Belonging to another! a maid marriageable —
  To wait, expecting next of kin unknown!
  This was the plea of justice to have urged,
  And you ought to have urged it.
Mic.   Not a bit.
  How could I plead against the side of him
  For whom I went the advocate? But. Æschinus,
  What is all this to you and me? Or why
  Should we be— Wherefore do you weep?
Æs. Father, I pray you, hear.
Mic.   My son, I have
  Heard and know all. I love you well, my Æschinus.
  And therefore intermeddle where I love.

Æs. My father, may your love for me be still
  Equal to my deserts and my repentance;
  For I am criminal, I grieve to say,
  And blush to stand before you.

Mic. I believe you;
  I know you have a fair, ingenuous mind,
  But reckless, negligent. Where do you deem
  You dwell? In Athens? You have wronged a maiden,
  Forbidden by the law; there the first breach,
  And, though a fault, yet not a turpid one;
  One which hath happened unto worthy men.
  But afterwards—what did you afterwards?
  Precautions for the future—did you take
  A step towards reparation of your fault?
  Did you acquaint me? Or, if shame forbad,
  Did you find others to do so? And thus,
  Ten months elapsing, and the wife and child
  Betrayed—betrayed by your irresolution—
  What, did you think that you might go to sleep,
  And let the gods take care, and from the skies
  Drop her in your cubiculum and home?
  I grieve to find you so improvident;
  Be of good cheer, for you shall lead her home.

Æs. Ah!

Mic. Be of good cheer, I say.

Æs. , Ah! mock me not,
  Dear father, I entreat you.

Mic. I mock you, I!

Æs. I know not; I am troubled in the spirit;
  My soul is all alive to fear, not hope.

Mic. Go home; beseech the gods to bring you home
  Your wife. Away!

Æs.   My *wife*, lead home my wife?
Mic. Ay, now.
Æs.   Now?
Mic.   Well, soon as we may.
Æs.   Father,
  May the gods hate me, if I love you not
  More than the light of day.
Mic.   What more than *her!*
Æs. As well as her.
Mic.   Well, that is saying much.
Æs. But where is that Milesian?
Mic.   He embarked,
  And has gone to the bottom of the sea.
  Away with you!
Æs.   Father, do you beseech
  Our gods for me; you better are than I;
  Your prayers will be the more acceptable.
Mic. I must go in, for I have what to do;
  If you are wise, go do what I have said.
Æs. [*Alone.*] Ah! this is to be a father—this a son,
  Or friend, or brother; what could he be more?
  Kind and beneficent. Ah! ought I not
  To cherish him within my inmost heart?
  Ah! I will take good heed, and walk a path
  Of circumspection, if to grieve him not.
  I must go in myself, and hurry too,
  Nor be the cause of my own more delay.

ACT IV.—Scene 6.—Demea.

I have walked till I am weary. May Jupiter
Confound that villain Syrus and directions—

The gate, the fountain—ne'er a baker's there.
Nor carpenter's—nor brother, could I find;
So here I am to wait for his return.

ACT IV.—Scene 7.—Micio—Demea.

Mic. I go to tell them now that we are ready.
Dem. Why, here you are! I sought you up and down.
Mic. And wherefore so?
Dem.   Offences more and more—
 Your excellent young man!
Mic.   Well, what?
Dem. Why, felonies.
Mic.   No, no.
Dem.   No, no; you know him not.
Mic. I know him well.
Dem.   You nothing know at all;
 You deem some matter with the Psaltrian.
 This is a crime against a citizen—
 A virgin.
Mic. Well, I know.
Dem.   And suffer it!
 You know it and you suffer it!
Mic.   I do.
Dem. Does it not drive you wild, nor make you mad?
Mic. No, I would rather——
Dem.   But a boy is born—
Mic. May the gods bless him!
Dem.   She has not a stiver.
Mic. Ay! so they say.
Dem.   A wife without a dowry.
Mic. It is so.

Dem.   Now, what is to be done next?
Mic. What to be done!   We must take the bride home.
Dem. O Jupiter!   Is that what you will do!
Mic. Nay, what more can I do?
Dem.   What more can do!
  Why, grieve—or make a semblance that you grieve!
Mic. I have betrothed the damsel, and to-day
  We celebrate th' espousals.   They are happy,
  Happy exceedingly.   I have done that.
Dem. Apparently, you like this matter, Micio.
Mic. I like it not; would it had never been!
  What is past help, is past all remedy.
  The life of man is as a game of dice :
  If you cannot throw sices, you must be
  Content with what turns up, and try and eke
  Out ill luck by *good* play, and so correct it.
Dem. Corrector! by your play—some twenty minæ
  Are lost upon the cast—this Psaltrian
  Has cost so much and now must be resold,
  And if no buyer, then the price is lost.
Mic. Ah! but good sooth I do not mean to sell her.
Dem. What do you mean to do?
Mic.   To take her home.
Dem. Faith of the gods! how so—a wife and mistress
  Together in one house?
Mic.   And wherefore not?
Dem. Now by my word I do not think you sane.
Mic. In truth I am.
Dem.   As the gods love me now,
  If you are not half-witted—you must mean
  To keep her as your minstrel.

Mic.   Wherefore not?

Dem. And then the bride may listen to her lays.

Mic. Ah! so she may.

Dem.   You dance a fling with them.

Mic. Just so.

Dem.   Just so!

Mic.   And you shall dance and sing,

   You shall be one of us.

Dem.   Fie! are you not ashamed!

Mic. I do entreat you, brother, to cast off

   This black and moody temper. Now look gay,

   And smile upon the nuptials of your son.

   I must go see the bride and then return.

Dem. [*Alone.*] O Jupiter! what life—what manners—

        madness!

   Wife without dower—and a Psaltrian there—

   A house of sheer expense and luxury—

   A dotard senior! Ah! if the goddess Health

   Should stoop to earth to save them, 'twere in vain!

ACT V.

Scene 1.—Syrus.—Demea.

Syr. Edepol, Syrè—you have taken care
  Of number one—yourself, and not done badly.
  I have stuffed full of everything within—
  Now I come forth to breathe a bit without.
Dem. Look at him there—a pattern for instruction.
Syr. Ah! here is our old man—our own old man.
  I say—what makes you glum?
Dem.   You, villain! dog!
Syr. Ah! are you talking proverbs—words of wisdom.
Dem. If you were mine!
Syr.   You would be rich, indeed,
  Ah! Demea, that would 'stablish your affairs.
Dem. I would make you an example to the rest.
Syr. And why—my tidy one?
Dem.   Why! because you're drunk—
  Because midst turmoil and midst trouble you
  Joy and are merry, all good fun to you.
Syr. Plague on it, wherefore came I forth, I trow.

ACT V.—Scene 2.—Dromo—Syrus—Demea.

Dro. Ctesipho, Syrus, calls aloud for you.
Syr. [*To Dromo.*] Be off.
Dem.   What did he say of Ctesipho.
Syr. Nothing.
Dem.   Why did he name him then?
Syr.   Not him—

Another parasite—young good for nought—
He named.

Dem.   Ah! I will see.

Syr.   Stop, stop—where are
You bound?

Dem.   Ah! let me go.

Syr.   I won't, I tell you.

Dem. Let go your hold—or I will break your head.

Syr. There he goes in—and edepol, a guest
Not over-welcome—least of all to Ctesipho.
What must I do the while of all this row?
I will creep in a corner and go sleep
Off the effects of wine—ay, that will I !

ACT V.—Scene 3.—Micio—Demea.

Mic. We are all ready, Sostrata, whene'er
You please—holloa! who kicks so loud at doors?

Dem. What shall I do—where go—where cry aloud,
Or where complain? O Heaven! O earth and seas !

Mic. He has discovered it—he bellows out—
Now they implead—I must unto the rescue.

Dem. Behold him, lo! corruptor of our youth.

Mic. Calm, calm yourself, anger now makes you mad.

Dem. Now I am calm enough, and let me speak,
I will not objurgate—but to the point.
It was agreed between us—you proposed it —
You should not interfere with mine, nor I with yours, ·
Was that not so?

Mic.   It was so—I avow it.

Dem. Then what doth he now, feasting here with you—
Why do you purchase him a slave girl, Micio?

Why deal you not with me as I with you?
I interfere not, neither so should you.
Mic. This is unjust now, Demea, faith it is:
You know the good old proverb that declares,
That all things should be common between friends.
Dem. Sarcastically spoken—do you run
To sarcasm now for aid!
Mic.   Hark ye, brother, mine;
If you are vexed at their extravagance,
Remember that you formerly regarded,
According to their narrow means, their fortunes,
And thought that they were limited to yours.
You thought that I would marry—think so still.
Go on the old routine—to pare and spare—
Close bind, close find; and all to leave them more.
To spare is then your cue—to spend be mine,
Since mine comes unexpectedly on you.
Your funds decrease not, do not then refuse
Good fortune that falls on you unawares.
Now turn this over, Demea, in your mind,
And save ourselves and them anxiety.
Dem. I care not for the money, but their manners.
Mic. Peace! I am coming on to that. There are
Points about men, by which you can discover
How, when two men run in the self-same road,
You may predict to one impunity
And danger to the other. Granted the facts
To be the same—the men are different.
Now to these sons of ours—I can see
Sufficient reason to confide in them,
And they will go all right. Good sense: they have
Intelligence—they have the gift to blush—

They are affectionate—love one the other—
And have good temper.   Men to be reclaimed.
You fear lest they be reckless of their weal.
Ah! Demea, Demea, in age we grow more wise,
In all things else save in amassing wealth.
That is the vice of age—then be contented,
For age is sure to make them covetous.
Dem. Cease to persuade me by such sophistry.
    Ah! Micio—you will ruin them, I fear.
Mic. Rest you contented : that will never be,
    Join then our feast to-day and smile again.
Dem. So be it then to smile and feast to-day,   ˙
    To-morrow at the rising of the dawn,
    I and my son are off unto the farm.
Mic. At midnight if you will—be happy now.
Dem. And that same Psaltrian must go with me.
Mic. Good tactics : and take care and keep her safe,
    So will you surely keep your son at home.
Dem. I will be careful—kitchen and the mill
    Will make her white and black with meal and smoke,
    And sprinkle her with ashes—to the fields
    At mid-day to reap stubble—till her face
    Is black as charcoal.
Mic.   Excellent! in faith,
    Both wise and equitable.   Then force your son,
    Whether he will or no, to couch with her.
Dem. Ah! can'st thou joke upon it—light of mood,
    I feel—
Mic.   Ah! there you go again.
Dem.   I've done.
Mic. Then come within, and join the sport begun.

ACT V.—Scene 4.—Demea.

Never did mortal wight devise a plan
To guide his steps aright, but fortune's freaks,
Or age, or something else would interfere
And mar his project—and would teach him this
That he knows nothing that he thought he knew.
All chosen plans he must repudiate—
And, even so, it happens to myself;
For standing now on life's extremest verge
Do I renounce my life of abstinence:
For now I see that nought is preferable
To fellow-man, than courtesy and kindness.
My brother and myself may prove that rule ;
For he has passed a life of merriment,
Courteous and kind, and loving and beloved ;
Whilst caring for himself—beloved of all.
I, rustic, rough, and frugal, took a wife,
With matrimonial miseries; and children—
Paternal cares; and laying up a store,
Toiling for them, I fall upon old age ;
And in old age what is my harvest home ?
Hatred from those for whom I toiled and moiled.
My brother reaps the harvest of their love :
They love him and consort him, and fly me ;
They ask his counsel, and they cherish it ;
And I look on deserted by them both ;
They pray for him to live—for me to die ;
Their education at my charge and cost,
He, without any cost, secures as his.
I sow the seed, and he reaps all the fruit.

Well! it is come to this—he challenges,
And I must arm—with smiles and benefits.
I will be loved and I will be esteemed,
My children shall esteem me; I will buy
And bid for it. If I exhaust my means,
It signifies to me no jot, for I
Am in my old age with no time to lose.

ACT V.—Scene 5.—Syrus—Demea.

Syr. Demea—your brother prays you not to go.
Dem. Who calls me? O, our Syrus—Syrus, hail!
  How do things go, all right?
Syr.   All right.
Dem. [*Aside.*]   All right.
  Three words are uttered all against the grain,
  As, " *O, our Syrus!—how go things?—all right?* "
  You are an honest fellow—I am glad
  To have the means to serve you.
Syr.   Many thanks.
Dem. I will indeed, and, Syrus, this is true—
  I will do something for your benefit.

ACT V.—Scene 6.—Geta—Demea.

Get. Mistress, I go to find them, that they may
  Bear home the bride. Ah! behold! Demea.
  Health, Demea.
Dem.   Say, who calls.
Get.   Why, Geta.
Dem. Geta, you proved to-day an honest man.
  You had your master's interest at heart,

A thing that I approve; to love your lord :
And in return—soon as occasion serves
I will reward you, Geta.
Get.   You are very good
To hold these sentiments.
Dem. [*Aside.*]   Thus I make my court
By affability, which answers well :
And first I win the Commons to my cause.

ACT V.—SCENE 7.—ÆSCHINUS—DEMEA—SYRUS—GETA.

Æs. Murdered am I by form and ceremony.
Why can't a man be married without this?
To waste a day in silly preparations.
Dem. What is the matter, Æschinus.
Æs.   My father !
Ah! are you there, my father ?
Dem.   Hush, I am—
Your father in the body and the soul,
And love you more than eyes the light of day.
Why do you not lead home the wife?
Æs.   I would fain
They wait the tibicina to precede,
And sing the hymenæals.
Dem.   Will you take
An old man's counsel ?
Æs.   What is it, my father ?
Dem. March them all off—the hymenæal crowd,
Torches, and the musicians : and knock down
That garden wall—down with it to the ground.
Carry her over, make it all one home,
Bring mother, bride, and servants all to us.

Æs. And it would please well dear father.

Dem.   See to it.

   Thus I grow affable.   My brother's house
Is pervious to all—they will burst in,
And eat and drink—and what is that to me?
He pays the cost, and I am affable,
They bow and give me thanks.   Bid Babylo
He fork out twenty minæ.   Syrus, Eh!
Why do you stand and stare? set off about it.

Syr. Anon!

Dem. Down with that wall—demolish—and,
   Geta, be off, and lead her thro' the gap.

Get. Gods bless you, Demea, for your benefits,
   Since so benevolent to us and ours.

Dem. You well deserve it all—you, too, my lad.

Æs. I think so also.

Dem.   This mode is better far
   Than bear a young wife in her parturition
   Thro' public ways.

Æs.   And nothing can be better,
   Dear father!

Dem.   Ah! ah! dear father; here is Micio.

ACT V.—Scene 8.—Micio—Demea—Æschinus.

Mic. My brother ordered it!   Where is he then?
   You ordered this thing—Demea!

Dem.   I did.
   In this thing, and all others, I desire
   To aid, to help, to cherish, and attach
   Their home to ours.

Æs.   Consent to it my father.

Mic. Oh! I do not object.

Dem.   But we are bound,
  I say, to do so : first, she is the mother
  Of my son's wife.

Mic.   And then?

Dem.   Modest and wise.

Mic. Ay, so all say.

Dem.   And aged.

Mic.   It is so.

Dem. Past child-bearing, and lone in widowhood.

Mic. What then?

Dem.   That you should marry her, and you
  [*To Æs.*] Should make him do so.

Mic.   What! I marry her!

Dem. You.

Mic.   I!

Dem.   Yourself I say.

Mic.   Go! you are mad.

Dem. Now, if you are a man, Æschinus, make him.

Æs. My father.

Mic.   And you, too, ass—go to—and heed him not.

Dem. You struggle in the net, it must be so.

Mic. You are crazy.

Æs.   Let me beseech you, father.

Mic. Are you mad, too—away!

Dem.   Brother I beseech you
  Do not refuse your son.

Mic.   You all are mad,
  For I am sixty-five, and she decrepit—
  You all are mad!

Æs.   Father, I promised her.

Mic. Promised !   Go compromise yourself !
Dem. But what will you reply—when we demand
  Something of moment?
Mic.   Which this is not at all.
Dem. Now pardon him.
Æs.   And grant us this small grace.
Mic. Leave off, I say.
Æs.   Nay, not till you consent.
Mic. This is abduction.
Dem.   Do not say so, Micio.
Mic. Absurd in the extreme doth it appear,
  I say, to me—depraved and stupid—
  But if you still insist—why, be it so.
Æs. Ah, thou dost well and rightly, I esteem you.
Dem. [*Aside.*] At him again—whilst in this yielding mood.
  [*Aloud.*] Our neighbour Hegio, Micio, is our kinsman,
  He is a very poor and worthy man,
  We ought to do some act of kindness to him.
Mic. Do what, what act ?
Dem.   You have a small estate
  Here in the suburbs.   Grant it him in fee.
Mic. Small—do you call it !
Dem.   Well, it is not large.
  Grant it in fee : for he has been a father
  Unto the bride—he is upright and honest,
  He is our kinsman, and he well deserves it.
  For I take up the proverb, Micio,
  You lately dropped.   " It is the vice of age
  To be enthralled with cares of property "—
  It is a proverb true — and it behoves
  That we, in sailing, should steer clear of it.
Mic. Do what you will, I yield.   Do what you please.

Æs. My father, thanks.
Dem.　　　　　　　　　　And now I recognize
　　We—brothers are, in body and in soul.
Mic. I am contented.
Dem.　　　　　　　　Stabbed with his own sword!

ACT V.—SCENE 9.—SYRUS—DEMEA—MICIO—ÆSCHINUS.

Syr. It is knocked down, as you commanded, Demea.
Dem. A trusty man, and edepol! I think
　　We ought to grant to Syrus—liberty.
Mic. Freedom to him—and wherefore?
Dem.　　　　　　　　　　　　Many reasons.
Syr. Oh! our Demea, you are good and just;
　　You know how I have tended both your boys—
　　Have tended and admonished them, and taught them
　　All the good precepts that I know myself.
Dem. Do I not see and know it—is the thing
　　Not self-apparent?　Thou hast taught them first
　　To love, and found them mistresses to feast.
　　Accomplishments, I say, that lie beyond
　　The usual bounds of mediocrity.
Syr. O worthy gentleman!
Dem.　　　　　　　　Besides—to-day—
　　To-day he bought that psaltrian; it was he
　　Who managed all, and it is only just
　　That he should have his recompense, and so
　　Encourage others in the path of duty.
　　And Æschinus desires it.
Mic. [*To Æs.*]　　　　　　　　Do you so?
Æs. And heartily.

Mic.   Syrus—come hither—there—
   Be free.   [*He gives the stroke of manumission.*]
Syr. My grateful thanks, indeed, to all,
   But, Demea, most to thee.
Dem.   I am rejoiced.
Æs. And I.
Syr. And also I; but still I wish
   My manumission were complete—my wife—
   My Phrygian wife—to share my freedom with me.
Dem. A most deserving woman.
Syr.   And the first
   That gave the teat unto your grandson, Demea.
Dem. That is sufficient—that is cause enough,
   Hercle, she must be freed.
Mic.   Freed—and for what!
Dem. For that—and I will pay her purchase sum.
   See, pay her worth.
Syr.   May the gods bless you, Demea,
   And grant you all your wishes.
Mic.   Syrus, eh!
   This day has been a lucky day to you.
Dem. Micio, it will be so, if you perform
   Your duty by him, and bestow wherewith
   To start him off in life; a man like him
   Will soon restore it.
Mic.   Not a rotten nut.
Æs. The man is trusty.
Syr.   I promise to restore it.
Æs. Come, father!
Mic.   Well! I'll think of it—I'll think.
Dem. So! that is done.

Syr.   My best friend.

Æs.   Father, thanks.

Mic. But brother how is this—and whence this change
   From niggardness to prodigality?
   Tell me the reason of this altered mind.

Dem. And I will tell you, brother, and lay bare
   The secret of my children's love to you.
   They love your easy and condoning ways;
   It is not they are either great or good—
   It is not they are noble, or are just;
   It is assent, indulgence, money, means,
   That wins you their compliance, Micio.
     Now, Æschinus, if my more rugged mode
   Of life be hateful to you, and if I
   Refuse condonance with your faulty deeds—
   I wash my hands.   Go on, and spend nor spare,
   Follow your passions, and I give you up.
   If, on the contrary, you choose to hear
   Advice which age can proffer unto youth,
   And to restrain its headlong, headstrong sway:
   If you will suffer me to reprehend,
   And, in due time, advise and rightly rule—
   Then follow me, and I will do my best.

Æs. Father, I, for the future, yield to you,
   Nor shall you henceforth find me blameable.
   But now what of my brother—what of him?

Dem. What's done cannot be undone, he must have
   Her he has chosen—may it be the last
   Folly he may commit.

Æs.   All right.
        [*To the audience.*] Applaud.

————————————

TEMPLE OF JANUS.

PHORMIO.

PERSONS.

Phormio—A Parasite.
Demipho—Father of Antipho.
Chremes—Brother of Demipho.
Antipho.
Phædria—Son of Chremes.
Phanium—Daughter of Chremes.
Geta—Slave to Demipho.
Davus—Slave.
Dorio—Slave Merchant.
Sophrona—Nurse.
Hegio
Cratinus } Advocates.
Crito
Dorcium—A Maiden.

PROLOGUE.

When the old poet * could not force the young †
To leave off writing plays and hold his tongue,
He set to work to ban by maledictions ;
And said his comedies were nought but fictions
Of meagre subject and oration trite ;
Because he never drew a crazy wight
Who dreamt he saw a deer which, chased by hounds, ‡
Sobbed and shed tears on his domestic bounds.
Now if that author would but understand
How much the actors helped him out of hand,
He would acknowledge that the author's credit
Depended on his friends and actors' merit,
And would have curbed the roughness of his tongue.
For if there be this audience among
Who think us aided by such hostile act
To write our prologue, we deny the fact ;
The palm of your applause is free to all
Who may excel in art theatrical.

---

* Lavinius, his predecessor poet. † Terence.

‡ A scene in a play by Lavinius. Terence often showing up his
blundering. He made Mercurius, as Losia, act indecorously for a slave ;
in Heauton. Prologue. In making the defendant open the case and
produce his own title deeds in the Eur. Prologue ; and in making the
deer seek protection with sobs and tears, as above.

But he would drive him hence to pine and starve.
We therefore seize upon the knife to carve;
And had our rival been but generous,
He should have shared a couch and fed with us.
It is his own fault—he must not look grim
In taking what he gave—good-bye to him.
But our request is that you lend us ears.
We bring a new piece on the stage, it bears
This name—Epidicazomenos *—in Greek,
In Latin, Phormio, because we seek
A parasite to bear the brunt, and show
The plot which he unravels as we go.
Lend us your ears, be favourably inclined,
Nor let that last occasion come to mind †
When tumult drove us hence, and in a rage
Chased actors and the poet from the stage;
Restored to which by your benignity,
We try to-day your equanimity.

---

* The claimant for the heiress.
† When the Hecyra was hissed off the stage.

PHORMIO.

ACT I.

SCENE 1.—DAVUS.

Geta, my best of friends and countryman,
Found me out yesterday.   It seems that I
Owed him some money; and he came to pray
Me to repay him.   Well, I got it him.
I hear his master is married, and no doubt
He wants it as a present for the wife.
Custom iniquitous—that we the poor
Must ever fee the rich! all, he has screwed;
His little savings swallowed at one gulp
By bowels void of pity—head of thought
How he slaved to obtain them!   It ends not here:
Another sop when she is brought to bed;
Another one when the first birthday comes;
Another at each feast: we fee the boy,
The mother bears it off.—Here Geta is!

ACT I.—SCENE 2.—GETA—DAVUS.

Get.   Now if one red-haired seek me—
Dav.   He is here!
   Spare yourself toil.

Get.   Eh! Davus; you, I sought.
Dav. Well! here it is—good weight and number—count.
Get. I love thee; thou art just; I give thee thanks.
Dav. You are in the right: the manners of to-day
     Make it superfluous to pay one's debts.
     But, notwithstanding, you methinks look sad.
Get. And reason, too.   I stand in peril, man!
Dav. Upon what score?
Get.   But can you keep a secret?
Dav. Go to, I am no babbler.   Can you doubt
     A debtor who has paid you in full weight—
     What should I gain by babbling now?
Get.   Then, listen!
Dav. Oh! don't be in a hurry.
Get.   Know you Chremes,
     Brother of our old master?
Dav.   Wherefore not?
Get. And Phædria his son?
Dav.   As well as you.
Get. Well! they are off, the old ones—both together—
     Chremes to Lemnos, and our own good man
     Unto Cilicia—to an old acquaintance—
     Allured by hopes of mountains made of gold!
Dav. What he, so rich already, covetous!
Get. Nay, 'tis his nature.
Dav.   Would I were a king.
Get. The two old boys are off, and leave me here
     The governor of their sons.
Dav.   Unhappy Geta!
     Hard governments—rebellious provinces!
Get. All will come right in time, I trust in that.
     My *genius* is offended through some fault:

I parleyed with them firstly: useless words!
But what of that: fidelity, I trow,
Is loss of labour!
Dav.   "Kicking against pricks:"
That motto often comes before my mind.
Get. And therefore I resolved to kick no more,
But let them have their way.
Dav.   As in the Forum.
Get. Now Antipho went right. But Phædria,
The day his father went, must needs go seek
A Citharistrian, and run mad for her.
A dealer owns her, vilest of his tribe.
We, empty pouches: the old fathers had
Taken especial care of that: and wanting means,
He fed his eyes; he followed her about
As she went to her lessons and returned.
For lack of better work, we followed him.
Now opposite the master's was a barber's:
We waited there. It happened, as we waited,
A boy came by in tears: we pitied him,
And he replied with fervour —" Never, never
Has poverty been burthensome till now.
A maiden weeps upon her mother's corpse,
She hath nor kith nor kin. A hired crone
Performs the rites ; and she herself so fair—
So exquisitely beautiful." Then Antipho,
For we were touched in heart, proposed to go
And visit her; and he consenting, led,
And so we went; and there she was indeed,
Divinely beautiful,—'twas beauty unadorned,
With naked feet, dishevelled hair, and grief ;
Tears and uncomely garb—becoming her.

Now he in love with his Fidicina,
Said, she was pretty; but our Antipho,
Poor Antipho!

Dav.   He fell in love with her.

Get. O'er head and ears—deep as the Hellespont!
He finds out the old woman, and entreats
To be allowed to see her. She refused:
She rated him with words. She was, she said,
An Attican, well born and bred: if he
Wished to espouse her, let him legally
Seek proper means: if he had other thoughts,
He was mistaken. And the poor boy longs
To wed the maiden; but he dreads his father.

Dav. Perhaps, if present, he would have consented.

Get. What! he consented—to a stranger girl,
Without a dower—quite the contrary!

Dav. What have you done!

Get.   There is a certain Phormio,
A loud and boisterous parasite—may gods
Confound him.

Dav. What did he?

Get.   Well! he advised:
It was the law, he said, that orphans should
Marry the next of kin: the self same law
Ordaining the same kin to marry them.
" I will make oath you are her next of kin;
And, as your father's delegate and friend,
Assign her to you. Now to Judgment Hall—
Father and mother, genealogy—
I will invent all that. All must go straight
If you oppose no obstacles; you wed,
Back comes the father—he impleading me;

I do not care a doit—the girl is yours,
  Espoused for ever."
Dav.   Audacious roguery!
Get. 'Twas said and done; they went—we were condemned—
  They wedded.
Dav.   What!
Get.   They wedded on the spot!
Dav. O Geta, what on earth will fall to you!
Get. I know not. I shall take it easily,
  Nor rack my soul about it.
Dav.   Now credit me,
  But I admire your courage.
Get.   Well! I trust
  In my resources.
Dav.   Good.
Get.   I shall go seek
  An intercessor, who with humble breath
  Will come and plead—"O pardon! I beseech you—
  Have mercy and compassion—if again
  He dares offend, et cetera;" going out
  He whispers in the ear, " Half-murder him."
Dav. So, like a pedagogue, he walks abroad
  And leads a Citharistrian!
Get.   Somewhat like.
Dav. He has not much to give her.
Get.   Heaps of words.
Dav. Comes Chremes back?
Get.   Not yet.
Dav.   And Demipho?
Get. I know not; but they say his letter lies
  Now at the port, and now I go to get it.
Dav. Have you more news, my Geta?

Get.   None—Farewell!
  All happiness.—Holloa! you urchin—boy,
  Come here—take this to Dorcium: off now —bolt!

ACT I.—Scene 3.—Antipho—Phædria.

Ant. 'Tis useless, Phædria, consulting me,
  I am in fear immortal, and I dread
  Return of him who cares the most for me.
  I have done stupidly—for otherwise
  I had expected him impatiently.
Phæ. Now what is this about?
Ant.   Ah! you know well—
  You witness were of my unhappy deed.
  Why, why did Phormio so counsel me?
  Headlong in evil have I plunged : my passion
  Would have evaporated in few days:
  My care will eat my heart up many days.
Phæ. I hear you.
Ant.   And now daily I expect
  Him home again, and loss of her I love.
Phæ. Most men bewail lacking the thing they love,
  And you bewail to hold yours in possession.
  Hercle! I would that I stood in your place.
  As the gods love me, nothing I desire
  More or so much, as to win her I love,
  And then to die, if die I must, with joy.
  Me obstacles oppose, and knock me down.
  Behold me, and go! joy in your success.
  Why you have wit, and beauty, and good birth—
  And without trouble, and without expense—
  All that the heart can wish, a girl above

The breath of scandal.   You are fortunate!
Her worth is as the daylight, palpable;
Success o'erwhelms you.   On the other side,
I have a greedy dealer; but I wot
One never is contented with one's lot.
Ant. And Phædria, I deem you fortunate:
You may advance, retreat, do what you will—
You do not stand committed to the chain.
I in the quagmire am, and floundering:
I neither can possess her; neither can
I e'er consent to lose her.   Geta comes,
And comes in haste: I trembling at the sight,
Dreading all news that he can bring to me.

ACT I.—Scene 4.—Geta—Antipho—Phædria.

Get. I am undone, annihilated, crushed!
Ah, Geta! You must seek good counsel straight.
Evils impend o'er your unhappy head;
I know not what to do, nor what to think.
Nor how to extricate—for—keep it secret,
That is downright impossible—downright.
Ant. What threatens now?
Get.   And not a moment's space
To think, for here my master comes ashore.
Ant. What evil is this?
Get.   Suppose now, he knows all,
How shall I meet his wrath—What shall I say?
When every word will but enrage him more—
Or silence, worse—excuses, worst of all.
It is not me alone; there is Antipho.
Ah! my soul bleeds for him: I pity him,

And solely for his sake do I stay here ;
Else had I run away—ay, long ago ;
And on our savage senior been revenged—
I would have girded loins, and cut and run.
Ant. What doth he say of girding loins and running?
Get. But where is Antipho? Zounds! I want Antipho.
Phæ. He calls for you.
Ant.   Some woe is imminent.
Phæ. You are all right.
Get.   I shall find him at home.
Phæ. Eh! call him back.
Ant.   Stop! Geta!
Get.   Words imperious,
   Whoe'er—
Ant.   Geta!
Get.   Ah! ah! the man I want.
Ant. Geta, what news?   Pronounce it in one word.
Get. I will.
Ant.   Say on.
Get.   From the Piræeus—
Ant.   Ah!
Get. There, lo! you now—
Ant.   I perish!
Phæ.   Hem!
Ant.   Ah! me—
   How now?
Phæ.   How now!
Get.   His father, sir, your uncle,
   Arrived at the Piræeus.
Ant.   .   All is lost—
   There is no remedy! O Phanium, Phanium,
   We shall be parted, and I wish to die!

Get. Ah! well then, things are at the worst ; so now
  Pluck up your courage—Fortune aids the bold.
Ant. I know not where I am.
Get.   Be present, then ;
  For if your father sees you in this fright,
  He will suspect you culpable.
Phæ.   He will.
Ant. I cannot help it.
Get.   How would you manage then
  In a case, difficult?
Ant.   E'en worse than now.
Get. O Phædria! Now will he ruin all—
  We lose our labour and our time—I'm off.
Phæ. And so am I.
Ant.   But if I simulate security,
  Will that suffice?
Get.   You cannot.
Ant.   Let me try—
  Behold! Will that do ?
Get.   No.
Ant.   Will this?
Get.   •   Why—better.
Ant. This ?
Get.   Ay, that would do. Can you command it,
  Responding word for word, unshrinkingly—
  When he shall browbeat?
Ant.   Yes.
Get.   Go answer him :
  You were enforced by law ; that judgment was
  Pronounced against you. Do you understand ?
  Here comes some old man—

Ant.   It is he—himself—
  I dare not meet him!
Get.   Eh! what! stop Antipho!
  Stop—stop—I say!
Ant.   I know, I recognize
  My fault; take care of Phanium for me,
  Good-bye my life.
Phœ.   Now, what shall we do, Geta?
Get. Well! you must stand the verbal strife, and I
  The whip and scourging. Phædria, I advise
  That we should do the like, as even now
  We counselled Antipho.
Phœ.   Confound advice—
  Say, what is to be done.
Get.   Go! brazen it;
  Declare her rights were incontestable—
  Indisputable—that law was on her side,
  And folly to oppose it.
Phœ.   I will do so.
Get. Add what comes in your mind—perplexing, subtle—
  Confuse him if you can.
Phœ.   •   I will do so.
Get. I will stand by, as force subsidiary,
  To help at need.

ACT I.—Scene 5.—Demipho—Geta—Phormio.

Dem. What! married! Antipho, without consent
  And braving my authority: authority—
  Displeasure, reverence. Graceless and impudent—
  Outrageous action! Geta! Monitor!

Get. [*Aside.*] Ay, I am there.
Dem.   What will they tell me—what!
  Reasons, excuses—
Get.   We have them all ready;
Dem. Go on—If obligation, by decree of law,
  On him unwilling—I will yield consent.
Get. Good.
Dem.   But if he yielded, unopposing, and
  Suffering default—
Phæ.   That would be hard indeed!
Get. I will accost him now.
Dem.   I am at sea;
  Nor know I how, in ignorance, to act.
  And far too angry for my soul to think.
  Such is the state of man : prosperity
  Should make him careful and most sedulous
  To ward attacks of fortune : and returning
  Home from abroad, then let him be prepared
  For evils—peril—loss—a wife deceased—
  A daughter sick—these, common are to all.
  Let him expect them : if they happen not,
  He may regard all as a gain for good.
Get. O Phædria, faith ! it is incredible
  How much in wisdom I surpass my master !
  Never on me fall evils unforeseen—
  I have anticipated this his return ;
  And, with it, grinding at the mill and stripes,
  Fetters and overseers—all these foreseen—
  And nothing unexpected unawares.
  So if they happen not, I hold it gain.
  Accost the old chap—gently at the first.

Dem. Ah! Phædria there—my nephew!

Phæ.   Uncle, hail!

Dem. And hail, my nephew! Where is Antipho?

Phæ. Welcome, returned—

Dem.   Yes, yes! but answer me.

Phæ. Right well, and here at home. Has business
 Prospered well?

D m.   I would so.

Phæ.   Would, uncle, what?

Dem. No humbug! Phædria. A famous marriage
 Has come off in my absence.

Phæ.   On that account
 Deem you of cause for anger?

Get.   Ah! the rogue,
 Excellent actor!

Dem.   Cause for anger, ay—
 Would he were present here to know and learn
 His father, unto him most lenient,
 Is now a parent most inexorable.

Phæ. And yet, my uncle, he hath nothing done
 Deserving punishment.

Dem.   Hark to him now!
 All—all alike! Birds of the self-same feather—
 Know one, know all.

Phæ.   Nay, not at all, my uncle.

Dem. When one has played the fool, the other stands
 Forth to defend him; and, in his own turn,
 Expects defence at need and finds it too.

Get. The man now speaks more truly than he deems.

Dem. For were it not so, Phædria, you could not
 Defend him thus.

Phæ.   Uncle! if Antipho
  Has done some wrong, careless of fame and duty,
  Be well assured that I would not defend him.
  Let him be punished.   But if some miscreant,
  Preying on inexperience and on youth,
  Has laid some snare, unhappily successful,
  Is it our fault?   Or is it not the judges',
  Who oftentimes, through envy, rob the rich ;
  Bestowing it, through pity, on the poor?
Get. His words almost deceive *me*.   Ah! the rogue!
Dem. But how can any judge do otherwise,
  Where there is no defence made ; Antipho
  Made no defence—judgment was by default.
Phæ. Alas! too oft, the fault of modesty
  Of youth ingenuous—of good birth—so oft
  Before the judges suddenly are dumb,
  Oblivious of their argument are mute.
Get. Most excellent advocate, I am contented with him.
  Hail! master.   Happiness for safe return!
Dem. Oh, oh! good keeper, hail!   Custodier
  Of house and home, and guardian of my son!
Get. Too long we suffer undeserved rebuke—
  We are not faulty, we have done no wrong—
  I, least of all.   The law does not allow
  A slave to plead, nor to give evidence.
  The courts of law were barred in this to me.
Dem. Agreed ; I make allowance for all that—
  Ingenuous modesty—and you a slave ;
  But wherefore did he wed her? for no law
  Compels to wedlock—only to pay dower,
  And wed her to another ; but he chose
  To take her dowerless and wed himself.

Get. Ah! that was not the reason; 'twas the lack
   Of money.
Dem.   Why, then, not take some?
Get.   Take some!
   Take what, or whence?   To take some is soon said.
Dem. Well, borrow, then, on usury.
Get.   Better yet!
   And who would lend to us the whilst you live?
Dem. No, no! this roguery shall not succeed,
   I will not suffer it; she shall not stay;
   He shall have his deserts.   Now, for the man.
   Who is he? and where dwells he?
Get.   Phormio.
Dem. Her patron—where is he?
Get.   I will go seek him.
Dem. Antipho, where is he?
Get.   He is gone forth.
Dem. Phædria, go thou and seek him, bring him here.
Phœ. I go directly.
Get.   Ay, to Pamphila.
Dem. I will salute my household gods: and hence
   Unto the Forum: get some advocate:
   When Phormio comes—so I shall be prepared.

ACT II.

Scene 1.—Phormio—Geta.

Pho. How, fled!   Afraid to face his father, eh !
Get. Just so.
Pho.   Abandoning his Phanium ?
Get.   Ay, ay.
Pho. And the old dad irate ?
Get.   Outrageously!
Pho. Ah! Phormio, Phormio—you are in for it:
   " As thou dost sow, so must thou reap," tis said;
   Well, then, tuck up.
Get.   Phormio.
Pho.   If he demand —
Get. We trust in you.
Pho.   I have it—he demands
   Her restitution.
Get.   .   May it come to that ?
Pho. I think so.
Get.   I will back you.
Pho.   Come away.
   Where is the old man ?   I have arguments
   All ready on my tongue.
Get.   What arguments ?
Pho. That Phanium is his wife: that Antipho
   Is all deserving: let him wreak his wrath,
   There upon me.   So be it.
Get.   Heroic man !
   Invaluable friend!   But, Phormio,
   Suppose this end in sending you to jail?

Pho. Ah! fear not that : past is the peril, when
  Clearly I see my way. How many men,
  Think you, that I have beaten unto death,
  Strangers and citizens? Ah! we old hands
  Work pretty safely. Geta, answer me,
  Or have you ever heard, or ever known,
  Me suffer condemnation—restitution ?
Get. And how comes that?
Pho.   Because men spread no nets
  For merlins nor for goshawks—birds of prey,
  And dangerous to meddle with—but polts,
  Fat and resistless, which repay the pains.
  So are the rich in danger—bags to bleed ;
  I possess nothing—and they know it well.
  Ah! but the jail : I am a cormorant—
  They know that also : neither do they choose
  To render me such benefit for ills.
Get. We shall be ever grateful unto you.
Pho. Nay, 'tis the contrary ; we can ne'er enough
  Be grateful to the benefits kings do.
  Let off shot free ; free unguents and free bath—
  With nought to think about, all—fancy free.
  Your master, meantime, bothering his brains.
  We laugh, he grumbles ; we enjoy ourselves ;
  Served first in meat, and drink, and dubious food.
Get. How, dubious food?
Pho.   Impossible to choose ;
  Variety, all excellent, all costly.
  Is it not plain you have a present god ?
  Is it not plain we ought to worship him ?
Get. Here is the old man : be upon your guard :
  The onset tells ; the after-fight is play.

ACT II.—Scene 2.—Demipho—Geta—Phormio.

Dem. Did ever any one or see or know
  Such wrong—such contumelious injury—
  As I sustain?   Come, aid me, I beseech you!
Get. He is in a rage.
Pho.					Hist, Hist; I'll tackle him.
  Faith of immortal gods!   Does Demipho
  Deny that Phanium is his kinswoman?
  Does Demipho deny his kinswoman?   Ah!
Get. He does deny it.
Dem. 'Tis doubtless he, the man.   Eh! follow me.
Pho. Denies he knows her father, who he was!
Get. Assuredly denies it.
Pho.					What, knows not Stilpho!
Get. Assuredly.
Pho.				It is because the maid
  Is poor and orphan'd he denies to know her,
  Will own her not.   Behold, now, avarice!
Get. Do you accuse my lord of avarice?
  There you are wrong.
Dem.					Audacity! 'Tis like
  He will begin the plea—accusing me.
Pho. For Antipho—I cannot blame the boy—
  He knew her not; the man was very old,
  Poor, and a rustic, wedded to his spot
  Of rented land.   He oftentimes complained
  How Demipho, his kinsman, oft expressed
  Contempt for him, how undeservedly.
  I never knew a man of greater worth.
  He rented of my father, so I knew him.

Get. What, that to us! I should much like to know.

Pho. Go, and be crucified!   But that I know
 · Him faultless, good, think you, I ask, that I
  Had drawn hostility on me and mine
  From one so powerful as yours, for her?

Get. Why, miscreant! continuing to defame
  My absent master.

Pho.   Well he merits it.

Get. Ah! Ah! you will.

Dem. [*Calls.*]   Geta!

Get.   Calumniator—
  Robber!

Dem. [*Calls.*] Geta!

Pho. [*To Geta.*]   Reply.

Get.   Ah! who is this?

Dem. Be silent, sirrah.

Get.   He ceases not to say
  The vilest calumnies against you—all
  Fitting himself.

Dem.   Be silent, sirrah.   Friend,
  With your permission, and with pardon craved,
  And, if it pleases you, reply to me:
  Who was this friend of yours, where did he dwell,
  And in what manner claimed he me as kinsman?

Pho. You ask me as though you were ignorant.

Dem. Not ignorant—what I—

Pho.   You are not ignorant.

Dem. But I deny it; and what you affirm
  Behoves it you to prove.

Pho. ·   What, know you not
  Your cousin-german!

Dem.   Zounds!—his name— his name—
Pho. His name—ay, doubtless—
Dem.   Ah! you know it not!
Pho. Bother it—I forget it.
Dem.   Now, then, now!
Pho. [*To Geta.*] Geta, if you remember, tell it me.
   O, stuff of nonsense! you pretend not know.
   To trap me by a question.
Dem.   Trap you, I!
Get. [*To Phormio.*] Stilpho.
Pho.   What signifies.   'Tis Stilpho.
Dem.   Who?
Pho. Stilpho, I tell you; as you know right well.
Dem. I never had a relative so named.
Pho. Astounding!   Are you quite devoid of shame?
   Had he but left ten talents—
Dem.   Gods, confound you!
Pho. You had been sharp enough with memory,
   Citing grandfather and great-grandfathers.
Dem. Just so: do you the same, and cite me now
   Their genealogies.   This damsel, now —
Get. Zooks! that's a poser!   Phormio, look out.
Pho. I did so, fully, at the proper time.
   Why did not Antipho deny it then?
Dem. Reminding me of Antipho—the fool—
   Folly beyond belief!
Pho.   But you are wise:
   Go to the magistrate, and try again
   The cause upon appeal: for I perceive
   That here you reign omnipotent, with right
   To adjudicate the selfsame matter twice.
Dem. The injury is done, and sooner than contend

And hear thee more, I am content to pay,
As though she were my relative indeed.
Hold! here are fifteen minæ, which the law
Assigns as dower.

Pho.   Ha! ha! ha!—excellent!

Dem. How, now!—Do I demand a thing unjust?
I but avail myself of public rights.

Pho. How so, I pray you?   Treat a freeborn maid
Like to a harlot, giving her her hire!
The law ordains—the orphan-citizen
To wed their next of kin, to save from want,
To save from shame.   Lo! what the law awards,
What you refuse.

Dem.   Ay, wed their next of kin,
Which we are not.

Pho.   Stuff!—do not debate it more—
The thing is done.

Dem.   I not debate it more.
Ay, till it is undone.

Pho.   O, stuff of nonsense!

Dem. I will—I will.

Pho.   In one word, Demipho,
Your son, and not yourself, must plead in this:
'Twas he who stood condemned in this—not you.
You are not at an age to wed a girl.

Dem. What I say, he says—he must say the same;
Or I will chase them, bag and baggage, forth.

Get. He's savage.

Pho.   Nonsense, you would not do so.

Dem. Avaunt! thou enemy—avaunt! I say.

Pho. Browbeat and frightened, in his own despite.

Get. A very good beginning.

Pho.   Hark you now :
  'Twere better to submit with a good grace—
  'Twere better also we continue friends.
Dem. The gods forbid it !—rather let me wish
  That I had never cast my eyes upon you.
Pho. If you accept her for your daughter, she
  Will be the consolation of your age—
  You stricken are in years.
Dem.   ·She pleases you—
  Pray take her to yourself.
Pho.   ·   Nay, calm yourself.
Dem. Mark you my words—for what I say, I do :
  Take off this woman, or I'll cast her forth !
  I have said it, Phormio.
Pho. Mark you my words : if you entreat her ill,
  I will find means to make you pay for it.
  I have said it, Demipho.
        [*And to Geta.*]   I shall be found at home.
Get. Good.

ACT II.—Scene 3.—Demipho—Geta—Hegio—Cratinus— Crito—(Advocates.)

Dem. Oh ! in what care and what solicitude
  Has my son cast me !—shackling himself and me
  In this cursed marriage.   Nor do I wish
  To see him yet, until I know his mind.
  Go seek him, Geta, if he be at home.
Get. I go.
Dem.   You see the mess wherein we stand—
  What say you to it, Hegio ?

Heg.   Demand
It, if you please, of Cratinus.

Dem.   Say, Cratinus.

Cra. Do you mean me?

Dem.   Yes—you.

Cra.   It is my wish
That you shall do the very thing that's right.
I think it is but just and reasonable
All wrong your son has done you in your absence
Should be restored in full. Such is the law.
I have said.

Dem.   Now, Hegio, what say you?

Heg. Cratinus has said well. Yet it is said—
"So many men, so many sentences"—
Each one according to his light. Now, I
Hold on the contrary: a judgment given
Cannot be so reversed; and, further, I
Deem it disgraceful to urge such a suit.

Dem. Speak, Crito.

Cri.   I think that the subject needs
Deliberation; for it is not small.

Heg. Do you require us more?

Dem.   I thank you—no.
I am perplexed worse than I was before.

Get. They say he has not returned.

Dem.   My brother comes—
He is expected; and he shall advise me.
I will hence to the port and ask about him.

Get. And I to Antipho, to tell him all.

ACT III.

Scene 1.—Antipho—Geta.

Ant. It needs must be admitted, Antipho,
   That you lack courage, and are blamable.
   Why did you flee and leave the thing to others?
   Could you not best conduct your own affairs?
   There is one thing, my boy, that you must do:
   Remember your beloved one in the house;
   Let not the faith she lent your promises
   Return to her unbidden—let her not
   Grieve with the thought that you are treacherous.
Get. Master! and truly we have grieved, and long,
   Your absence, and condemned you.
Ant.   I sought you.
Get. And yet we never doubted of your cause.
Ant. Tell me, I pray you, how stand my affairs—
   What is my destiny—my father—what?
Get. Why, no.
Ant.   Is there then hope?
Get.   I know not.
Ant.   Ah!
Get. But Phædria, as I know, pleads well for you.
Ant. He always does so.
Get.   And Phormio, also,
   Has shown himself a man—careless of thunders.
Ant. What has Phormio done?
Get.   Confuted has
   Your irate father, with good arguments.
Ant. Good Phormio!

Get.　　　　　　　　　And I too, what I could.
Ant. Good Geta! and I love you.
Get.　　　　　　　　　　　　Things stand now
　Thus in abeyance, silently.　Your father
　Waits for your uncle to confer with him.
Ant. With him?
Get.　　　　　　　He will take his advice, he says.
Ant. How dreadful to me, now, seems his return!
　My happiness depending on his word.
Get. Lo! here is Phædria.
Ant.　　　　　　　　　　Ah! where?
Get.　　　　　　　　　　　　Behold
　Him issuing from—from his palæstra, there.

ACT III.—Scene 2.—Phædria—Dorio—Antipho.

Phœ. Dorio, hear me, pray!
Dor.　　　　　　　　　I will not hear.
Phœ. One moment.
Dor.　　　　　Let me go.
Phœ.　　　　　　　　　Listen to me.
Dor. Your thousand-time-told tale is wearisome.
Phœ. My present tale is new, and happier.
Dor. Then tell it.
Phœ.　　　　　Can't you wait three days? do not go.
Dor. I guessed as much that you have nothing new.
Phœ. What! you will not believe.
Dor.　　　　　　　　　　Just divination!
Phœ. My word.
Dor.　　　　Trash! trash!
Phœ.　　　　　　　　You said yourself
　That you would do this for good usury.

Dor. Words—words!

Phœ.   By Hercules! upon my word
   You never shall repent.

Dor.   Phantoms and dreams!

Phœ. Try—but three days.

Dor.   Ever the self-same song.

Phœ. And be my father, uncle, and my friend.

Dor. Bah! bah! bah! bah!

Phœ.   .   Inexorable man,—
   Is it in nature that hearts are so hard,
   Nor prayer nor pity can lay hold of them?

Dor. And are there, Phædria, men such simpletons
   To think to purchase and to pay with words?

Ant. It is pitiful.

Phœ.   Ah! he is in the right.

Get. How truly both of them perform their parts.

Phœ. And Antipho, whilst he holds his desire,
   And I must pine for mine.

Ant.   What is it, Phædria?

Phœ. O happy Antipho!

Ant.   What, I!

Phœ.   Yes, you:
   You have at home, and in possession, her
   Whom you adore: you have not got to deal
   With merchantmen.

Ant.   Ah! Phædria, at home
   I hold the wolf, as some say, by the ear,
   And dare not keep my hold, nor let him go.

Dor. And even so I stand myself with him.

Ant. Courage, then, Dorio! and hold him fast.
   What has he done?

Phæ.   He has sold Pamphila—
   Inhuman monster!
Get.   What! sold Pamphila?
Ant. Sold, do you say?
Phæ.   Ay, sold!
Dor.   A dreadful fact,
   To have sold her I purchased with my brass.
Phæ. He will not wait three days. I have besought him
   But for three days' delay—the whilst I gather
   Loans that are promised me from many friends.
   If, after three days' space, I ask for more,
   Believe me not.
Dor.   You bother me.
Ant.   Dorio,
   Three days—no more. He will repay you well,
   Requiting double.
Dor.   These are only words.
Ant. Will you deprive us, then, of Pamphila?
   And will you separate two lovers thus?
Dor. Nor I, nor thou—
Get.   May the gods pay thee off,
   After your own deservings.
Dor.   Look you, now:
   This long time, to my injury and loss,
   You weep and promise, but do not perform.
   To-day I find a tearless purchaser,
   Who pays his way. You must give way to him.
Ant. And yet, methinks, if I remember right,
   You named a day hereafter for the purchase,
   Pre-emption granting Phædria.
Phæ.   It was so.

Dor. Do I deny that?

Ant.   Is the day passed by?

Dor. No; but the purchaser has come before.

Ant. Do you not redden at a broken word?

Dor. No—not with payment.

Get.   Ah! dunghill knave!

Phœ. Ah! Dorio, is it right to use me thus?

Dor. Such as I am—make use of me, or not.

Ant. Ah! to deceive him so.

Dor.   No, Antipho,
  He deceives me: he knew me what I was.
  I knew not him.   I trusted to his word,
  And he deceived me.   I never tried to seem
  Other than what I am.   This will I do.
  The soldier pays to-morrow: if to-day,
  You bring the money—you shall have the girl;
  That is my law and custom.   I will sell
  To the first purchaser with cash!   Farewell.

ACT III.—Scene 3.—Phædria—Antipho—Geta.

Phœ. What shall I do? nor can I raise the money
  Thus in a moment's space, for none at all,
  In sooth, have I.   I trusted in three days
  To find the means.

Ant.   Come, Geta, lend a hand;
  You have fought well for me—now fight for him,
  And let us strive to aid him in his need,
  And to return the benefits we owe him.

Get. Well, that would be right enough.

Ant.   Up then, and aid,
  For you alone can save us at this pinch.

Get. What can I do?

Ant. What do! why, get the money.

Get. I would do so; but how? Inform me that.

Ant. My father here.

Get. I know it: and what then?

Ant. A word's enough unto the wise.

Get. I know.

Ant. Of course.

Get. Hercle, you reason well; and I
　Ought to be thankful.　I have not got through
　The quagmire of your marriage, and now I
　Must run a rig for him, and risk the cross.

Ant. Too true.

Phæ. Do you regard me, Geta, then,
　But as an alien?

Get. Quite the contrary.
　And do you count as nought the old man's rage—
　Shall we go irritate him more, and close
　The door for ever to our franchisement?

Phæ. A soldier carries off before my eyes
　My Pamphila, to die in foreign clime.
　Then, farewell! Antipho, farewell! we greet
　In word and action now for the last time.

Ant. Why so, and wherefore?

Phæ. Wheresoever they
　Shall bear her, I will follow, or will die.

Get. May gods protect you! but don't hurry so.

Ant. Can you assist him?

Get. If—and what—and how—

Ant. O Geta, try: I supplicate—entreat you,
　Arrest these cursed matters that afflict us.

Get. Arrest—well! that is feasible; but then
　I put myself in peril.

Ant.   Never fear;
    We will divide the peril and the gain.
Get. How much do you require?
Ant.   Thirty minæ.
Get. Thirty! she's very dear.   O Phædria.
Phæ. Dear! she's dirt cheap.
Get.   Well, well; I'll find the means.
Phæ. Good fellow!
Get.   Well! be off then, and away.
Phæ. I want them now.
Get.   Go, go—and you shall have them.
    But send me Phormio here; I must have him.
Phæ. Bid him meet me at home.
Ant. He is there.   Ah! he is the staunchest friend—
    The boldest advocate.
Get.   Away, then, to him.
Ant. Can I be of assistance?
Get.   None—away!
    Go and console your mistress—weeping now—
    Half dead at your long absence; go to her.
Ant. With all my heart and soul.
Phæ. What will you do?
Get.   I tell that on the march—
    Now cut along.

ACT IV.

Scene 1.—Demipho—Chremes.

Dem. Brother, have things gone well: returned from Lemnos,
    Say, do you bring your daughter?
Chr.   No.
Dem.   How so?
Chr. Her mother was impatient at my absence.
    My child was nubile; therefore they set sail
    With household, and came hither, seeking me,—
    So they report of her.
Dem.   Then why did you
    Delay return?
Chr.   Zounds! I fell sick.
Dem.   Of what?
Chr. Old age—the worst of sicknesses. I learn
    From mariners, who bore them, they are here.
Dem. Know you the escapade my son has played?
Chr. It knocks all my intentions on the head!
    For if I give her to another man,
    I must make declaration who she is.
    You, I can trust—trust as I can myself;
    A stranger now would hold me at his mercy,
    And if I quarrelled with him might betray me;
    And if my wife should know it, I may flee.
    I stand alone, with nobody to help me.
Dem. It is so—and I am the more concerned:
    I will not leave a single stone unturned,
    Until we bring to pass—that I have promised.

ACT IV.—Scene 2.—Geta.

Get. I never came across a cleverer man
　　Than Phormio.   I found him out, and said
　　We wanted money: asked how to obtain it.
　　I asked, he answered; neither did he brag,
　　But lauded me.   He seeks now the old man,
　　He renders the gods thanks, permitting him
　　To testify that he loves Phædria, too,
　　As well as Antipho.   Straightway he goes
　　To meet our old man.   Ah! here he is himself.
　　Who comes with him?   Pol! it is Phædria's father.
　　Why am I scared with fright?   Is it because
　　He holds two gudgeons in the lieu of one?
　　Now we can choose in an alternative,
　　And if I lose my venture with the one,
　　Then for the other: so about it straight.

ACT IV.—Scene 3.—Antipho—Geta—Chremes—Demipho.

Ant. I waiting am for Geta; and behold
　　My uncle with my father.   How I dread
　　Their conference, and its results to me.
Get. I'll board them straight.   Chremes, our master, hail!
Chr. Hail! Geta.
Get. 　　　　　Your safe return is gladness.
Chr. I hope so.
Get. 　　　　　Is all well?
Chr. 　　　　　　　　Not so.   Returning,
　　I hear some bad news.
Get. 　　　　　What, of Antipho?
Chr. It is so, even so!

Get.   He has told you all.
  Ah! Chremes, what misfortune to our house.
Chr. We talked of it e'en now.
Get.   And, hercle! I
  Talked of it with myself, and have discovered,
  Methinks, a remedy.
Dem.   Geta, what remedy?
Get. When I last quitted you it so fell out,
  I hit on Phormio.
Chr.   What Phormio?
Get. He who imbroiled us with this——
Chr.   Ah! I know.
Get. It came into my mind to question him.
  I drew him first aside, then said to him,
  Why, Phormio, do you not devise some means
  To compromise this matter? Master now
  Is liberal, and hates a court of law;
  Whilst every friend and neighbour, one and all,
  Are urging him to chase the woman forth.
Ant. What does the fellow say—what does he mean?
Get. You say, " if so, the law will punish him."
  " But, that's the question. Many learned heads,
  And eloquence in plenty, on my soul,
  Will make you sweat. But let us grant, you win
  The cause—what then? a matter 'tis of money,
  Not life or death;" and when I saw him waver
  I said, We are alone, speak plainly out,
  What must we give you now to take her off,
  To rid us of this baggage—suit and all?
Ant. Have the gods turned his head?
Get.   For I know well
  If you are just and reasonable, you

Will find my master just; and in three words
The matter may be settled.
Chr.   Very good;
It leads us to the matter on our hand.
Ant. I perish—slain.
Chr.   Go on.
Get.   He made a row,
And strode about——
Chr.   Ay, ay! What did he ask?
Get. What? Oh! too much, and more than he will get.
Dem. Yes; but how much?
Get.   He said, if we would give
The larger talent.
Chr.   Curse him; may he choke,
Unblushing beast.
Get.   The very thing I said.
I said : a dowry for his daughter, only child,
Could not be more; and small avail to him
To have no daughter, since this one, ready made,
Comes for a dower.   To cut my story short,
And leave out his impertinencies, lo!
This was the end : "Once on a time," quoth he,
"I had myself resolved to wed with her—
Child of my nearest friend. I pitied her,
And thought it right; for it came in my mind
How poverty is brought to servitude,
Purchased by wealth.   But to tell you the fact—
Frankly and openly to tell the truth,
I want a wife with dowry, for my debts.
If Demipho consents to dowry her
At what I want, then will I marry her.
I love her more than any other woman."

Ant. Oh! is this malice or stupidity
  Propense or thoughtless, I should like to know.
Dem. But if, forsooth, he owes his soul and body.
Get. "I have a field in pledge, pledged for ten minæ "—
Dem. Well, well! then, let him wed her; I will give them—
Get. "A house for ten——"
Dem.   Enough, enough; no more.
Chr. I will redeem it; I will pay ten minæ.
Get. "A slave to wait upon my wife—and some
  Trifle of furniture--the wedding feast—
  Put all together, make ten minæ more."
Dem. Rather six hundred suits of law. I say
  I will give nothing—Does the fellow think
  I am his zany?
Chr.   I will give them; hold!
  And let him wed her, whom you wish, you know.
Ant. Geta, your lies have ruined me downright.
Chr. This is my matter, and I ought to pay it.
Get. But let me know, he said, without delay,
  That I may know my course with her and him.
  The matter is on hand to-day—conclusive.
Chr. He shall receive it. Let him ransom her,
  And let him marry her.
Dem.   And break his heart
  Or head.
Chr.   Now, happily, I have with me
  The money ready—product of the lands
  My wife possessed at Lemnos; I will use
  Them now at need, and settle it with her.

ACT IV.—Scene 4.—Antipho—Geta.

Ant. Geta!

Get.   Ah!

Ant.   What hast thou done?

Get   Done the old men,
  And got the cash.

Ant.   Enough?

Get.   That I know not,
  But what you asked.

Ant.   Nay, answer me; in terms
  Directly to my question.

Get.   .   What do you ask?

Ant. What do I ask!   I tell you I'm undone—
  That you have ruined all.   Gods, goddesses,
  The gods above, below—confound and make
  Example of you!   And you the only man
  To serve one at his need!   Why touch upon
  The subject of my wife, and given hopes
  Unto my father to get rid of her?
  And Phormio—if he receive the dowry,
  Will marry her.

Get.   He will not marry her.

Ant. What! will he go to jail—for love of us—
  Keeping the money?

Get.   There is nought, Antipho,
  Which cannot be perplexed in its narrating,
  When men will view things other than they are.
  Now hear the other side.   If Phormio takes
  The money, he must take the girl—agreed;
  But all this takes some time, to call the guests,

To offer sacrifice.   Meantime we get
The money we are promised, and Phormio
Will give her back to us.
Ant.   I understand not.
Get. Not understand !   Excuses by the thousand—
A neighbour's black dog entered by my door ;
A snake fell off the roof into the court ;
Or a hen crowed ; or else the soothsayer,
Or the haruspex vetoes till the spring—
All lawful good impediments, d'ye see ?
Ant. Will these pass ?
Get.   These will and shall do so.
Here comes the money, and the man ; be off,
And bear the news to Phædria.

ACT IV.—Scene 5.—Chremes—Demipho—Geta.

Dem. Rest you contented.   I will take good care
That there shall be no roguery in this.
This money does not go forth from my hands
But before witnesses: to whom and why.
Get. How wise he is, when all is done and over.
Chr. Do so, but hurry, if he change his mind,
Or if this other one betrothed, appear,
It all may end in nothing.
Get.   It may so.
Dem. Then let us lose no time.
Get.   Behold me ready.
Chr. When you have done so, pass on to my wife
And let her catch the girl ere she go forth,
And let her tell her she is Phormio's bride,
Nor to be angry, for he suits her best ;

Tell, that they are akin and know each other,
That we have done our duty, and have given
The dowry he demanded.
Dem.　　　　　　Now what signifies
That rigmarole?
Chr.　　　　　　Much, Demipho, I say.
Dem. Say, is it not enough to do our duty
But all the world must know and praise it too?
Chr. Let it be seen and known as voluntary,
Not that we chased her forth.
Dem.　　　　　　　I can do that
Without your wife to aid.
Chr.　　　　　　A woman best
Manages women.
Dem.　　　　　I will make the request.
Chr. And I go find the while these Lemnian dames.

ACT V.

Scene 1.—Sophrona—Chremes.

Sop. I know not what to do, or where to find
  A friend or counsellor to ask for aid,
  And to confide a secret of such weight.
  I am afraid my mistress will be wrathful—
  Indignant at unworthy injuries;
  The father of the youth inexorable.
Chr. Who is this—this old lady—coming forth
  Out of my brother's house?
Sop.   Ah! poverty
  Has pushed me into this; although I knew
  Such marriages were insecure, I counselled
  Advising this: good sooth! in need of bread.
Chr. By Pollux! if my eyes do not deceive me,
  It is our nurse.
Sop.   Neither have we discovered
  Who is his father.
Chr.   Shall I hear more, or
  Shall I confront her?
Sop.   Could we discover that
  We should be heart-whole.
Chr.   Eh! Sophrona—nurse!
Sop. Who challenges by name?
Chr.   Nurse, look at me.
Sop. I do beseech you—art thou Stilpho? say.
Chr. No.
Sop.   Do you deny it?
Chr.   Sophrona, come you here

Away now from that door, and take good care
Never again to call me by that name.
Sop. Are you not he, whom they declared you are?
Chr. Hist!
Sop.   Fear you these doors?
Chr.   Ay, for I have therein
A fearful wife.   Therefore I took the name
That you should not by inadvertency
Betray me, and disclose our mystery.
Sop. Pol! that is wherefore we have asked in vain.
Chr. But tell thou me, what is it you do here—
Here, in this house: where are your mistresses?
Sop. Ah me! ah me!
Chr.   Say, are they both alive?
Sop. Your daughter lives.   Your wife, alas! alas!
Has fallen the prey of misery and death.
Chr. Unhappiness!
Sop.   And I alone and old,
Poor and unknown and friendless, have conjoined
In wedlock's tie your daughter to a youth
Inhabiting this house.
Chr.   To Antipho?
Sop. 'Tis he—himself.
Chr.   What, married to two wives!
Sop. What, what!   Ah! nay; he married is to one.
Chr. Where is the other then—his kinswoman?
Sop. 'Tis she herself.
Chr.   What do you say—'tis she!
Sop. It was done so expressly; her lover so
Obtained her without dowry.
Chr. Faith of immortal gods! how rashness oft
And inadvertency can serve us well,

Beyond one's utmost hopes.   I find my child
Wedded to him to whom I destined her,
And this poor woman inadvertently
Performs a task, we have essayed in vain.
Sop. Let us take counsel now.   The sire returns,
　As they report, most wrathful 'gainst the marriage.
Chr. All is quite right, fear not; but I entreat,
　Implore, let no one know she is my child.
Sop. None shall for me.
Chr.　　　　　　　　　Then follow me within.

ACT V.—Scene 2.—Demipho—Geta.

Dem. By human faults does wickedness succeed
　The whilst men vaunt and boast their righteousness.
　Lose not in travelling the sight of home,
　Says the old proverb.   Was it not enough
　To suffer wrong and injury, but we must
　Offer him money for subsistence and
　More villainies?
Get.　　　　　　　　It is most truly said.
Dem. They win the prize who swear that black is white.
Get. They do.
Dem.　　　　　　We have done very foolishly.
Get. Except he means to take the damsel off.
Dem. Is that in question?
Get.　　　　　　　　Hercle! he is a man
　Who might forswear.
Dem.　　　　　　　　How then—forswear?
Get. I do not know.   I spoke the thought at hazard.
Dem. I shall do as my brother has advised,

To set his wife to parley with the woman.
Go you and intimate to her, we want her.
Get. [*Alone.*] Money is found for Phædria.   No thunders yet,
　They sleep in silence : we have taken measures,
　The wife of Antipho remains at home.
　What more is there to do and to be done ?
　Ah ! Geta, you are ever in some scrape ;
　You change your bail, you but delay the day ;
　I bear the stripes, nor see I sure redemption.
　To Phanium now, to set her soul at rest
　Nor suffer it to quell at Phormio.

ACT V.—Scene 3.—Demipho—Nausistrata—Chremes.

Dem. Hence, dear Nausistrata, we pray you use
　Your ordinary tact, and let her know
　We wish her welfare ; try what you can do
　To cause her to depart.
Nau.　　　　　　　　　I'll do my best.
Dem. Now aid me with your wit, as heretofore
　You have done with your wealth.
Nau.　　　　　　　　　　Pol ! not so much
　As I could wish.   It is my husband's fault
　If he keeps me deceived.
Dem.　　　　　　　How so ?
Nau.　　　　　　　　　　　Because
　He has no right to my paternal lands,
　Which, whilst my father lived and managed them,
　Produced two talents yearly.   Oh ! difference
　'Twixt man and man !
Dem.　　　　　　　Two talents !

Nau. Ay, no less—
  When money was worth more.

Dem. Hem!

Nau. Tell me true,
  What think you of it? I would I were a man
  I would—

Dem. No doubt.

Nau. Soon show the compact which—

Dem. I pray you now—reserve your forces now
  To war with this young woman in the house.

Nau. I will do so. Lo! here my husband comes.

Chr. Hem! Demipho. Say, have they got the money?

Dem. I have ta'en care of that.

Chr. I wish it were not given.
  Zounds! there's my wife. I fear I've said too much.

Dem. Why, Chremes?

Chr. Nothing.

Dem. Say, have you told the girl
  Nausistrata is coming?

Chr. I have.

Dem. Well!
  And what said she?

Chr. She will not hear of it.

Dem. How, will not? Eh!

Chr. Both of them are in love.

Dem. Well, what of that!

Chr. Much—and I have discovered
  She is our kinswoman.

Dem. Go, go! you are mad.

Chr. Good faith! good faith! Now bear in memory
  That which I told you.

Dem.   Tell me, are you sane?
Nau. Eh! I beseech you heartily, take care—
    Wrong not a kinswoman.
Dem.   Pooh! she is none.
Chr. Her father bore another name—and so
    We were deceived.
Dem.   Does she not know her father?
Chr. Ay! doubtless.
Dem.   Wherefore, then, another name?
Chr. Ah! you are dull and stupid—understand—
Dem. How can I understand?
Chr.   Then you go on.
Nau. Now, what does all this mean, I marvel much?
Dem. Well, I know not.
Chr.   Then know, if you insist:
    By Jupiter! there is none nearer her
    Than you are and myself.
Dem.   Faith of the gods!
    Let us go seek her—all of us, and clear
    This mystery up.
Chr.   Ah!
Dem.   What's the matter now?
Chr. What, will you not believe my word?
Dem.   Believe!
    Will you I shall not ask; inquire—so be it.
    But this child of our friend—then what of her?
Chr. Nothing.
Dem.   We paid her off.
Chr.   Why not?
Dem.   The other stops.
Chr. Just so.
Dem.   You may go now, Nausistrata.

Nau. Pol! it is better for us, one and all,
  That the child should remain. Don't send her off;
  She is of gentle blood, it seems to me. [*She goes out.*]
Dem. What does she say?
Chr.   Has she shut to the door?
Dem. She has.
Chr.   O Jupiter, the gods are placable :
  My daughter and your son are man and wife!   ·
Dem. What contract—how ?
Chr.   Come in.
Dem.   I am with you.
Chr. Take care and keep it secret e'en from them.

ACT V.—Scene 4.—Antipho.

Ant. Though my affairs go badly, I rejoice
  That Phædria's speed well. Ah ! it is wise
  To entertain no wishes, other than
  May reach one in bad fortune. Now, Phædria's
  Have fled and vanished by the force of money.
  I find no remedy for my disease.
  Whilst it is in abeyance I'm in care,
  And when it is discovered I'm in dread.
  But Phanium lures me ever to this home.
  Geta, where art thou, Geta? I must learn
  From thee what time to meet my father's face.

ACT V.—Scene 5.—Phormio—Antipho.

Pho. I had the money—I have paid the merchant—
  I have the girl; or Phædria has got her,
  Whom he can marry. She, thus manumitted,

One thing remains—a week to feast and drink
At cost of the old men.   I must have that.
Ant. Phormio, how now?
Pho.   What?
Ant.   What must Phædria do?
How can he now reap fruits in his possession?
Pho. Why, do as you did.
Ant.   What?
Pho.   Why, flee away—
Avoid his father: and you must do as he,
And fight his battle with his father—so—
He comes to me to supper, and I feign
To go to Sunium, to market there
The girl that Geta told them I should buy.
So they will rest in peace, nor dream that I
Have filched their money bags.   Who comes?
Ant. 'Tis Geta.

ACT V.—Scene 6.—Geta—Antipho—Phormio.

Get. Fortuna! Fors Fortuna! what a gush
Of benefits have you bestowed this day
Upon my master, Antipho!
Ant.   Eh! what?
Get. And eased his friends from fear : why dally I —
Why not snatch up my cloak to find him out,
And tell him the good news?
Ant. [*To Pho.*]   Do you comprehend him—
Pho. Do you?
Ant.   Not I.
Pho.   Nor I.
Get. I will to Dorio's—they are there, no doubt.

Ant. Hola! Geta.

Get.   Hola thyself—lo! now
   Called back, e'en as I cut away; 'tis odd.

Ant. Geta.

Get.   Hark to him—and I am stone-deaf.

Ant. Geta, I say.

Get.   Some scurvy messenger
   Is calling me. May you be whipped—away!

Ant. Whipped you shall be, unless you stop directly.

Get. Some boon companion chaffing: let me see—
   Ah!—is it he, or not—'tis he himself.

Pho. At him at once.

Ant.   Now what is this about?

Get. O man of men, who dwell upon the earth,
   Favoured, most favoured by the gods above;
   Who love you, Antipho, and none but you.

Ant. So it be. Now, what is it? speak away.

Get. Are you content to wallow in delights?

Ant. You torture me.

Pho.   Come, come; quit promises.
   Go on to facts.

Get.   Ah! you here, Phormio.

Pho. I am—therefore go on.

Get.   Well, listen then :
   When we gave you the money on the forum
   We went straight home. As soon as we got there,
   The master sent me off unto your wife.

Ant. Well! why? why? why?

Get.   Ah! that I will not tell you,
   For truly it has nought to do with it.
   When I approached the bower, lo! the boy
   Midas, behind me caught my cloak: I turned

And asked him why he did so.   He replied,
It was forbidden all to enter now,
For Chremes and Sophrona both were there
In conference.   When I heard this and that
I went on tiptoe : crouching at the door,
I held my breath and opened all my ear;
I listened and I heard—I strained to hear.
Ant. What, Geta?

                O, wonderful ! twice three times
Wonderful !—I almost screamed for joy.
Pho. What was it ?
Get.   What do you think ?
Ant.   We know not.
Get. Ah ! more than wonderful ; 'twas wonderfullest.
Your uncle is the father of your Phanium.
Ant. What do you say ?
Get.   Her mother was his concubine
In Lemnos.
Pho.   Stuff and nonsense.   Do you say
She knew not her own father ?
Get.   Ay, Phormio.
We know but part—not all; think you that I
Could hear each syllable outside the door ?
Pho. I have heard something like it : similar—
Get. Let me go on with probabilities :
Your uncle went out, and returned again
Accompanied by your father.   Both declared
That they consented you should have your wife,
And ordered me to seek and take you there.
Ant. Why do you not, then, Geta, swoop me off ?
Get. Come on, then !
Ant.   O my Phormio, farewell !

Pho. And farewell, Antipho! Rejoiced am I,
 As the gods love me now, this fortune falls
 Where least it was expected. Phædria,
 This is a chance for you; for we will dupe
 The old ones, and get money for our need,
 Nor importune our friends. Ah! good at need,
 This money falls despite of them, and ne'er
 Shall they behold it more. Another robe,
 And face, and manner I will now assume.
 Now will I lurk in ambush, and pounce out
 Upon them as they pass. Eh! excellent—
 No more of Sunium, or slave-market there.

ACT V.—Scene 7.—Demipho—Phormio—Chremes.

Dem. To the great gods do I return my thanks,
 Affairs have issued all so prosperously.
 Now need we only to find Phormio,
 And to retrieve from him our thirty minæ
 Ere they be spent.
Pho.   I must discover straight
 If Demipho be home.
Dem.   We, Phormio, too,
 We are in search of you.
Pho.   No doubt—no doubt;
 On the same quest.
Dem.   By Hercules!
Pho.   I thought it:
 Why take that trouble? 'twas ridiculous.
 Think you that I am not a man of word?
 Lo! now—however poor I am and may be,
 I have and ever will keep my good name.

Chr. [*Abstractedly.*] Is she not exquisite, as I reported?
Dem. She is assuredly.
Pho.   'Twas therefore I
  Now sought you, Demipho.   Behold me ready,
  Desirous to take her to wife, directly.
  I have postponed all other minor things,
  Knowing how strongly you had this at heart.
Dem. My brother here has altered his intention:
  He dreads the rumour out of doors.   He says
  That, when a virgin, you refrained to take her;
  Now she is married we must not expel her.
  It were a deed disgraceful.   Every plea
  That you adduced before we echo now.
Pho. You treat me without ceremony.
Dem.   How?
Pho. How, do you ask!   Have I not lost the other—
  How can I ask again her I rejected!
Chr. [*To Dem.*] Besides that, Antipho will not resign her,
  Nor she herself consent.   Inform him so.
Dem. Besides, my son is resolute, nor will
  Resign the wife, unless the law compel him.
  So now unto the forum—to retrieve
  The money, Phormio.
Pho.   What! take again
  The money I have paid my creditors!
Dem. Why did you so?
Pho.   Give me the maid you promised:
  Lo! I am ready to take her for wife.
  If you retain the wife, release the dower—
  You, Demipho—because you have deceived me,
  Rob me as well.   It was at your behest—

At your requirement, I refused the other
And lost her dowry—equal sum to yours.
Dem. Go down to Stygian—with your boasts and brags—
  You runaway! Think you that we know not
  Your antecedents!
Pho.   I am getting savage.
Dem. Dare you to wed the girl, were we to give her!
Pho. Try and prove me.
Dem.   That Antipho may live
  With her in your house—is that your design?
Pho. What are you babbling of!
Dem.   Give me my money.
Pho. Give me my wife.
Dem.   Off to the magistrate.
Pho. Off to the magistrate! If you proceed—
  If you will carry on this odious strife—
Dem. What then?
Pho.   You think that I can patronize
  Only the orphan dowerless—I will show
  That I can patronize the dowered wife.
Chr. What's that to me?
Pho.   Nothing. I know a wife
  Whose husband had—
Chr.   Eh!
Dem.   What's the matter now?
Pho. A concubine in Lemnos—
Chr.   Annihilated!
Pho. Whose daughter reared in secrecy—
Chr.   I am slain!
Pho. I can relate it all—eh! through and out.
Chr. Do not, I pray you!

Pho.　　　　　　　　Oh!—is it you, then?
Dem. He fools us.
Chr.　　　　　　We release you—go away.
Pho. No bit of it.
Chr.　　　　　　What want you more?　The money?
　We condone it.
Pho.　　　　　　I hear—I hear.　Wherefore
　Do you entreat me thus?　Wherefore cajole me
　Like to an urchin lad?　I will—I won't;
　Again I will, again I won't—you yield,
　Resume again, pronounce and unpronounce,
　What was is not, and done must be undone.
Chr. How learnt he all of this?
Dem.　　　　　　　　I know not, I;
　I never mentioned it to mortal man.
Chr. As the gods love me this is wizarddom.
Pho. I puzzle and perplex them.
Dem.　　　　　　　　Zounds! this fellow
　Will jeer us and walk off.　I'd rather die.
　'Twere better pluck up courage to resist.
　The thing is known and bruited far and wide—
　You cannot hide it from your wife.　Believe me,
　Chremes—make virtue of necessity
　And tell her all, or e'er she learn from others;
　And then avenge ourselves on this accursed—
Pho. I must look out for squalls—they heave ahead
　Like gladiators, combatting to death.
Chr. She'll not be pacified.
Dem.　　　　　　　O, fear you not;
　You shall return to grace.　Besides you know
　The Lemnian woman's dead.
Pho.　　　　　　　Conspirators!　.

And not such bad ones. Hercle! Demipho.
You would absolve your brother at my cost;
And, Chremes—you, a stranger, and imagining
To put a gross affront upon a woman,
One of high rank, and wash it out with tears!
But I will kindle such a bale of fire,
Shall blaze, altho' you melt away in flood.
Dem. May the good gods and goddesses confound you!
Does such audacity impel a man,
And shall we not expose it—banish it
To desert isle?
Chr.   I am perplexed—nor know
I what to do.
Dem.   I know. The Court of law.
Pho. The Court of law—so be it—why not here!
Dem. Stop him, till I call help.
Chr.   I cannot single-handed.
Pho. I have one suit with you.
Chr.   So be it—so.
Pho. Another one with Chremes.
Dem.   Haul him off.
Pho. Now then for action. Ah! Nausistrata.
Chr. Gag him—his mouth—
Dem.   Scoundrel! how strong he is!
Pho. Nausistrata, Eh! Eh!
Chr.   Wilt thou hold thy peace!
Pho. No—no.
Dem.   Then hit him in the ribs—the wind—
Pho. Thrust out my eyes—I'll be revenged on you.

ACT V.—Scene 8.—Nausistrata—Chremes—Phormio—
Demipho.

Nau. Who calls me?
Chr.   Hem!
Nau.   Husband, what is it, pray?
Pho. Will you reply—why not!
Nau.   Who is this man—
  Reply!
Pho. He cannot answer, herele! look at him,
  He knows not where he is.
Chr.   Believe him not.
Pho. As cold as marble stone—Oh! touch and try.
Chr. It is nothing.
Nau.   Nothing—who is this man?
Pho. Hear, then, and know.
Chr.   Believe him not at all.
Nau. I have heard nothing yet.
Pho.   He is in fear—
  Out of his wits.
Nau.   Husband, what is the matter?
Chr. Out of my wits!
Pho.   Go on, then, tell your tale—
  Tell it yourself.
Dem.   Villain! at your requirement!
Pho. Ah! take your brother's part.
Nau.   Husband! my husband!
  What is all this about?
Chr.   But—
Nau.   But what?
Chr. Nothing important, wife.

Pho.   Ah! not to you.
   Important, though, to her.   At Lemnos—
Chr.   Stop!—
Dem. Be silent.
Pho.   Secret—
Chr.   Ah!
Pho.   He took a wife.
Nau. My husband, contradict it—gods forbid!
Pho. 'Tis even so.
Nau.   I am undone.
Pho.   A girl—
   Without your pains and peril—then was born.
Nau. By the immortal gods! unworthy deed,
   And infamous!
Pho.   And true.
Nau.   Oh! never, never,
   Before to-day, was deed so infamous!
   Now, Demipho, my question is to thee.
   I blush beholding him.   Was it for this
   You made your voyages and stays at Lemnos?
   For this—bad crops and murrains evermore
   Ate up my dowry.
Dem.   I, dear Nausistrata,
   Own and admit my fault, which yet, I hope,
   You will call pardonable.
Pho.   She hears you not.
Dem. For it was neither negligence nor hate
   Induced the deed.   Some fifteen years ago,
   After a feast, he met her on the road,
   Compressed, and had, indeed, a daughter by her;
   But never wooed her more.   And she is dead;
   And, therefore, I beseech you in this matter,

Bear it with equanimity and patience,
Such as are native to you.
Nau.   Equanimity!
  Patience! I—All bonds are burst betwixt us.
  What could I hope!—would age—access of years,
  Bring him access of wisdom!   He was old
  When this occurred; and, Demipho, am I
  Youthful as I was then?   Why do you, then,
  Counsel me " equanimity and patience "?
Pho. Whoe'er would see the exequies of Chremes,
  Let him make haste, the funeral rites appear.
  So let it happen to the foes of Phormio;
  So let them fall like Chremes.   Let him make
  A peace, if possible; my wrath is stilled.
  His wife from henceforth will assail his ears.
Nau. Perchance it was my fault.   Ah! Demipho,
  Can one recount my benefits to him?
Dem. I know them well.
Nau.   And did I merit this?
Dem. Nay, not at all; but it will nought avail
  Now to complain: and he avows his fault,
  I pray you, pardon him.
Pho.   But, before that
  I have a word to say for Phædria.
  Before Nausistrata—you make reply.
  Give me a hearing.
Nau.   Speak.
Pho.   I thirty minæ
  Got, somehow, from them for your son, and he
  Purchased his mistress from the broker.
Chr.   Eh!
Nau. Eh! he so young, and you so old a man;

He with one mistress, and you with two wives;
And dare you to condemn him—Answer me!
Dem. He shall obey your will.
Nau.   This is my will—
Nor pardon, neither acquiescence, till
I have beheld my son; for he shall be
The arbiter of this—he shall decide.
What he says I will do.
Pho.   Nausistrata,
Ah! wise and prudent, thou.

Nau.   Are you contented?
Pho. Throughly, most throughly: more than I can say.
Nau. What is your name?
Pho.   Phormio—the friend
Hercle! of all your family—and most
Of Phædria.
Nau.   Phormio, depend upon me;
As your good mistress, you may count on me
In all your needs.
Pho.   Benignant lady! thanks.
Nau. Pol! thou deservest well.
Pho.   Nausistrata,
Would you do me a pleasure, and, at once,
Enrage your husband much?
Nau.   Most willingly.
Pho. Invite me, then, to supper.
Nau.   Pol! I do.
Dem. Let us go in.
Nau.   But where is Phædria,
Our arbiter?
Pho.   Ah! he will present be,
I promise that.   Applaud, and fare ye well.

EUNUCHUS.

PERSONS.

PHÆDRIA.
PARMENO—Slave of Phædria.
THAIS.
ANTIPHO.
CHÆREA—Brother to Phædria.
GNATHO—Parasite.
THRASO—A Soldier.
PYTHIAS—Maiden of Thais.
CHREMES—Brother to Pamphila.
DORIAS—Maid to Thais.
DORUS.—Eunuchus.
SANGA—Slave of Thraso.
SOPHRONA—Nurse.
LACHES—Father of Phædria and Chærea.
PAMPHILA.
SIMALIO
DONAX } Slaves of Thraso.
SYRISCUS

PROLOGUE.

Is there an author studious to indite
What may please all and do to none despite,
Your author is the man.   But if another,*
Finding himself used roughly, cannot smother
His peevishness, then let that man be told
That he was the aggressor and too bold,
And that the plays he travestied from Greek
Into the Latin were but poor and weak.
He was the man translated from Menander
"The Phantom" and "The Treasure ;" † like a gander
Making defendant read the deed's recital,
Before the plaintiff pleads to prove his title
By which he claimed the treasure in the tomb.
Now let him not deceive himself, his doom
Depends on what he does, not what he says.
If he go on in his infernal ways,
I will have at him ; he shall not escape,
But truss him as a viper by the nape.
Now when the Ædiles bought Menander's play,
"Eunuchus," which we offer you to-day,

---

* Lavinius, his predecessor poet.

† "The Phantom" is based on a youth mistaking a maiden sacri-
ficing, for a spirit or goddess—"The Treasure" is somewhat like to our
Heir of Lynne, but the treasure in the tomb and letter of advice have
passed with the tomb by sale to a miser, who, though defendant, opens
the pleading by producing his deed of purchase.

He asked permission to examine it.
And when the magistrates were met to sit,
He bellowed out, a thief, and not a poet,
Presents this drama, by this fact we show it,
The " Colax," parasite and soldier, caught us,
The property of Nævius and Plautus.*
We poets sometimes with imprudence glide
Down the same flowing current side by side ;
You must decide if this be robbery.
Menander wrote the Colax, wherein he
Portrayed the soldier and the parasite,
The characters we represent to-night
In the Eunuchus, from Menander's Greek ;
That is as true as I am here to speak ;
And to deny, in tone that is most flat in,
That they have been translated from the Latin.
If it be not permitted to repeat
A character which one may elsewhere meet,
How can we ever lawfully portray
A faithful servant or a runaway,
A matron or a meretricious dame,
A parasite, a warrior of name,
Maidens and boys and old men, or to seek
Some tale of love or hatred, not in Greek?
Ah, there is nothing new beneath the sun,
Whatever is, or may be, has been done ;
Bear and forbear awhile with nothing new,
And what the Ancients did now let us do.
So sit at ease and listen to our play,
And hear what the Eunuchus has to say.

---

* Probably translated.

EUNUCHUS.

ACT I.

SCENE 1.—PHÆDRIA AND PARMENO.

Phæ. What shall I do—shall I not go to her,
  Now that she bids me of her own accord?
  Or, rather, shall I brace my spirit up,
  And bear no longer meretricious wiles?
  She shut me out, she calls me back again;
  Shall I return? No, not though she entreat me.
Par. Hercle! if so you can, nought better were,
  Nought worthier; but if you hoist your sails,
  And let them drop again—if you return,
  Conquered by passion, she expecting not,
  With broken truce, unable to bear absence,
  Showing you doat, and cannot live without her,
  It is all up—you perish—she will fool
  You merrily, when she has vanquished you.
  Therefore, let us take counsel whilst we may.
  Master, these matters neither counsel nor
  Experience permit,—they are not ruled
  By counsel. In love are many consequents
  Of evil import—injuries, suspicions,
  Hates, jealousies, and war—and peace again.
  Now, if you try to make unstable counsel

Stable by reason's rules, you only add
To madness, and are reasonably mad.
So, what you now deliberate in rage—
As, shall I go to her? who him? who me?
Who not? I'd rather die; nay, she shall know
What stuff I am; and all this manly bluster
Melts and dissolves before one little tear,
Unreal, squeezed out of eye with effort strong,
And rubbing it: then you accuse yourself,
And cry for pardon.

Phæ.   Oh! unworthy weakness;
Ah! she is false, and I am miserable;
I wearied am, the whilst I burn with love;
Seeing and feeling fall a willing prey;
Nor know I what to do.

Par.   This is to do—
Redeem yourself, a captive, as you can,
At any cost: at small, if possible,
And save yourself.

Phæ.   And do you so advise?

Par. If you are wise: and add not unto love
Ills needless to be borne; meantime to bear
The needful patiently.   Ah! here she comes—
The bitter hail-storm that consumes our crops.

ACT I.—Scene 2.—Thais—Phædria—Parmeno.

Tha. Unhappy me!   I fear lest Phædria
Has taken unto heart more than he ought
His yesterday's repulsion.

Phæ.   Parmeno,
I shake and tremble on beholding her!

Par. Be of good cheer; approach yon blazing fire:
  You will be warm enough.
Tha.   Who is't that speaks?
  My Phædria, and art thou here!   But why
  Stand here and enter not?
Par.   Ah! not one word
  Of yesterday's exclusion.
Tha.   Silent, my Phædria?
Phæ. Truly, your doors are ever open to me,
  And I with you stand first.
Tha.   Dismiss such taunt.
Phæ. Dismiss—O Thais, Thais; would to heaven—
  Or that your heart responsively met mine,
  Or that you grieved to grieve me as I grieve,
  Or that my heart was stony hard as yours!
Tha. Nay, I beseech, my soul, my Phædria,
  Do—do not doubt.   It is not that I love
  It is not that I cherish aught but you;
  But that affairs—affairs of weight—compelled me.
Par. No doubt, no doubt, poor child!   For very love
  You shut him out of doors.
Tha.   Fie! Parmeno,
  Do you condemn me?   Hear me, Phædria,
  Why I besought you now to visit me.
Phæ. I hear.
Tha.   But, tell me, ere I tell my tale,
  Can he keep counsel?
Par.   I—excellently well.
  But on condition: what is true, I hold
  Firm as my faith and secret: what is false,
  Vain, or fictitious, that I blurt abroad:

Falsehood, like water, flows through all my chinks.
Speak truth, and I am trusty.
Tha.   A Samian
My mother was, but dwelt at Rhodes.
Par.   And I
Can keep that secret.
Tha.   There a merchantman
Gave her a child he took in Attica.
Phæ.   A citizen ?
Tha. We think so ; but we know not.   The young girl
    Could tell the names of father and of mother,
    But not their dwelling-place, nor knew her age.
    The merchant purchased her—or so he said—
    From pirate boats at Sunium, captured there.
    My mother took her and instructed her,
    As though she were a daughter : many thought,
    Indeed, she was my sister.   For myself,
    I quitted Rhodes with him.   He loved me well,
    And gave me everything that he possessed,
    I ne'er knew man, save him.
Par.   I overflow—
    Two chinks of falsehood.
Tha.   And what may they be ?
Par. " All you possess," and " he your only lover "—
    For one did not content you ; and for wealth,
    Much was my master's.
Tha.   Both of which are true.
    And now let me proceed.   He went to war,
    Draughted to Caria : then met I you.
    Since when you know how dearly I have loved you,
    And gladly have confided all to you.
Phæ. Neither will Parmeno be secret here.

Par. No, that flows forth.
Tha.   Now, listen, Phædria.
  My mother died at Rhodes.   Her brother, who
  Is parsimonious, seeing in the child
  One fair, well-formed and featured—playing, too,
  Upon the strings—resolved to sell her, and
  Fortune, then kind, sent my same captain there
  To purchase her for me, by accident;
  He did not know his purchase.   He came here,
  And, when he heard of you, he took offence;
  Refused the promised gift.   For jealousy
  Laid hold of him, to see himself supplanted;
  And I, accepting her, rejecting him.
  And, to conclude, I fear he loves the maiden.
Phæ. Nought further passed?
Tha.   Nought, for I questioned him.
  And now, dear Phædria, she is my sister—
  At least was deemed so—and I wish, indeed,
  To render her to freedom and her friends;
  Therefore to purchase her.   I am alone—
  Nor friend, nor parent: whom I might regain
  Through her, by deed of benefit like this.
  Therefore, I pray you, help me.   Suffer him,
  For a few days, to dwell in preference,
  I do entreat you.   Do you not reply?
Phæ. Reply—Iniquitous! to words like these.
Par. Right excellent! I praise you; riled at last.
Phæ. In faith, I cannot see at what this drives.
  A girl was kidnapped; by your mother bred
  As her own child, and passing for your sister.
  Now you would purchase her, to yield her up

To friends unknown.   It simply ends in this—
You thrust me forth to make a way for him.
Wherefore?   Because you love him better, and
You fear the maiden may lure him away!
Tha. I dread not that.
Phæ.   What is it that you dread?
Is he the sole one who presents you gifts?
Or is my hand asleep?   When you desired
An Æthiop maiden, did I not, quitting all,
Search till I found one?   When you wished an eunuch,
Which queens alone possess, I found one, too.
But yesterday I paid down twenty minæ,
And am to-day thrust forth.   I wearied not,
I pined for you, and you care nought for me.
Tha. Then, I renounce her, Phædria.   I desired,
With passion, to obtain her; and I might,
With small renunciation on your part, do so.
Rather than have you wrathful, I obey you.
Phæ. Would that were true! Oh! that those words were
          sooth!—
" Rather than have you wrathful."   What is there
I could not suffer—what could not endure.
Par. He yields.   One word— no more; so quickly conquered.
Tha. I speak not sooth?   What is there, I beseech you,
In earnest or in frolic, I refused you?
Yet you will not accord me two day's space!
Phæ. If but two days—I fear they would be twenty.
Tha. In truth, two days, or—
Phæ.   Or—or what?—say on.
Tha. No more.   Your fears are groundless—very vain.
Phæ. But I must yet concede the thing you wish.
Tha. Thanks, Phædria; I love you, and I thank you.

Phæ. Into the country I; and kill the time,
　And weep and sigh, for Thais wills it so.
　You, Parmeno, remain, and lead them hither.
Par. Ay, ay.
Phæ.　　　　　Thais, farewell! And, for two days, farewell!
Tha. My Phædria, and thou. Would'st nothing more?
Phæ. Ah! Thais; when the soldier's by your side,
　Think of me absent; day and night desire me;
　Dream of me, and expect me; think of me;
　Hope and anticipate; be all mine own,
　And let your soul be mine, as mine is yours.

ACT I.—SCENE 3.—THAIS.

Unhappy I! He judges me by others,
Nor credits my true speech. Pol, but I know
I have spoke nought but truth; I love him more
Than I love any other. What I have done
Has been for the poor maiden; and I think
I have found out her brother: a citizen
Of birth and good repute. He comes to-day,
And I go in, preparing to receive him.

ACT II.

Scene 1.—Phædria—Parmeno.

Phœ. Do as I bade you do; conduct them there.

Par. It shall be done.

Phœ.   And quickly.

Par.   Quickly done.

Phœ. Early?

Par.   Ay, ay.

Phœ.   Do you quite understand?

Par. I think so. It is difficult, no doubt.
    Ah! master mine, I wish you were as sure
    To find a treasure, as to lose those slaves.

Phœ. Ah! I lose that—that unto me is dearer—
    Lost my repose: I mind not other loss.

Par. Nor then will I: I will perform that bidding.
    Have you aught else to bid me?

Phœ. Grace with the gift of words, my gift of price,
    And do your best to chase him from her house.

Par. I should have done those of my own accord.

Phœ. Into the country I—there to abide.

Par. Good.

Phœ.   But, hearken!—

Par.   What?

Phœ.   Do you believe that I
    Can do so for so long?

Par.   Well, I do not.
    Either you will return directly, or—
    After a sleepless night—at peep of dawn.

Phœ. But I will work, and, wearying myself,
  Will sleep in spite.
Par.   Wearied you'll watch again,
  And watch in wearying.
Phœ.   Ah! say not so,
  My Parmeno. Hercle! I must cast off
  This softness of the soul. What, can I not
  Command myself for three days, if I will!
Par. Three days of absence—Eh! consider.
Phœ.   And I have.

ACT II.—Scene 2.—Parmeno.

Good gods! what a disease. Is it possible
That love can so pervert the mind of man,
It is not to be recognized. His soul was firm—
None firmer; steady, strongly self-reliant.
But who is this? Ah! Gnatho, parasite
Unto our soldier. And he leads a girl,
A gift to Thais. Papæ! she is gentle.
I shall have small thanks for my wrinkled eunuch.
Thais is not so comely as this maid.

ACT II.—Scene 3.—Gnatho—Parmeno—Pamphila—
Ancilla.

Gna. Immortal gods! How man surpasseth man!
  And how intelligence surpasses folly!
  That sentiment was upmost in my mind,
  Encountering an acquaintance—an old neighbour,
  Honest, not covetous, with wasted wealth.

I marked him squalid, pale, and miserable.
"Hola! How now?" quoth I.   "Ruined!" quoth he,
"Of property and of my prosperous friends."
I cast my eyes on him from top to toe—
"Most despicable man! are you so fallen
As to retain no hopes?—have you lost all
Your money and your soul? For, like to you,
I, too, lost all; but cast your eyes on me:
Colour and smoothness—raiment—lustyhood—
What have I lost that I do not retain?
What lacking, do I lack?"—He made reply:
"I could not suffer poverty, nor slavery,
Nor play the mime."—"Nor was occasion, friend;
That mode of getting bread is very old—
Old as our grandfathers. I first found out
A better mode to set the snares for woodcocks.
There is a human race believes itself
Superior to its fellows. Shallow race!
To them I cringe, but not to make them smile,
Though I smile at them, and admire their wit.
What they assert, I praise—and if again
They contradict that praise, I praise again;
Deny what they deny, or yield assent
To aught which they assert. If you do so,
You have discovered a short road to wealth."
Par. Hercle! a learned man, a sort of man
    Who makes a madman of a fool.
Gna. And, talking thus, we run upon the market;
    And, running to me, in the lust of gain,
    Delighted stall-holders of meat and fish,
    Hunters and fowlers, and confectioners,

Remembering days of my prosperity,
And custom since, they hasten to salute me,
Delighted to behold, invite to supper.
When my good man in difficulties sees
Me gain a livelihood so merrily,
He craves to follow me, I bid him follow;
For, as the sects of the philosophers
Adopt the appellations of their founders,
I fain would found a parasitic school --
Gnathonian.

Par.   O blessed gift of ease
To live on others!

Gna.   But behoves me now
To leave this damsel at the home of Thais,
And ask her to our supper.   Ah! Parmeno,
Our rival's servant, standing by her door,
And moody—that is right; the atmosphere
No doubt is cold.   Now must I play the rogue.

Par. They think to purchase Thais by their gifts.

Gna. Health unto Parmeno, from his best friend--
From Gnatho; and how now?

Par.   Well, I am here.

Gna. I see it.   Do not you see something, too,
You do not like?

Par.   Thee?

Gna.   Well, me—and something else.

Par. Why do you ask?

Gna.   Because you look so sadly.

Par. Eh! not the least.

Gna.   That's right.   Eh! Parmeno,
What of this purchase?

Par.   Hercle! not so bad.

Gna. I rile the man.

Par.   He is wrong.

Gna.   Thais, methinks,
 Will like this gift?

Par.   He thinks to buy us out.
 All mortal things are subject unto fortune.

Gna. For six months, Parmeno, I grant you rest—
 Nor hurry by the day, nor watch by night.
 Do you not thank me?

Par.   Papæ! truly—thanks.

Gna. I love to serve a friend.

Par.   Benevolent!

Gna. But let me not detain you if you're busy.

Par. O, not at all.

Gna.   Then I will be beholden
 To you, for introduction unto Thais.

Par. Her doors will not be shut against your charge.

Gna. Shall I send some one to you out of doors?

Par. [*Alone.*] Patience! I say—it is but for two days—
 For two days' space you may with little finger
 Open that doorway—after that your heels
 Shall not prevail, and you will kick in vain.

Gna. [*Returning.*] What, Parmeno, still here upon the guard:
 Have you some dread some messenger may pass
 In privacy to Thais from the soldier!

Par. Said cheerily, and quaintly; just the phrase
 To please a soldier. Ah! ah! our younger son—
 What doth he do away from the Piræus?
 He was on guard there: he is steady, too,
 And rushing here in haste, regarding round.

ACT II.—Scene 4.—Chærea—Parmeno.

Chæ. Murder! lost sight of her! I neither know
  Where she has gone to, whither I have followed,
  Nor in what path pursue, nor whom to ask,
  But this I know, that such resplendent beauty
  Cannot be hidden.   A celestial face!
  I wipe from off the mirror of my soul
  All other women, and will worship her.
Par. Behold! another votary of love.
  Master, unfortunate old man, if this
  Runs riot in his madness—all as yet
  Has been but twaddling in the scenes of love.
Chæ. May gods and goddesses curse that old wretch
  Who held me in his prate, and curse myself
  For suffering it!   Ah! salvè, Parmeno.
Par. Why are you moody? whither in such haste?
  Whence come you?
Chæ.   I do not know at all,
  Nor whence, nor where; for I am off my head.
Par. Why, I beseech you?
Chæ.   For I love—
Par.   Ahem!
Chæ. Now, Parmeno! now show yourself a man.
  Now, Parmeno, accord me promised aid:
  You ofttime said to me—when, Chærea,
  You need my aid, depend on me to give it,
  And filch for you all in your father's house.
Par. Go to—you dream!
Chæ.   Hercle! it is no dream.
  I have discovered her you spoke about,
  So lend assistance; she is worthy of it.

s 2

She is not like our girls, with falling shoulders
And pent-up bosom—slender as a reed.
If they are plump, they are called pugilists,
And put upon short commons; artificially
They bend like canes, and men admire them.
Par. And what is yours like?
Chœ.   Ah! superlative!
Par. Papæ!
Chœ.   Ah! fair and firm, with health superfluous.
Par. How old?
Chœ.   Sixteen.
Par.   The very spring of youth.
Chœ. Ah! Parmeno; by force, or fraud, or prayer,
    Win her for me—I reck not of the cost.
Par. Then who and where is she?
Chœ.   Ah! that I know not.
Par. From whence?
Chœ.   I know no more.
Par.   Where does she dwell?
Chœ. I do not know.
Par.   Where did you meet her, then?
Chœ. Here in the street.
Par.   Wherefore not follow her?
Chœ. 'Tis that enrages me.   I am unlucky;
    And all my lucky chances fall out ill.
    It drives me to distraction.
Par.   What occurred?
Chœ. Coeval with my father, Archidemidas,
    Do you know him?
Par.   Do I not—
Chœ.   Caught hold of me
    When I was in full chase.

Par.   That was unlucky.

Chœ. 'Twas misery and not mishap.   O Parmeno,
  This six or seven months I have not seen
  Aught equal to her; neither can I live
  Without her; and I think it ominous.
  What do you think?

Par.   'Tis very probable.

Chœ. He ran to me from far, all bent and doubled,
  With open mouth, and panting.   Chærea, oh!
  I want you—so I stopped—do you know why?
  I know not—say.   To-morrow is my plea:
  I want your father's aid as advocate.
  So he went on one hour.   At the last
  I got away, and saw the damsel last
  Here in this place.

Par. [*Aside.*]   Her they have given to Thais.

Chœ. Yet here I find her not.

Par.   But who had charge
  Of her?

Chœ.   A parasite and maiden.

Par.   Ah!
  It is herself.   Cease to be troubled so.

Chœ. You mind me not.

Par.   I mind you very well.

Chœ. But know you where she is—tell me, I pray you?

Par. I know, have seen, and know where she is now.
  She is here with Thais; and a gift to her.

Chœ. And who so rich as to bestow such gift?

Par. The soldier Thraso, rival to Phædria.

Chœ. Hard lot for Phædria.

Par.   That is very true.

If you beheld his gift opposing this,
You would confess so.

Chæ.   What gift?

Par.   Eh—an eunuch.

Chæ. That wretch he purchased yesterday?

Par.   '   The same.

Chæ. He will be kicked out with his semi-male.
I never knew that Thais was our neighbour.

Par. But latterly.

Chæ.   I never saw her.   Tell me
Is she as beautiful as rumour speaks her?

Par. She is very beautiful.

Chæ.   But not like mine?

Par. Oh! quite another thing.

Chæ.   Ah! Parmeno,
Contrive that I may have her in possession.

Par. I will do my best, and aid you all I can.
Do you want nothing more?

Chæ.   Where go you now?

Par. Home first, and thence to leave the slaves with Thais,
As Phædria commanded.

Chæ.   Eunuch, thrice happy!

Par. And wherefore so?

Chæ.   Ah! do you ask? to wait
Attendant upon her, to behold her face,
To see, to touch, to live in the same house:
To eat with her, to sleep in her own room.

Bar. Then why not you?

Chæ.   How? Parmeno. Reply.

Par. Assume his vestments.

Chæ.   Vestments, and what then?

Par. Assume his place.

Cha.   I comprehend.

Par.   Assert
  That you are he.

Chæ.   I will.

Par.   Possess his reign—
  To eat, to view, to touch, to laugh with her,
  To couch in the same room.   You may do so ;
  None of these women know you ; for your chin
  You may pass safely for him whom you seem.

Chæ. Well thought and well advised !   I never heard
  A better thing devised.   On—on, and in !
  Array me—clothe me—lead me thither straight !

Par. What do you do ?   I did but speak in jest.

Chæ. Yes ; now you do.

Par.   I am undone and ruined,
  For what do you propose ?   I pray you quit
  Your purpose, or quit me.   Farewell ! I say.

Cha. Off, let us go.

Par.   You will ?

Chæ.   Ay, resolute !

Par. Beware ! the path is perilous.

Chœ.   Away !

Par. You will get quit ; my back must bear the beans.

Chæ. Ah !

Par.   'Tis a flagitious deed !

Chæ.   Flagitious deed !
  Is it flagitious to burst wide the doors
  Of such a one as preys upon our youth,
  Taunt us, enrage us by all wiles and guiles ;
  To treat them as they treat us constantly ?
  Or should I rather treat my father so,

And suffer blame from all the world? the while
The world will vaunt my very name for this.
Par. Nay! if you will, you will.   About it then,
But do not cast the blame on me, I pray.
Chæ. I will not.
Par.   Now command me!
Chæ.   I command you,
I order and compel you: nor will I
Ever deny it was my act and deed.
Par. About it then.   Gods grant us good success!

Europa Sidonia.

ACT III.

Scene 1.—Thraso—Gnatho—Parmeno.

Thr. Thais, no doubt, returns me gracious thanks?

Gna. Ay, mighty!

Thr.   And tell me, was she merry?

Gna. The giver, not the gift, has touched her most;
  She is triumphant.

Par.   It is about the time
  I should present our slaves.   The soldier!   Ah!

Thr. Fortune was kind to me: whate'er I do
  Is gracefully accepted, as bestowed.

Gna. I ever noted it.

Thr.   Why the king himself
  Would thank me hugely, and would snub another.

Gna. Ah! eloquence will walk off with the praise
  Which others gain with toil; that gift you have
  In an extreme degree!

Thr.   Good!

Gna.   Then the king
  Regarded you with—

Thr.   He did so.

Gna.   Honour

Thr. Entrusting me with the sole conduct of
  The army and his counsels.

Gna.   Wonderful!

Thr. And when the king was sick of business,
  Wearied with being bothered, when he would
  Repose, you know—as—understand?

Gna.   Right well.
  To chase the courtier nuisance from his mind.

Thr. Ay, and then bade me sup with only him!

Gna. Ah! you describe a jewel of a king.

Thr. One who is overchoice in his selection.

Gna. Hating the whole world, loving only you!

Thr. And envious courtiers, grinding of their teeth—
I snapped my fingers at them—animals!
But one, who ruled the Indian elephants,
Chafed out of bound. "Tell me, I pray you, Strato,"
I asked, addressing him, "Are you so fierce,
Because you govern beasts?"

Gna.   Thrice excellent!
Mehercle! Sapient, papæ! too. Why that
Twisted and cut his windpipe! What said he?

Thr. He was dumb.

Gna.   Dumbfoundered? Ah!

Par. [*Aside.*] Faith of the gods!
Here's a soul lost—lost utterly. Ah! villain.

Thr. But, Gnatho, I have never told you, how
I treated once a Rhodian at a feast.

Gna. Never—[*Aside.*] A thousand times—I beg and pray
You to recount it.

Thr.   'Twas one night at a feast,
The youngster Rhodian, whom I told you of;
I had my mistress with me; he began
To play the fool and chaff. "Oh, oh!" quoth I,
"A hare yourself, and hunting after game."

Gna. Ah, ah, ah!

Thr.   Eh, eh?

Gna.   Clever, famous,
Marvellously good! I never heard a better.
But tell me, pray, was that same saying yours?
I thought it ancient.

Thr.   One you had heard before?
Gna. Often, and much admired.
Thr.   Mine, I assure you.
Gna. I grieve for that young Rhodian—gently born—
Par. The gods confound you!
Gna.   How did he endure it?
Thr. Smashed up! and all the others laughed to death.
  Since then, they 'ware of me.
Gna.   Good reason why.
Thr. But tell me, ought I to explain to Thais,
  I care not for the girl—allay suspicions?
Gna. The contrary, arouse them.
Thr.   Wherefore so?
Gna. Wherefore!   Because when she names Phædria,
  And praises him—but to do you despite—
Thr. I have it.
Gna.   You have her on the hip—aha!
  She will name Phædria, you immediately
  Name Pamphila; so if she says invite
  To supper Phædria, shout out for Pamphila
  To sing unto us.   She praises forsooth him,
  Then vaunt her beauties forth; whate'er she doth,
  Do thou the like--until she bite her lips.
Thr. Ah! if she loved me, Gnatho, that would do.
Gna. She loves your gifts: nor can there be a doubt
  She loves yourself—expects you.   Have no fears,
  She will not chafe with you, lest you should go
  And carry off your presents in your hand.
Thr. And that is true, indeed; I overlooked that.
Gna. You thought not of it; did not overlook it.
  Had you but thought a moment, it had come.

ACT III.—Scene 2.—Thais—Thraso—Parmeno—Gnatho
—Pythias.

Tha. I heard my hero's voice, and here he is—
  Salvè, my Thraso!
Thr.   Salvè, Thais mine!
  My joy of joys! and how goes all with you?
  Love you me, for the player on the harp?
Par. Hark to him! hark how cheerily he greets!
Tha. I love you for yourself!
Gna.   To supper then.
Par. Hark to another of them.
Tha.   I am ready.
Par. I will accost them as if just from home.
  [*Aloud.*] Departing, Thais, whither are you bound?
Tha. Ah! Parmeno, at happy time.   I go—
Par. Where?
Tha.   Oh! hist, do you not see the soldier?
Par. I see and I enrage.   When, if you please,
  May I present the presents Phædria sends?
Thr. Come on; what stops the way?
Par.   Hercle! I pray,
  Permit us to present the gifts to Thais,
  And grant a moment's time for conversation.
Thr. Incomparable gifts, eclipsing ours!
Par. They answer for themselves.   Hey! bring them here,
  Advance and quickly; from far Æthiopia
  This damsel comes.
Thr.   And worth about three minæ.
Gna. About that.
Par.   Come hither Dorus, forward here you have
  An eunuch in the flower of his youth.

Tha. As the gods love me, an ingenuous face!

Par. What say'st thou, Gnatho? something to despise.
   What thou, O Thraso?   Nothing.   That is praise.
   Make your essay in letters or in speech,
   An orator and musician, instructed full
   In liberal lore.

Thr.   I try him? nay not I.
   He may pass muster.

Par.   The giver of these gifts
   Demands not you should live for him alone,
   For him expelling others; neither vaunts
   His battles and his wounds; neither besieges
   You, as some one does, importunately;
   He is contented to abide your will,
   And when you suffer him, he is rejoiced.

Thr. Servant of an impoverished master this
   In purse and will.

Gna.   No doubt none other one
   Could suffer that, if he could purchase better.

Par. Peace! viler than the vilest of mankind;
   Say what you would not do to cram your maw!

Thr. Let us be off, I say.

Tha.   I will go in,
   Dispose of these, and straight be back again.

Thr. I go; wait you for her.

Par.   It doth not suit
   The grandeur of a General, to walk
   Beside his mistress in the public ways.

Thr. What shall I say to thee? like man, like master!

Gna. Ha, ha, ha!

Thr.   What are you grinning at? I say.

Gna. At what you said to the young Rhodian
   It flashed across my mind—I could not help it.
   Here Thais comes.
Thr.   Go and get all prepared.
Gna. It shall be done.
Tha. [*to Pythias.*]   Mind, Pythias, what I say.
   Should Chremes haply come—first bid him stay.
   If stay he cannot—bid him come again.
   If he will not do that, bring him to me.
Pyth. It shall be done.
Tha.   And, Pythias, have a care
   Of the young damsel.   Keep yourself at home.
Thr. Let us be going.
Tha.   Follow me—you others.

ACT III.—Scene 3.—Chremes—Pythias.

Chr. The more I think of it, the more appears
   Thais—some day—will do me some ill turn.
   She lays her meshes for me – she invites me
   To visit her—to see her.   All will ask
   What I do here.   I do not know the woman.
   I came, and she sought pretexts to detain me—
   A sacrifice: and afterwards. discourse
   Of moment great—and I had my suspicions
   Of trickery.   She sat herself beside me
   And asked me of my parents—were they dead?
   I answered, long ago.   Then wished to know
   If I had once a house at Sunium,
   And how far from the sea.   I think she wants
   To purchase it and wheedle it from me.
   Whether I had a sister, who was lost ;

Her age—her dress—and, lastly, who was with her—
Could any recognize her.   Why all this?
Methinks that she is bold enough to dare
Pass off herself as this lost child.   But if
My sister lives—she is but sixteen years
No more—Thais is old as I.   Again
She sends for me to see me ; and again—
But for the last time—I obey.   Holloa!
Pyth. What is it?
Chr.   Chremes, it is I.
Pyth.   Ah! well—
    You're a fine fellow.
Chr.   Lo! my fears were just—
    This is some trick.
Pyth.   Thais begs and prays
    You will return to-morrow.
Chr.   No; I go
    Into the country.
Pyth.   Do not, I entreat you.
Chr.   I can't, I tell you.
Pyth.   Will you wait awhile
    Till she return?
Chr.   Still less and less, I trow.
Pyth. Why so, my Chremes?
Chr.   Baggage! hence away.
Pyth. But if you cannot wait, nor come again,
    Say will you kindly follow where she is?
Chr. With all my heart.
Pyth.   Eh! Dorias—quickly
    Lead him unto the soldier's.

ACT III.—Scene 4.—Antipho—Chærea.

Ant. Some friends at the Piræus yesterday
    Agreed to meet to-day, and dine together,
    And Chærea was commissioned to provide.
    We gave our rings in pledge, named time and place.
    The time has passed and nothing is prepared,
    And he is absent, and I am perplexed.
    They bid me find him out, and therefore I
    Seek him at home.   Why, here he is himself,
    And coming forth from Thais.   What on earth!
    Why, how is he equipped!   What can this mean!
    I will withdraw awhile and look about.

Chæ. Is the coast clear?   It is—doth any follow
    Out of the house?   Nay, none.   May I shout out
    My triumph and my joy.   Proh Jupiter!
    Now is the time that you may strike me down,
    Nor let the leaven of the after time
    Corrupt and mingle this.   Should any one
    Now see me, follow me, and pester me
    With questions wherefore I am mad with joy;
    Or ask me whence I come or where I go;
    Wherefore I wear this garb, and what I seek,
    And whether I am in my wits or no.

Ant. I will address him: he shall have the wish
    Ejaculated acted.   Chærea, why—how now—
    Whence comes this joy and triumph?   Why are you
    Garbed in such sort, and wherefore mad with joy?
    Ah! whether are you in your wits or no?
    Why gaze you at me?   Wherefore answer not?

Chæ. O festal day of man!   Salvè! my friend,
    You are the person upmost in my thoughts!

Ant. And wherefore so, I pray you?

Chœ.   I pray you
  To listen.   Know you my brother's mistress?

Ant. Thais?

Chœ.   Herself.   To-day was sent to her
  A girl of a—I won't describe her beauty.
  You know I am fastidious in beauty!
  Nor without judgment in its attributes;
  But her's astonished me.

Ant.   Ah! is it so?

Chœ. You will confess so much when you have seen her.
  I fell in love, fortune befriending me.
  It chanced that Phædria bought, to give to Thais,
  A certain eunuch, to be sent to her.
  Then Parmeno gave counsel which I followed—

Ant. What!

Chœ.   I will proceed—to change my vestment
  With him, to take his place, and represent him.

Ant. An eunuch's!

Chœ.   Even so.

Ant.   And wherefore so;
  What profit could accrue from such a deed?

Chœ. What profit! none—to be with her I loved?
  So it fell out.   Presented unto Thais,
  She led me to the damsel, and committed
  Her to my care.

Ant.   Ah! truly, a safe guardian.

Chœ. She bade me not to let another man
  Have access to her: bade me not to quit her,
  To guard her in the chamber far remote;
  And I held down my head, and bowed assent.

Ant. Poor boy, poor boy!

T

Chæ.   I sup in town, she said.
    She took her damsels with her, leaving me
    Some novices, who then prepared her bath.
    I bade them hurry. She in the conclave sat
    Meantime, and gazed on a depicted tale
    Of Jupiter and Danaë; how once
    The god descended in a golden shower
    Into her bosom. I looked at it too,
    And joyed to see the metamorphosed god
    Fall through the pluvium of another's house,
    To teach a mortal humble as am I
    The thing I had to do. It pleased me well.
    Meantime the damsels led her to the bath.
    She went and she returned, then languid lay
    Upon the couch the whilst the maidens bathed.
    I stood expecting what my duties were,
    When one, "Eh! Dorus, take this fan, and breathe
    Upon her gently." I took it moodily.
Ant. A wondrous spectacle of impudence,
    Handling a fan with limbs so asinine.
Chæ. Away they ran to bathe, all joy and riot,
    As maidens wont to do, the mistress absent.
    She slumbered, and I gazed down silently
    Beneath the fan. I looked—we were alone:
    I thrust the bolt——
Ant.   What then?
Chæ.   Idiot! what then!
Ant. Well, I confess it.
Chæ.   Occasion brief, unhoped for,
    To pass away—desired and obtained.
    I was not that, that I appeared to be.
Ant. Well done! and now what of the rings and supper.

Chæ. All is prepared.
Ant.   Why, good again! and where?
Chæ. At our freedman's—at Discus.
Ant.   Far away.
Chæ. Ah! we will run.
Ant.   But change your garb.
Chæ.   Ah! change—
 I cannot do so, and I am undone.
 I am shut out from home: I fear my brother—
 I fear my father should he be returned.
Ant. Come home with me.
Chæ.   I will, and readily;
 Moreover, I would take advice of you
 How I may hold my capture.
Ant.   Willingly.

ACT IV.

Scene 1.—Dorias.

As the gods love me well, I am afraid
That there will be an outbreak with this soldier
And our Thais.   When I led Chremes there,
The brother of our maiden, Thais asked
Admission for him; then the soldier flared,
Commencing by refusal.   Nevertheless,
Thais insisted,—seating him by her
And waiting opportunity to speak—
And Thraso ended by inviting him.
My mistress meantime fain to talk with him;
Our captain thought he smelt a rival there,
And bellowed forth in rage, "Eh! boy, go bring
Pamphila here, for she will cheer us up."
Thais as loudly said, "Do no such thing;
What, bring her to a festal!"   He insisted,
And then they quarrelled.   She has taken off
These ornaments of gold for me to bear,
A proof that she will follow speedily.

ACT IV.—Scene 2.—Phædria.

Departing for the country, I began,
Among the lanes, to meditate upon
This thing and that, and to view everything
With miserable view.   Shortly to speak:
I passed our house unwillingly—returned,
With sickness at my heart.   I reached our gate

Upon the road, and there I stood to dream :
Two days alone—two days to dwell without her.
But if I be forbidden to approach her,
I am not to behold her with my eyes ;
To gaze is not forbidden me.   In love,
The smallest boon is better far than none.
But what is this—our Pythias in trouble !

ACT IV.—Scene 3.—Pythias—Phædria—Dorias.

Pyth. Where shall I find the villain—Ah ! ah me !
  Where seek for him—O most flagitious deed !
Phœ. I die ! nor know I what to fear.
Pyth.   The scoundrel
  The villain has abused her unawares ;
  Has rent her garments, and torn out her hair.
Phœ. Hem !
Pyth.   Ah ! if I come across him, ravisher !
  I'll set my finger nails in eyes and cheeks.
Phœ. Some great calamity has fallen here :
  What is it Pythias ; what afflicts you so ?
  Whom seek you now ?
Pyth. Whom—Phædria do I seek—
  Go, where you ought to go—you and your gifts !
Phœ. What is the wrong ?
Pyth.   What is the wrong do y' ask—
  The eunuch whom you gave us has abused
  The virgin whom the soldier sent a gift !
Phœ. What ?
Pyth.   I am undone !
Phœ.   Tipsy, not undone.
Pyth. I wish my enemies were both as I.

Phæ. Pythias, you rave—for how could he do this?

Pyth. I know not, I—but that the thing is so
  Facts, and the maiden's sorrow, indicate;
  She dares not answer to our questions. He,
  Scoundrel, is fled—perhaps a thief as well!

Phæ. Impossible!—weak in his frame and spirit.
  If he be fled, it must be to our house.

Pyth. I pray thee see then.

Phæ.   That will I presently.

Dor. Undone! undone! I pray you, did ere one
  Hear ever of a such flagitious deed!

Pyth. Pol! I have heard it said they are lascivious—
  Crazy for womankind. I had forgotten it,
  Else I had never given him the child to ward.

ACT IV.—Scene 4.—Phædria—Dorus—Pythias—Dorias.

Phæ. Come forth, you scoundrel, come! you fugitive!
  A pretty purchase, you!

Dorus.   Ah! I beseech you.

Phæ. Behold him, hangman! with his jaws awry.
  Why, sirrah, are you here—what garb is this?
  Speak, scoundrel! Pythias, one moment more
  And he had fled. I caught him, baggage packed.

Pyth. Ah! have you got him?

Phæ.   Ah! I have.

Pyth.   Good, good.

Dorias. Pol! and I am glad, too.

Pyth.   And where is he?

Phæ. Where is he—there!

Pyth.   There! Where? I do beseech you.

Phæ. He.

Pyth. He! that man?

Phœ.   Ay—to-day presented you.

Pyth. I tell you, Phædria, these eyes of mine
  Ne'er beheld him before.

Phœ.   Ne'er beheld him before!

Pyth. I do beseech you tell me—do you think
  This man was led to us?

Phœ.   What other else—
  I have none other.

Pyth.   This was not the man,
  Nor can compare with ours.   He was proud
  Of bearing, features of nobility.

Phœ. Garments—they were garments of divers colours,
  Which set him off; he shows now shabbily.

Pyth. Peace! I beseech you; there is no mistaking:
  The youth you sent was pleasing to the sight:
  This, Phædria, is old, decrepit, tawny.

Phœ. This is mysterious!   Fellow, answer me;
  First, tell me truly did I purchase *you*?

Dorus. You purchased me.

Pyth.   Now bid him answer me.

Phœ. Ask him.

Pyth. [*To Dorus.*]   Were you sent home to us to-day?
  He shakes his head.   It was another came—
  A boy of sixteen years with Parmeno.

Phœ. And now reply to me.   Where did you get
  That vestment which you wear?   You answer not.

Dorus. Chærea is come!

Phœ.   My brother?

Dorus   Even so.

Phœ. When?

Dorus.   But this day.

Phæ.   How long ago?

Dorus.   Just now.

Phæ. With whom?

Dorus.   With Parmeno.

Phæ.   Know you him before?

Dorus. No; nor did I ever hear say who he was.

Phæ. How did you know, then, that he was my brother?

Dorus. Parmeno named him; we exchanged our clothes.

Phæ. I am struck down!'

Dorus.   He dressed himself in mine,
   And they went forth together.

Pyth.   Ay, I am tipsy, I;
   And not undone.   Ay, it is sure enough
   The virgin is abused.

Phæ.   Be silent, beast!—
   Do you believe that fellow?

Pyth.   Have I not reason, I!
   The facts speak for themselves.

Phæ.   Fellow! come here.
   Repeat me now again what you have said:
   That Chærea took your clothes.

Dorus.   He took my clothes.

Phæ. And dressed himself in them?

Dorus.   And dressed in them.

Phæ. And led hence in your stead?

Dorus.   Led in my stead.

Phæ. Great Jupiter! audacity of man!

Pyth. And I unhappy!   What! you don't believe
   That we have suffered this indignity?

Phæ. I do not marvel you believe his words—
   I know not what to do.   Now hark you, sirrah,
   [*Aside to Dorus.*] Deny all you have said.

[*Aloud.*]   How shall I wrench
  The truth from you.   Have you seen Chærea ?
Dorus. No.
Phæ.   Without the scourge he will not tell the truth.
  Follow me, sirrah!   Now vouch, now deny—
  [*Aside.*] Pray mercy.
Dorus.   I entreat you, Phædria.
Phæ. Enter, I say.
Dorus. [*As if smitten.*] Hohi!   Ohee!
Phæ.   None other way
  Than beating, to extract the truth from him.
  [*Aside.*] If he speaks truth, I perish.   Scoundrel! knave!
  To practise roguery at our expense.

ACT IV.—Scene 5.—Pythias—Dorias.

Pyth. As sure as I'm alive, this is a trick
  Of Parmeno's.
Dorias.   It is—it is.
Pyth.   Pol! I will find a way
  To pay him off before the day be passed.
Dorias. About the virgin?
Pyth.   Ay, what about her—
  Shall I divulge the deed or hold my peace?   ·
Dorias. Pol! Pythias, if you're wise, you will know nought
  About the matter, Dorus, or the maid ;
  You won't get into trouble, nor displease
  Our mistress Thais—say only he is fled.
Pyth. I will do so.
Dorias.   And look when Chremes comes,
  Thais will come anon.

Pyth.   How do you know?
Dorias. They had begun to squabble when I left.
Pyth. Bear in the gold then, I will meet him here.

ACT IV.—Scene 6.—Chremes—Pythias.

Chr. Hercle! they have deceived me.   Wit is out
     When wine is in.   Now, as I lay reclined,
     I was all right enough; but when I sought
     My feet to stand upon, my head swam round.
Pyth. Chremes!
Chr.   How now—Ah! Pythias my fair,
     You are sweeter looking than you were just now.
Pyth. Pol! so are you in a far better humour.
Chr. The saw is true—Ceres and Liber banished,
     And Venus freezes.   But Thais is returned.
Pyth. Has she then left the soldier's?
Chr.   Long ago;
     They were at fisticuffs.
Pyth.   Did she bid you
     To follow her?
Chr.   No, but she nodded to me.
Pyth. Eh! is not that enough?
Chr.   But I knew not
     What it might signify; that want
     Was filled up by the Captain, by the shoulders
     Who put me out of doors.   Ah! here she comes—
     I marvel how I am so long before her.

ACT IV.—Scene 7.—Thais—Chremes—Pythias.

Tha. Upon my life I do believe that he
  Will come to take the girl.   Well! let him come,
  If he touch but her finger I will dig
  My fingers in his eyes.   His brags and boastings
  I can bear very patiently; but if he come
  To force and action, let him look about.
Chr. Thais, I wait this long while.
Tha.   Chremes, mine!
  I have expected you.   Ah! do you know
  You are yourself the cause of this ado;
  And that this matter's yours?
Chr.   Mine!   How and why?
Tha. I strive to render unto you a sister,
  And to restore her to you; and for that
  I suffer all that you have seen me suffer.
Chr. Where is she?
Tha.   In my house.
Chr.   Ehem!
Tha.   Fear not
  She educated is, and very worthy.
Chr. What do you say?
Tha.   I say the simple truth,
  I give her unto you; nor ask reward.
Chr. But you shall have it, I assure you, Thais—
  Thanks and reward.
Tha.   But, Chremes, have a care
  You lose her not before you have possession;
  For it is she the soldier comes to seize.

Pythias, go bring the casket with the proofs—
Proofs—for her recognition.

Chr.   Is he near, Thais?

Pyth. Where is the casket?

Tha.   Dullard! in the press;
Accursed dulness—

Chr.   Atat! what a troop
The Captain brings with him!

Tha.   Eh! fear not him—
You are not timorous?

Chr.   Question it not;
Me timorous—no no—no man less so!

Tha. We need a champion.

Chr.   You deem ill of me.

Tha. Do not dispute; but bear in mind that he
Is but a stranger—you a citizen
With many more to aid at need than he.

Chr. I know all that, but it is very stupid
To meet an evil that you can avoid;
And better far than vengeance is prevention.
Go bar the doors. I to the forum go
And seek for friends to aid me in a fight.

Tha. Stay.

Chr.   I'd better go.

Tha.   Stay.

Chr.   And be back in a second.

Tha. We need no help, my Chremes; only say
The damsel is your sister, a lost child,
Whom you now recognize and now retrieve,
Here are the proofs.

Pyth.   The casket—here it is.

Tha. Take it; and if he menaces, away
  To judgment hall.   You understand.
Chr.   Ah! well.
Tha. Speak to him dauntlessly.
Chr.   I will.
Tha.   Your pallium
  Is dropping off.   My champion, ah!—he needs
  A champion himself.

ACT IV.—SCENE 8.—THRASO—GNATHO—SANGA—DONAX—
      SIMALIO—SYRISCUS—CHREMES—THAIS.

Thr. What, Gnatho! shall I suffer such affront?
  I would rather die.   Holloa! Simalio,
  Donax, and you Syriscus—follow me!
  I will assault the house.
Gna.   Right excellent!
Thr. I will bear off the girl.
Gna.   Eh! better still!
Thr. And I will punish Thais.
Gna.   Best of all!
Thr. Donax, come with the lever to the van
  And form the main; Simalio, to the left;
  Syriscus, the right wing.   Where are the rest?
  Where the centurion Sanga, with the band—
  Brigade of thieves?
San.   Here we are.
Thr.   How, fellow, how,
  With a cook's dishclout here!
San.   Ah! noble captain,

There will be bloodied noses and cracked crowns,
Where'er you combat; this will slop it up.
Thr. And where are all the rest?
San. Where all the rest!
Why, Sannio only stays to guard the house.
Thr. Sound for the onset. I bring up the rear,
And issue the commands.
Gna. Ah! in the rear.
There wisdom and there safety is in that.
Thr. Pyrrhus was first to hold himself in rear.
Chr. Thais, do you see this, how he commands?
I gave you good advice to bar the doors.
Tha. Oh! fear not him. He is a very braggart—
A coward.
Thr. Gnatho, look out!
Gna. O for a sling,
And fighting from afar and in the rear,
And from an ambush, till they take to flight!
Thr. Behold her!—Thais.
Gna. Shall we charge on her?
Thr. Wait; let us parley. For a wise commandant
Prefers a treaty to a combat; for who knows,
But she may grant us all the terms we ask.
Gna. Faith of the gods above! sagacious man—
I never can come near you, but I reap
A store of wisdom!
Thr. Thais! now answer me.
Did you not promise, when I gave that damsel,
That you would give yourself to me these days?
Tha. What then I pray?
Thr. What then I pray! dost ask—

Before my very eyes obtrude your lover,
And then walk off with him ; what for, I pray ?
Tha. It pleased me so.
Thr.   Give me back Pamphila,
Unless you wish me to take her by force.
Chr. Give her to you—or you take her by force—
Basest of men !
Gna.   Oh ! peace ; be not so rash.
Thr. Eh ! what not take my own !   The girl is mine.
Chr. Thine—furcifer !
Gna.   Zounds ! have a care, I say ;
You know not whom you curse.
Chr.   Be off from this,
Know you the rights of this ?   For if to-day
You make a riot here, be sure of this—
You never shall forget this day nor place.
Gna. Ay, but you grieve me, drawing on your head
Hostility like his.
Chr.   I'll cut your head
Short of the shoulders—if you be not off!
Gna. Is it thus, dog—I ask you is it thus ?
Thr. Who is this man ?   Who are you ? and what right
Have you in her or this ?
Chr.   That she is free.
Thr. Hem !
Chr.   A citizen of Attica.
Thr.   Ah, ah !
Chr. My sister.
Thr.   Brazen face !
Chr.   Soldier, take heed !
Commit no violence.   Thais, I go to seek
The nurse Sophrona ; she must see the proofs.

Thr. May I not touch a girl who is my own?

Chr. I tell you no.

Gna.   Enough! we have heard him call
    Himself a thief; that is enough for you.

Thr. Thais, do you say this?

Tha.   Do not ask me.

Thr. And now, what shall we do?

Gna.   Well, I advise
    That we go home, and let her send for us.

Thr. You so advise?

Gna.   Of course I do.   The wit
    Of women runs capriciously.   You will,
    They won't; again you won't, they will.

Thr. Right! you are right.

Gna.   Disband the legions, then?

Thr. Ay, ay, disband them.

Gna.   Sanga, disband the legions,
    Let them repose beside the household hearth.

San. My soul is in the platter—has been long.

Gna. You are good at trencher.

Thr.   You, follow me.

———————————

ACT V.

Scene 1.—Thais—Pythias.

Tha. Cease, naughty one! to trouble me with fears.
  You know, and do not know—have heard, and not—
  Speak plainly, wench, and tell me what you know.
  The girl has garments torn, is silent, weeps,
  The Ethiopian fled! Wherefore, and where?
Pyth. How can I tell you what I do not know.
  They say the eunuch was not what he was.
Tha. Who, then?
Pyth.   Who! Chærea.
Tha.   Who is Chærea?
Pyth. Brother to Phædria, he—
Tha.   What beldam, what?
Pyth. I tell you truly.
Tha.   Wherefore did he come
  To us, I say;—what was it brought him here?
Pyth. I know not, but think, love for Pamphila.
Tha. Ah! I am slain downright, if this be true:
  And therefore doth she weep.
Pyth.   Truly, I think so.
Tha. O sacrilegious wretch! how dared you go
  And quit her, contrary to my command!
Pyth. By your command I yielded her to him.
Tha. Beldam, you gave the lamb unto the wolf!
  Oh! you have shamed me past the power of words!
  What sort of man is he?
Pyth.   Peace! here he is.
  Hush! Madam, hush!

Tha.   Where is he?

Pyth.   Hush! he is
 At your left hand; do you not see him there!

Tha. I do.

Pyth.   Shall we arrest him?

Tha.   Fool, be still!

Pyth. Be still, you bid me! Look now, I beseech you,
 How he looks brazen—

Tha.   Not a bit of it!

Pyth. And with what confidence approaching here!

ACT V.—Scene 2.—Chærea—Thais—Pythias.

Chæ. Father and mother both of Antipho
 Returned, as if expressly, to the house;
 Nor could I enter it unknown to them.
 And whilst I thus was standing at their door,
 One known to me approached me. When I saw him,
 I made off—as I might, turned corners, cut
 Down lanes and alleys, fleeing like a thief.
 Thais!—can that be Thais? It is she.
 What shall I do now—how proceed with her!
 Eh! I care not. She can do nought in this!

Tha. Address him. Honest man! Dorus, salvè!
 So you, it seems, thought fit to run away?

Chæ. Mistress, I did.

Tha.   And think you it was right?

Chæ. No.

Tha. Or to escape unpunished?

Chæ.   Pardon, Thais.
 If I offend again, then let me die.

Tha. Did you think me severe?

Chæ.   No.

Tha.   Wherefore then ?—
Chœ. 'Twas she I feared—lest she accused me to you.
Tha. What have you done then?
Chœ.   Ah! one trifling fault.
Pyth. A trifling fault!   O graceless!—trifling fault—
    To vitiate a virgin citizen.
Chœ. Truly, I thought she was my fellow slave.
Pyth. Your fellow slave—you monster!   I know not
    What now restrains me to dig out your eyes—
    Mocking your neighbours.
Tha.   Pythias, go away.
Pyth. Why should I go away—the furcifer!
    And he acknowledging to be your slave.
Tha. Pythias, have done!   Chærea, indignantly
    Have you entreated me.   Say, I deserved it,
    The deed is very shameful to yourself,
    Unworthy your position.   And, by my word,
    I am in deep distress about this virgin.
    You have upset my plans.   I know not what
    To do.   I wished to have restored her so
    As to have claimed their gratitude and thanks;
    Performed to them a solid benefit.
Chœ. Thais, I trust from hence, for evermore,
    There will be happiness.   Often it occurs
    A deed of rashness turns the contrary,
    And grows a blessing; if a god so wills.
Tha. Pol! that it may be so.   I wish it well.
Chœ. And, Thais, I beseech you do not think
    I meditated an affront to you,
    Or that it was not love.
Tha.   I do believe it,
    And I pardon you.   For, Chærea, my heart

Is soft and human, and, alas! I know,
By hard experience, of the wiles of love.
Chœ. As the gods love me, but I love you, Thais.
Pyth. Pol! mistress: then beware, if he speaks true
He is a perilous lover.
Chœ.   Deep respect!
Pyth. I would not trust you, I.
Tha.   O, silence! Pythias.
Chœ. I do most earnestly entreat you, Thais,
That you will my adjutor be in this:
O be my patroness, and hold my faith!
Thais, or I must wed her, or I shall die.
Tha. Your father—
Chœ.   Will consent, I am assured,
She is a citizen.
Tha.   Then wait awhile—
Her brother presently will bring her nurse:
You shall be at their meeting, Chærea.
Chœ. I will wait ever.
Tha.   Then let us enter in:
Not stand before the door.
Chœ.   I wait on you.
Pyth. Faith of the gods—what, Thais, do you do!
Tha. What mean you?
Pyth.   After that—what—go with him!
Tha. Ah! silence, I entreat you!
Pyth.   He is audacity—
He will do some disorder!
Chœ.   I shall do none,
O Pythias!
Pyth.   I will not trust you, Chærea,
Unless you stand committed.

Chœ.   Pythias, I will,
  Committed to *your* custody.
Pyth.   Not mine—
  I will not have you, nor shall any other—
  Take yourself off.
Tha.   Here, happily, the brother.
Chœ. Hercle! I am undone—Oh, take me in—
  Let him not see me standing in the street
  Clad in this garb!
Tha.   What! Chærea, bashful!
Chœ. Truly, I am.
Pyth.   Truly—Ah! Pamphila.
Tha. Go on—I follow you. Pythias, remain,
  And bring in Chremes and the nurse to us.

ACT V.—Scene 3.—Pythias—Chremes—Sophrona.

Pyth. Ah! how that fellow haunts my very mind;
  Would I might give him payment for his presents!
Chr. Nurse, stir your stumps.
Soph.   I do.
Chr.   Yes, but you don't progress.
Pyth. Have you shown her the tokens?
Chr.   All.
Pyth.   And did
  She recognize them?
Chr.   Instantly.
Pyth.   That's well—
  I love the maiden. Enter, if you please,
  My mistress is awaiting. Ah! Parmeno,
  See with what insolence the fellow comes!
  If the gods prosper me, I have a way

To excruciate him.   Let me first satisfy
My curiosity within, and I will forth
To satisfy my vengeance, here, without.

ACT V.—Scene 4.—Parmeno—Pythias.

Par. I come to see how Chærea gets on.
 Faith of the gods! if he has won the prize,
 What praise for Parmeno—love gratified,
 Despite of avaricious courtesans—
 Despite of difficulties, and of all
 Trouble or money.   And, more than all that,
 I give my master here an insight to
 Manners of courtesans, which, known betimes,
 Will be detested ever and a-day.
 They walk abroad in modest dress and mien:
 They banquet with exceeding delicacy;
 And they at home are gluttons—ravenous
 Of black bread, steeped in soup of yesterday.
 Much it behoves a young man to know this—
 Earlier the better.
Pyth.   I will be square with you
 For deeds and words, you good-for-nothing knave;
 You shall not mock at us and unavenged.

ACT V.—Scene 5.—Pythias—Parmeno.

Pyth. Faith of the gods! Ah! horrible—poor boy!
 Accursed Parmeno, who brought him here!
Par. What now?
Pyth.   I weep and wail his hapless fate—
 I have come forth to weep—Unhappy boy:
 Example terrible to future time!

Par. O Jupiter, what is this misery !
  I perish ! I must speak.   Hey, Pythias,
  What is all this about ?   Example what ?
Pyth. Dost thou demand, O most audacious slave—
  Did you not bring a young man in the stead
  Of Ethiopian, whom your master gave ?
Par. How so ? say what has happened.   Eh ! say what.
Pyth. The virgin who to-day was given Thais
  Is Attican, a citizen—her brother,
  A nobleman.
Par.   I know not that.
Pyth.   Then I
  Teach it you, fellow ! and he has abused her.
  Her brother, who, most rash and violent
  When he aware—
Par.   What, what ?
Pyth.   He bound him hard,
  In manner piteous to behold —
Par.   Bound ?—eh !
Pyth. Despite of Thais and her piteous prayers,
  Entreating for his youth—
Par.   What is all this ?
Pyth. They menace now to treat him as they treat
  Adulterers.   A thing I never saw,
  And never wish to see.
Par.   He dare not do it—
  Why, what audacity !
Pyth.   Audacity ?
Par. Audacity—unheard of, past belief !
  Adulterer—in house of Meretrix !
  Notion preposterous !
Pyth.   Ah ! I know not—

Par. Ah! you know not—then know this, Pythias,
  He is my master's son.
Pyth.   Eh! I beseech you—
  What! is that so?
Par.   Let Thais see to it;
  And bar all violence.   But I—
  Why should not I myself pass in the house?
Pyth. Ah! have a care what you do, Parmeno;
  You fail to aid him, and are caught yourself.
  They say you counselled him to what he did.
Par. Unhappy devil I! what shall I do?
  Ah! here our master is returned to town.
  Shall I tell him, or shall I not tell him?
  Hercle! I will tell him, whate'er betide
  To me myself.   'Tis he must succour him.
Pyth. Good!—I will go away—Tell him the whole,
  Exactly and precisely as it is.

ACT V.—Scene 6.—Laches—Parmeno.

Lac. What comfort to have country villa near!
  City nor country ever wearies me.
  I walk from one unto the other, as
  The humour takes me.   Ah! Parmeno,
  Our Parmeno—himself!   What doth he there?—
  What dost thou, Parmeno, before this door?
Par. Who calls me?—eh!   Ah! salvè, master, I
  Rejoice to see you well!
Lac.   What do you here?
Par. I choke—speechless my tongue with fear.
Lac.   How, now?
  You tremble, and are dumb.   What is it? say.

Par. First, master, let me beg you to believe
Whate'er has happened here or come to pass,
Did not occur by any fault of mine.
Lac. Say what.
Par.   Rightly you ask me what.   Behoves
To tell the tale—narrate the facts.   You see,
Our Phædria bought an eunuch to present her.
Lac. Whom?
Par.   Thais.
Lac.   Purchased, I perish! at what cost?
Par. At twenty minæ.
Lac.   All is up!
Par.   Moreo'er
His brother, Chærea, loves a flute-player.
Lac. He—love! what he—Doth he already know
What women are!   Is he returned to town!
Ill upon ill!
Par. Master, frown not on me.
It was not by my counsel these were done.
Lac. Leave yourself out, O furcifer; for if
I live I——.   Tell now honestly the whole.
Par. They led him there to Thais as the eunuch.
Lac. Led as the eunuch!
Par.   Yea, and treat him as
They treat adulterers.   He is bound hard.
Lac. I die!
Par.   Audacity of harlots—Eh! behold!
Lac. Have you poured forth your budget of bad news?
Is there no more behind?
Par.   No; that is all.
Lac. Why do I not break in?
Par. [*Alone.*]   Ah! past a doubt

But I must catch it; but I had no choice—
It was a stern necessity to tell.
The baggages—they, too, will meet their due.
Our Master long time held them in despite:
Now they will answer it, as he has cause.

ACT V.—Scene 7.—Parmeno—Pythias.

Pyth. I never, edepol! was tickled more
  Than when I saw the old man, out of breath,
  Come tumbling, on fool's errand, in the house,
  Out of his wits; and all the rest perplexed;
  For I alone knew what he thought and feared.
Par. What is all this?
Pyth.   Now I seek Parmeno:
  And where to find him—
Par.   Ah! she seeks for me.
Pyth. Eh! Parmeno.
Par.   Dunce say, how now—you laugh.
  Laugh on—don't stop.
Pyth. My sides are split—'tis you
  That causes me to laugh.
Par.   How so?
Pyth.   Do you ask,
  Because you are a fool?—the biggest fool—
  Pol! that I ever met. Why, what a farce
  Have you enacted for our merriment!
  And you—I ever thought astute and clever.
Par. How?
Pyth.   You would believe anything you heard.
  Must you first harm the boy, then tell his father.
  Now think—what was the father's state of mind

When he beheld his son dressed as a slave !
Eh ! it's all up with you.
Par   You female hag,
What is't you say—do you not lie ! You grin—
Is it so liquorish to jest at me,
You jade !
Pyth.   Immense.
Par.   If with impunity—
Pyth. Well, yes.
Par.   I will pay off old scores.
Pyth.   Do so—
That is hereafter ; your score is to-day.
My poor, poor Parmeno upon the cross !
Now, did one ever hear—mislead the youth,
And then proclaim it to the father ! Both—
Both will have at you.
Par.   . . . . annihilated I !
Pyth. For your fine present to us—take you that.
Par. I, like the mouse, betrayed by my own squeak !

ACT V.—Scene 8.—Gnatho—Thraso.

Gna. How now, what hope, what counsel leads us here—
What, Thraso, do you mean ?
Thr.   I come to yield
To Thais, at discretion to submit.
Gna. How ?
Thr.   So Hercules served Omphale ; I too.
Gna. An apt example—very quaint. Shall we
Behold her sandal and your head acquainted ?
Why creaks her opening door ?

Thr.   . Again undone!
  Another rival—never seen before—
  And coming forth, tumbling o'er head and ears.

ACT V.—Scene 9.—Chærea—Parmeno—Gnatho—
Thraso.

Chæ. My countrymen, was ever mortal blest
  As I am blest to-day?   Ah, hercle! never!
  The gods have clubbed all their benignities
  To shower them in storm divine on me.
Par. Wherefore so joyful?
Chæ.   O, my Parmeno,
  Author of all my joys, of fortune great—
  Inventor, and contriver, and perfector—
  Know you in what I am beyond my wits—
  My Pamphila, a citizen of Athens!
Par. I have so heard.
Chæ.   That she is my betrothed?
Par. As the gods love me—it was right well done.
Gna. Do you hear that!
Chæ.   Moreover, Phædria
  Possesses Thais tranquilly in love;
  Henceforth our home will be her domicile.
  She cast herself into my father's arms
  Imploring his protection, and she yields
  Herself entirely unto us.
Par.   And Thais
  Wholly your brother's?
Chæ.   Wholly.
Par.   Hurrah! hurrah!
  The soldier is thrust out of doors.

Chœ.   Quick then,
    Inform my brother, wheresoe'er he be,'
    Of this, directly.
Par.   I will go seek at home.
Thr. Now, Gnatho, now ; am I not wholly lost ?
Gna. Faith ! but it seems so.
Chœ.   Now, whether of we two
    Deserves the palm of merit.   He who devised ·
    Or he who put in practice the conception :
    Or yield the palm to Fortune, at the helm,
    Who steered our bark to so much happiness :
    Or to my father for beneficence ?
    O Jupiter ! confirm this happiness.

ACT V.—Scene 10.—Phædria—Chærea—Parmeno—
                    Gnatho—Thraso.

Phœ. Faith of the gods ! 'tis all incredible.
    Where is my brother, Parmeno ?
Chœ.   Lo, here !
Phœ. I am delighted.
Chœ.   I believe it well ;
    Brother, there is none worthier than Thais,
    The benefactress of our family.
Phœ. No need to pour her praises in my ears.
Thr. The less I am in hope, the more in love.
    Gnatho, I pray thee—I trust still in thee.
Gna. What would you have me do ?
Thr.   O get for me,
    By payment or by prayers, a part of Thais !
Gna. 'Twere difficult.
Thr.   You can—and if you will—

  I know you well—if you effect it, Gnatho,
  Ask what you will, and have your own reward.
Gna. In faith?
Thr.   In faith!
Gna.   Then you must grant me this:
  Absent or present, that your house shall be
  Free to me always—without invitation.
Thr. I give my word of faith.
Gna.   I gird my loins.
Phœ. Hail! Thraso.
Thr.   Hail!
Phœ.   Perchance you do not know
  Things which have come to pass.
Thr.   I know.
Phœ.   Then why
  Do I behold you here?
Thr.   Trusting on you.
Phœ. Know you on whom you trust? Soldier, I say—
  That if henceforth I find you in this place—
  Go, babble not it was by accident—
  Or friend—you sought—for by my word, you die!
Gna. This, Phædria, is unjust.
Phœ.   But it is said.
Gna. I knew not you were so peremptory.
Phœ. But you will find it so.
Gna.   Well, well! ere you
  Decide, grant me an audience; if you please—
  One word.
Phœ. We hear.
Gna.   Thraso, withdraw a space.
  Howe'er I may obtrude myself in this.
  First, I beseech you, give me credit due—

Whate'er I do is for my own advantage :
But if it chance our interests run together,
It were a folly to reject my counsel.
Phæ. Say on.
Gna.   The soldier ought to be received,
I think 'twere wise.
Phæ.   How ought to be received?
Gna. Consider, Phædria, your future means :
You love good cheer, and Thais loves good cheer ;
She demands much, and you have but small means ;
You cannot hold her long without some cost ;
Therefore, behoves to seek one to defray them.
Now one of smallest wit and largest means
Presents himself—a body without soul—
Snoring by night and day—aversion of
The woman, and—kicked out whene'er you will.
Phæ. What shall we do in this?
Gna.   Another thing
Has influence with me ; for nobody
Has better board, unniggard, than hath he.
Phæ. A sort of man convenient at need.
Chæ. So he appears to me.
Gna.   You rightly judge.
I have one other prayer to make to you :
Receive me in your flock—for, by my soul !
Too long I roll this stone.
Phæ.   My servant be.
Chæ. And willingly.
Gna.   Now I commence my service :
Take him, then, Phædria—take him, Chærea.
Devour and deride him as you will.
Chæ. I am contented.

Phæ. He is worthy.

Gna.　　　　　　　　　　Thraso,
　Approach, if 'tis your pleasure.

Thr.　　　　　　　　　Now, how go
　Our matters, I beseech you?

Gna.　　　　　　　　Even thus:
　They did not know you, nor appreciate;
　I have explained your worthiness; your deeds
　Of valour in the field they recognize.

Thr. You have done well, and I return you thanks.
　Where'er I go I stumble thus on friends—
　Here most of all.

Gna.　　　　　　I told you so—he has
　A fund of elegance, quite Attican.

Phæ. Now all is over, let us hence depart;
　We bid, Farewell! Do ye applaud our art.

"*RESTITVERE.*"

PRINTED BY WILLIAM CLOWES AND SONS, DUKE STREET, STAMFORD STREET,
AND CHARING CROSS.